Circus Rex

Angela,

Here it is —
enjoy every
digression.

CALUMET EDITIONS

Minneapolis

First Edition August 2023
Circus Rex. Copyright © 2023 by William Loren Niemi.
All rights reserved.

This is a work of fiction. All of the characters, names, incidents, organizations, and dialogue are either the products of the author's imagination or are used fictitiously.

Printed in the United States of America.
10 9 8 7 6 5 4 3 2 1

ISBN: 978-1-960250-93-3

Cover design by Mike Sommers
Book design by Gary Lindberg

Circus Rex

Loren Niemi

**CALUMET
EDITIONS**
Minneapolis

Memory begins to qualify the imagination, to give it another formation, one that is peculiar to the self.

–N. Scott Momaday

For

Kevin and Mike
Thanks for twenty-five years of building the world

Sandy Spieler
For thinking it could be done

Also by Loren Niemi

Inviting the Wolf In: Thinking about Difficult Stories
The New Book of Plots
What Haunts Us
Point of View & The Emotional Arc of Stories

Poetry:

Coyote Flies Coach
Vote Coyote!
A Breviary for the Lost

Prologue–Before We Begin

You asked, and I'll answer as truthful as a mostly self-educated man might, or at least as my memory and penchant for a language that is more colorful than precise will allow. After all, it was some time ago. Thirty-some years now. Maybe more. At this point, the "what" happened back in the day and, more to our present recounting, my feelings about what happened as I reconstruct those fabled events may be jumbled but well-intentioned.

I best acknowledge that after we account for a memory steeped in time and conscience seeped in a bit of single malt to ease the starting, what I'm going to say may be subject to some judgment about the veracity of the events. Often enough, what's factually "true" makes little sense and requires some improvement to swallow whole.

You might make me out to be what is called in literature an unreliable narrator. Perhaps I am, but we'll be a long way down the rutted road of recollection before either of us should come to any conclusions about the accuracy of what I speak.

I might draw my words from whatever sources come to mind, but trust me, the truth of my story is not in poor pitiful facts. More likely, the truth is in what the facts direct us to consider. Huzzah! Look over there... It's like the way a good bird dog stands—it's not whether the right or left leg is forward, though those are surely facts, but instead, the meaning of those facts as an indication of a bird in yonder bush that ol' dog is pointed toward.

I trust you will see for yourself "what is what" as we go along because, while back in the day I might have done this or that, might have felt some kind of joy or loathing at the time I did a particular thing, in retrospect I might want to approach what was done then and how I felt about it now cautiously, without rancor. Let bygones be bygones, as it were. Sleeping dogs, that sort of thing…

Yes, what's done is done and gone. Done so long ago, some of the innocent might have already served their time or passed from this realm, but what it meant then and should mean now is still subject to some cautious judgment and perhaps also to a substantial reconsideration of why I undertook that less traveled fork in the road in the first place. Even so, or especially when I tell the facts of this tale as I recollect it, a considerable portion is subject to having been polished by casual repetition in the telling of the parts I like. Fact is, I appreciate a good yarn as much as the next fellow.

I'll leave it to your own judgment as to whether you can validate my testimony with interviews of the living, séances with the dead, piles of invoices, articles published back in the day or whatever smidgen of evidence you might collect, but in my a priori defense I'll say there is little room for guilt or shame in my telling. If anything, I'll want to be forgiving of the sins of others, be neglectful of blame and entertaining enough to make it worth my time for the telling and yours for the hearing. As Mark Twain said, "Supposing is good, but finding out is better."

I'll also admit before I launch in full tilt, as you might already suspect, I am prone to digression. I'll make a few detours in the telling, but don't worry yourself, I'll come back to the main line sooner or later. As I used to say when I was calling the strolling midway crowd to those "two bits, four bits, six bits a dollar" sideshows, "You pays your money, you takes your chances."

1—The Call

I swear by a cold six-pack of cheap beer on a sweltering August day, when I answered the phone, I wasn't wishing for Opportunity's golden knock, but there it was. The one and only Flat Frank, a reliable fixer-upper of broken dreams, had found me in Mad Town and was offering me a long-legged beauty of a job as the Ringmaster and majordomo of the Rex Terrestrial, Celestial & Nautical Circus.

The "what" you might ask, or at least I did. "What kind of name was that?" slid to the tippy top of my tongue, but before the question could slip out, I got caught on that last word—Circus. It ricocheted in my ear. It settled in my brain like a warm slice of sweet something with ice cream on top. The *smell the greasepaint* and *taste the popcorn*—mmmm, yes—the circus. The very word shimmered rare and beautiful in the way that last dream does before you wake. Truth was that I was already a little bored with my sojourn as a late-night disc jockey at a Madison radio station where the ad rates were cheap and so was my paycheck. Frank's offer would be as good a way as any to pass time between not enough money and well-deserved sloth.

Holy Mother of Mercy, if I had known how hard it would be, I might have turned it down, but we seldom know how the story will end when it begins.

He called. I answered. At first, it seemed like a small potatoes deal when I heard him lay it out. Easy as falling off the couch, he says.

3

As Ringmaster, you call the acts and keep them on time. You give the marching orders to move the whole kit and caboodle along one stop after another by the schedule. Then he says, the stops and schedule is already fixed. You don't have to sell a thing, just check the boxes. You do a little PR along the way, polishing the tempting fruit of Eden's tree when you arrive in town, but you don't have to shake the tree, just offer the apple. My girl Lucy is on that one. The interviews get set up beforehand, so all you have to do is pillow talk an audience into the bleachers using your well-honed rhetorical skills.

He was pouring it on thick as fresh tar on gravel.

Frank continued along that cursive line of flattery and fact, saying you're an old salt, been in the touring business for more years than this operation has been in existence. You've got some very valuable experience to offer them. I'm telling you all you have to do is get them packed up and out the door, Buzz, up and out the door making money, or at least not losing too much, from start to finish. Then he delivers the coup de grace, Buzz, these people surely need a man like you.

In those days, and I suppose in these days as well, I was a sucker for the "saving" game. Might have been a holdover from my Bible reading days with Big Daddy. It was like I was some latter-day Moses standing before the fuckin' Burning Bush being told to lead the Israelites out of Egypt when I heard him say that. Not that Flat Frank is God. Far from it, Frank is closer to the devil you know, but the way he said it, the bright temptation of knowing what I desired, was right there. He had known me long enough to know that I liked the puzzle of doing what couldn't be done.

I mean, how hard could it be to do a twelve-state, six-month circus tour? Easy as falling off a couch, indeed! Take something that probably wasn't what you'd call a blue-ribbon moneymaker and manage by hook or crook to make it worth the blood, sweat and inevitable tears that would follow. I could do that.

Common sense should have said walk away, but at that moment, my common sense was in another room, and the Devil of Big Dreams was whispering, "What the hell, it's more interesting than anything else on the table." That was true enough. It was more interesting than another night of playing requests from manic-depressives who thought the only thing between them and the long goodbye was you putting John Coltrane's "A Love Supreme" on the turntable. Or worse, requesting "Stairway to Heaven" every hour on the hour.

If common sense had come back into the room, it might have said while this wasn't the only thing on the table, but it was a paying job that would take me down the Muddy Mississippi to the Big Easy. If nothing else, I'd be getting paid to arrive someplace warm for the winter.

I said, give me the directions to get to where they are now, Frank, and I'll go see if this dog will hunt. I'll call you back with an answer after I take a peek.

2—Alma

That next morning, I went up to Alma, Wisconsin, to look it over. On the map, it looked to be a small town on the banks of the Mississippi, just far enough from anywhere to afford some privacy. That's where they, whomever they were, were rehearsing the show, whatever it was.

Drove my classic, slab-sided, '68 Lincoln out of Madison, up one of them too-narrow state highways snaking through Wisconsin farmland till I got to La Crosse and headed north on Highway 37 until I came to Alma. Not a bad-looking town if you ignored the old school, coal-fired power plant on one end. Drove past neatly trimmed shops. Mostly ignored the tourist junk but did count how many bars lined Main Street. It looked like there was enough to slake the thirst after a day's toil with two or three real meat and potato cafes in between. It was at the too-soon arrival of the other end of town that I stopped by the trestle bridge that spans the Buffalo River where it empties into the mighty Mississippi, the big river I thought of as the great ditch of time.

Squint and Time slips away
Squint and the channel markers
The floodwalls disappear
The wild and dangerous river that steamboat passengers
On their excursion trips to the wilderness
Paid handsomely to traverse, returns.

6

Squint and the wandering sandbars,
The deadfalls of the fickle river,
That made Sam Clemmons consider
Another line of work return.

Squint and the river the Ojibwa saw
From their birch bark canoes years before
Longfellow imagined their romantic nobility
Or Europeans re-named their geography is manifest.

Squint and the real river returns to its eternal
And uncaring form, life coursing to the sea,
From glacier to flood to ocean, its current sweeping
History before it...

On the Mississippi side of the road was a small strip of neglected park overlooking a succession of backwater islands and, beyond that, the wide channel of commerce with twelve barge tows heading to or from the nearest lock and dam. On the right was the junction of some other even smaller state or county highway that followed the Buffalo along a narrow valley with marsh and cattails on one side and what looked to be mostly birch running up the side of the wooded bluff on the other. That was the road I wanted.

I turned and headed into a Territory Incognito.

No sooner did the road curve away from the river when there was a sign saying "SLIPPERY WHEN WET" and no sooner do I read it thinking it meant wet with rain or snow when my son of Henry Ford wiggled sideways, crossing a green sheen of cow poop that smelled like it had just been applied. Holy rock and roll! I gripped the wheel like the last thing I needed was to wrap my vintage black beauty around a telephone pole on a slick of contented cow excrement. No, thank you. I figured it came with the territory but resolved to drive a bit more careful because I didn't want to dent the Lincoln. I mean, that car was my pride and joy, a straight-off-the-production-line beauty the very last year they were made with suicide doors. It was the single thing of value I had to show for my many years of incidental employment.

April was already lush with the green of too many promises pointing to summer and heat, but I wasn't really looking at the scenery. I was turning over like a nervous man's coin whether I would or wouldn't take this gig. I wasn't sure that I needed a one-ring pastiche of artfulness, even for six months of a steady paycheck. Of course, that was a lie. I needed a steady paycheck as much as the next man Jack, but the contrary thought had lodged itself in my cerebellum that performing before two hundred small town faces night after night might get as boring as watching paint dry after a couple of weeks. Focus on the first, on the adventure of touring with a circus, I said to myself, and forget the second till it could not be denied.

Suddenly, I was as lost as a hummingbird in a plastic flower factory and needed to find myself a way. I had forgotten to pay close attention to the chicken scratch directions of how to find this one-ring wonder that I had scrawled on the back of the envelope when Frank called and decided I had better stop at the next place of commerce to check where I was. And just my luck, that would be Junior's Tap. How convenient, because when faced with a problem to adjudicate, there is nothing like taking time over a bump and a beer to refresh the overheated synapses as you consider your circumstances.

The guy I presumed to be Junior was standing behind the bar, idly polishing a glass by the light of an old Grain Belt beer sign. He was all of three hundred or more pounds of bald and big-toothed—front-loaded as they say—the classic advertisement for the product he poured and cinched tight with a belt as well as suspenders. When I asked where I might find the circus staging grounds, I got the glassy-eyed look of a man who didn't have a clue what I was asking, much less the answer. He turned his head in a clockwise motion as if winding some internal mechanism that would allow him to speak, then blurted out in a voice as small and irritating as a cuckoo clock, Ask Ma.

With that, she appeared wearing a flour-dusted apron, yarn falling from her pudgy fingers. If Junior was front-loaded, she had all her weight behind. I figured that woman would never need a seat cushion as she rocked back on her heels and scratched her head with a knitting

8

needle. Finally, she allowed that there had been a lot of commotion up around the Wheeler spread, but she thought that was because the barn had burned down. Or at least that's what she'd heard. Still, there was a bunch of guys she didn't know coming around in the evenings, and I was welcome to go look for myself or wait for them to show up to ask directly. Two miles up the county road, she said, just past where the school had been.

Back in the car, I drove the requisite two miles up the road but didn't see much more than trees and mailboxes next to rutted driveways. Another look at my map, and I realized that myself being halfway to dyslexic, when I had drawn it, I had exchanged the left and right sides of the road. By the map, Junior's would have been on the east side of the highway, while it was obvious from experience that it was not. That would make the turn-off on the other side of the road from where I was peeping. I slowed down and looked harder.

Three beats to the bar up the road, just about the time I was going to give up, a small hand-painted sign nailed to a mailbox post said, "Circus Mail Here." I turned onto the gravel road and nudged the Lincoln up a small rise shaded by newly green oaks. My sudden wondering if this had been worth the drive was held in suspension by the scene that manifested itself when I came over the crest of that hillock for my first glimpse of the Rex Terrestrial, Celestial & Nautical Circus.

Above the drive, a banner fluttered in the breeze, a white field with sun and stars, a crudely rendered globe with bright yellow lettering across the length of the banner spelling out Terrestrial, Celestial, and Nautical, as if the Earth, air and water deserved gold plated highlighting. It was a vision of tattered ballyhoo and razzle-dazzle so familiar that made me laugh out loud.

My first question, given the name, was where was the fourth classical element, the Fire? Was it in the belly or smoldering in an ash heap, waiting for a little breath to set the spark? Gone up in smoke? Damn—if you're going to invoke three of the four eternal verities, do it right and invoke them all. That's what I thought, but I let that go. I wasn't about to fight a battle over the name. I had bigger fish to fry.

9

As I surveyed the yard, my second thought was the name was dammed near as big as the tent… if there was a tent. From my vantage, I could not see one.

At the end of the driveway, scattered in a semicircle around an impressively large white three-story Victorian farmhouse with green trim, was a rag-tag collection of half-ton pickups with campers and older model sedans with rust and dents of the kind I usually associated with fly-by-night carnival operations. They all had the look of cars that needed work. Sell them now, I thought, or leave a trail of abandoned Chevys with broken axles and blown gaskets all the way from here to Memphis. But the house was pretty and looked to be in good repair. Beyond the house, I saw a couple of old school buses rebuilt as gypsy homes parked next to a small meadow. One was painted sea-foam blue and had a chimney coming out the back end. The other looked like a happy hippie love-in that had taken the wrong turn after Woodstock. I had done my time with the "toke 'em if you got 'em" crowd and knew what was what when it came to scraping the bowl, though they would not think so looking at me.

Call me David—I know a large Philistine waiting for a rock when I see one. Call me Ahab—I can obsess over metaphoric conundrums of white whales with the best of them. Call me anything, what trips off the tongue. It matters little, for I am a man of some guile and considerable patience, who has often managed to find my way through the valley of the Shadow of Death and come out bruised and bleeding but still very much alive on the other end. The truth being told, I know of what I speak.

There was an eighteen-wheeler that looked like it could carry a big tent parked next to a massive, weathered wood barn. And though it was tilting precariously toward the driveway from a stone foundation, the gray barn clearly had not burned down. If the barn was leaning, the foundation was made of solid, massive limestone blocks set into the soft slope of a hill with several corrals haphazardly arranged along the back side opening directly onto the small meadow. I could see a camel leaning against the fence chewing its cud with the banal disregard for the world that every one of those evil fuckin' beasts harbored. Sweet Jesus, of all the livestock you could populate a circus with, my last choice for necessary entertainment would be a camel. I wondered if I would smell elephants or big cats when I rolled the window down. I did, and nothing came but the smell of old camel and wildflowers running rampant along the edge of the meadow.

In that meadow, a circus ring was staked out with a small-canopied bandstand holding a couple of amplifiers next to it. Three poles stood upright where the main supports for a tent that was not yet erected would be, and those poles held what minimal trapeze and high wire rigging there was to be seen above the single ring. There were no hanging lights visible, so I guessed that they weren't doing any night rehearsals, or else they rigged the cans as they needed them. That was a bad sign. Too little equipment to spare meant everything had to be set up and taken down frequently, an invitation for accidents that would cost not only time but unplanned expense money.

A scattering of long-haired and bare-chested young guys wandered around the place without seeming to have anything particular to do. Their tans were already like soft Italian leather. One or two carried tool belts, but most seemed to be in conversations that required them to lean on fenders or fences. In front of the house, two or three naked or barely diapered babies played in the dirt, tended by a young woman with black hair in a bun. She sat at a sewing machine in the shade of a tree. The creeping doubt rattling around my brain now said maybe this wasn't going to be one of them firm-tits, long-legged adventures after all. That seamstress was offering the alternative—a Momma with three rug rats whining for something they don't have. Yes, sir, that was the feeling, and if that was the case, it would be long months of me trying to mind kids, whatever their age asking for what we couldn't afford and still get the groceries paid for.

Reaching back to my growing-up days for another Biblical image, I thought maybe you best call me Job. Bring on the dung heap and the holier-than-thou naysayers who wanted to know why God had inflicted these woes upon my head. How the hell did I know what prompted this misfortune? I would answer them with my long-suffering silence.

No, that wasn't even close. Job's silence, my ass! I'd have plenty to say. I always have plenty to say except when there's a reason to say little or nothing. As them old sideshow guys used to say, "When you're in charge, you'd better be large," and if I was going to take this on, there would be no room for Job's longsuffering whatever.

Some kids dream about running away with the circus, but let me tell you that running away is not all cotton candy and trapezes. There is a thrill when you are on a trapeze, swinging above the crowd, dressed in silks and letting go of the bar to fly. Oh, that is such a sweet feeling—moving through the tent's light and shadows, leaving one bar behind with the other just out of reach. Mmmm, it sure moves those endorphins.

But once you've had a taste of the real deal, tasted that daring do, at some point, you come to that terrible thought that someday that catch bar is not going to be at the end of your grip. You missed it by a beat. Close, so close, but just not close enough. That's when you find out for yourself what the real price of the thrill is.

Then you'll pray that as you fall, you'll ask whatever God you bow to that the net was rigged right. If it is, you'll bounce. If it isn't— well, enough said.

I know of what I speak. I've done that running away and gripping that bar to find out for myself more than once.

Year after year, I had chased one siren song of a sawdust trail after another under the ballyhoo bright lights and worn canvas looking for my last best gig, working everything from the penny ante carnival slick to late-night radio disc jockeying. I've done every Herculean labor available to the self-educated showman, from itty-bitty sideshows to sidewalk barking at hoochie-coochie clubs in convention towns. No sin in work, even if it is on the margin. I tried my hand at some legal stuff whenever that could put ready cash in my pocket. All the time, my eye was peeping for the next thing. Something. Anything. I was always looking for that which would make good use of my few but precious talents.

Just when it looked like all them years spent chasing the next Franklin for my too-skinny wallet had come short, the phone rang with Flat Frank offering me this nickel-and-dime thrill.

Not that there's anything wrong with a nickel tour. I've been there before. Guys like Frank call me when the job requires someone who can make nickels become dimes. I had a reputation for not dipping my hand in the till and was, as Frank said, "a dollar's worth of sweat for a buck" guy. If I signed on the line, I'd be touring again. If I had turned the Lincoln around and driven away, I might never have seen any of what you're asking me about. If I admitted what was in my heart at that very moment, it was that I dreamed of doing right by a circus for more years than I could recount, and this was, no matter how small and bedraggled, a real-as-it-gets circus.

Behind the wheel of the big Lincoln, the Rex Terrestrial, Celestial & Nautical Circus would have to do. I surveyed the landscape once more and made myself a promise then and there. I would take the reins in hand and make the circus be what I needed—no, what I *wanted* it to be. I would play God and make my Adam from common mud. I would be Frankenstein animating the cadaver on the slab, and when the Rex twitched and stood, I, too, would exclaim, "It's alive!"

Then I wrote Frank's number on the back of my hand. I would drive back down to Junior's that very evening and give Flat Frank the affirmative call.

3–Dr. Buzz Testifies

I suppose it is only natural that you wonder how I came to this. When did I fall under the spell of painted canvas and colored lights strung beneath a warm summer sky? That story begins in a far country called Texas. A country so flat and mean that I tried to get out of it from the moment I saw a map and could measure the distance from where I was to anywhere else...

The first time I knew what truly different looked like, I was walking alone through the County Fair midway with the smell of sawdust, grease and cotton candy, the smell of sweat and cologne from bottles reserved for Saturday night hanging in the tepid air. I might have been Paul on the road to Damascus. Lord, what a revelation! Struck dumb with wonder, I was witnessing another world previously unimagined and, when finally made manifest, fiercely present. Each booth offered the promise of pleasure and another way to fail. The rows of plates with a thin coat of oil that heartbroken coins skipped across, the stacked bottles waiting for a lopsided baseball to make them shiver, shake, but not fall. The walls of pink bears, a perpetual come-on to try again. I was taken, as if in rapture, by the sight of the crowd—the men dressed in their summer-weight, short-sleeve shirts and the fresh-faced girls in their tease-the-boys dresses strolling arm in arm along the trail of temptation.

I was seeing something I knew nothing about, and yet I felt as if I had come home. Every cheap trick and garish color sent a shiver up my spine. I could hear its tinsel heart happily beating nickels out of the hands of my wide-eyed contemporaries hanging on to their mother's hand and dollars out of men too eager not to be taken in by such nonsense. I could imagine the kisses stolen from local girls and the fistfight blood when their boyfriends caught them behind the booth with their lipstick smeared and their skirts riding up the greasy jeans of some carnival Romeo. I was ten, maybe eleven, at the time, but my fate was sealed. I knew what I wanted more than anything in the world when I heard the come-hither lilt of the pitchman's patter:

Huzzah. Huzzah. Huzzah. Step right up.
Come closer, don't be shy. You don't want to miss it.
No, you don't want to say that you did not partake of what I
have here—
The rare, the beautiful, the precious grail that makes all new.
This is what you have longed for, have sought after,
What you have only dreamt of. What you did not believe was
possible,
The eighth wonder of the world, ancient or modern...

What did it matter that it wouldn't be half of what it was cracked up to be? What strange vision of Paradise had I expected after listening to some old guy, a beer belly hanging over a too-tight belt, the shabby pastel suit, a size too big or too small, squinting at me in the cotton candy light and taking the cigar out of his mouth just long enough to say that he'd be glad to discount the price of admission if I brought my parent or guardian along. Did I really expect to see a two-headed man from Borneo, the famous Fiji mermaid wiggling in salt water or a woman with an hourglass figure turning into a snake before my eyes? That was what the illustrated walls proclaimed, but you had to believe enough, or want to, to pay the price to see what was inside.

Maybe I did believe but knew even at that tender age that what was behind the curtain wasn't the fact of it. It wasn't the bait and switch that made the trick work but the desire to see what was not

15

there. Or, more likely, though I could not have said it then, the desire to not see what was already there.

The problem of truth was far from my mind at that moment. Boy Howdy, I was all about the wonder of illusion, the caprice of gullibility satisfied. I wanted every doubt to be shamed by spectacle so I could say by all that was holy on Sunday that this was worth the knowing. Did I imagine that they wouldn't eat or sleep, that they never read the newspaper or laughed at some corny joke?

It would be several more years before I got to thinkin' about what the rubber band contortionists, the sword swallowers, the fire eaters with tongues aflame did when they stepped off the stage to slip behind the tents. By the time I did think about it, I was already in the trade and knew the answers applied to me as well as to any sideshow turn. By then, I was halfway past gone.

The Midway of that first youthful exploration was crowded with hopes and fears, a rough canvas universe exploding with giddy possibility, all riotous colors and calliope siren song. The tent banners presented the lithe curves of impossibly well-endowed women bursting from their too-tightly painted dresses or muscled giants of men grappling with rats as big as a car. Even the crudest illustrations promised something that was magical, exotic and certainly not the commonplace of farm chores, Sunday church pews and dinner-table conversation. What followed when the precious coins came out of my fearful grip, when the admission was paid, when I entered the musty darkness, was not just another guy making a buck or a woman who was more interested in the meatloaf cooking in the stove of the trailer behind the tent than any promised satisfaction of my wonder. In that first blush of first love, I only saw what was different. And it was a difference that I wanted to be mine.

Call me Isaac after the binding, though Pa would have called me a fool if he had known the life I craved instead of the one he had ordained as a fitting sacrifice on the stone of dull labor. To his mind, I should have recognized that the Midway was a hollow promise and denied my joy. If I was a good God-fearing Christian, I should have turned my back on the Carnival Devil, returned to plow and pew a better man for swallowing the bitter truth.

16

Far from it—I was already an apostate and would always be. I saw my future in that sleight of hand and knew that I would become the man in the rumpled suit, slicked-back hair beneath a battered fedora, smoking a five-dollar cigar while I rolled the vagaries of the mother-tongue through a hand-held mike.

Say Carrot Top, you look like a smart fellow.
But I bet a dollar I can tell you where you got your shoes.
Sure, I can. Chump change, but it's soooo easy I would feel bad
Taking you for more than a buck.
Tell you where you got your shoes. The very city and street.
Can't be wrong. Won't be wrong.
Are you a bright boy, a man who appreciates useful knowledge,
Willing to make that small wager to learn
How I know this fact?
Well, thank-you. Thank-you. I'll just hold that dollar now and
Give it back with one of its ilk if I'm wrong.
There you go, just put your old George Washington next to
mine.
Here it comes. Tell you true as your God is my witness
Here it is.
You got your shoes on your feet, right here
On the Midway of the County Fairgrounds.
Thank-you, thank-you...
I'll take that look on your face as a very small price for your
education,
For your tuition in the school of useful truth,
Now move along.

4—Family Stories

My pa, he always liked cows better than people. He'd sit for the better part of the day and sometimes a good bit of the night at the far end of the barn smoking his pipe in a broke down armchair that my ma made him take out of the house. Once in a while, he'd fiddle with the pipe, cleaning it or loading it from packets of close-out cherry blend tobacco he bought when one of the local drug stores went out of business. He'd pinch a little bit of graying tobacco and shove it in the pipe with his finger, then pinch another bit and repeat the process. Always used his little finger to pack it in. During that ritual nuisance of loading the pipe, he would grudgingly accept any question I might proffer about chores or the world. He'd offer a half-hearted comment on the weather or remind me of some Bible chapter and verse, but that was the extent of his fatherly advice.

Everything that was my life was nonsense to him. Everything that was anything but toil was foreign and not to be trusted, especially if it was in a mother tongue uttered by a banker or lawyer, preacher or politician, or for that matter, by Ma or me.

When he put the pipe back in, the only sound that followed would be the creak of the chair and the rustle of the cows in the stall. I'd watch the puffs fill the silence and the thin smoke rising through the shafts of light seeping through the cracks in the barn wall and tell myself that it wasn't only me. He never talked much to anyone. I used to think that it was an act of rebellion to run my mouth like I do, but I realized long ago that he hardly even noticed, or if he did, he never cared enough to have a conversation. The plain fact was that my old man didn't really like people. Didn't like talking to them. Didn't like being around them. It's a wonder he ever sired me, though more than once, I suspected that I looked more like his brother, Ray, than I looked like Pa.

He wasn't surprised that I left. When the day finally arrived, he looked up and said that he always figured it would be the army or jail, not a two-bit traveling carnival that I'd pack my bags for.

My ma, on the other hand, liked people, or at least liked the idea of people, though she was judgmental as hell about them. She would sit in church on Sunday and scribble little notes to herself in the prayer book about the way other people dressed or acted. She'd say hello to whomever she approved of that week in a voice so soft and sweet you'd think it was honey. Didn't fool anyone, but in our Sunday meeting community, we all pretended to have charity and good manners. Them that knew she had passed judgment on their trespasses tended to avoid her lest she get in one of her holier-than-everybody moods, break the polite façade and deliver a public scolding for sins real or imagined. Them that didn't know where they stood with her didn't come round any more frequently than obligation required. I could never figure out how anyone got on her good side once she condemned them to that prayer book. Maybe she just forgot what she was mad about, or they would manage to do something that won her approval. I never saw her remove a name from the book, but after she died, I took a good look at it and saw that more than a few had actually been erased.

At home, she ruled with a cast iron skillet. Ma measured the world by what she could cook and whether or not you ate it up. She was one of the founding mothers of the clean plate club, and under her rule, I left home heavy and have been wasting away ever since. When she died, Pa lost what little interest he had in eating, so he gave me the cast iron. I went home from my long exile in the land of idolaters and casual fornicators for the funeral and came back with the family skillet. I didn't have the nerve to cook with it for the first year, just carried it from town to town and set it on the back burner of whatever stove or hotplate was to be found as an altar to her devotion. Yes, that first year after her passing, I just dog-sniffed that black well of memory, longing for the taste of her pancakes.

After that, I used it, knowing those elemental pancakes were done and gone.

5—Introductions

I got out of the Lincoln, put my suitcoat on, straightened my bow tie and began introducing myself as the guy who had been hired to help out. When they asked how, I'd ask if they would introduce me to the next closest person I had not met or asked back what they did, quick as a rabbit darting away to outrun the fox. Not that I was avoiding the question of how I was going to help—I just didn't want anyone to start off thinking I was the new boss. Not yet, anyways.

My appearance hinted of insurance adjuster or accountant as much as anything else and was intended to do so. Rumpled gray suit, sensible shoes, white shirt and a plain bow tie. Not quite a fashion plate, or even fashionable, but suggestive of early '60s business class. I took off the Ray Bans and made a point to smile while I looked every one of 'em in the eye.

Not until I gave Flat Frank my final answer did I want to announce I was there to crack the metaphorical whip, and I wasn't going to signal Frank until I got a really good look at who and what the rag-tag company was. I needed at least a couple of hours of walk and talk before I would know whether there was really any point to get behind the "how" I would help or if I even had a clue as to where to start.

Met quite a few that was there that day. To my surprise, most of who would end up being the actual touring company was on the farm that day. I won't go into all the names and histories now. Hell, for most of the tour, the core was at least twenty-five performers, a half dozen road rats for the tent heaving and truck loading, another half dozen performers' kids in and out of diapers or old enough to be in school but weren't. I didn't know then which of the undetermined number of extras who were also present were wives, girlfriends, boyfriends or some vague relations who might or might not have been filling in the bit parts or just hanging around for company when they weren't coming or going. There must have been thirty or more warm bodies present that day, and I was of a mind to shake every one of their hands.

It's hard enough for me to keep track of who was who when the names aren't stuck like peanut butter to white bread and near impossible to say on first sight. I'd like to say that it got sorted out once we were on the road, but the truth is, all the way down to New Orleans, there was some of my asking, who is that guy carrying the amp or the girl I saw putting on the fish suit.

There were at least two dogs, and one of them had a wooden leg.

Suffice to say that halfway through my walk and talk, I had already started dividing everyone I met into two groups: those that did the work now and would do the work later and everybody who didn't do much now and could be left behind when it came time to head on out. Say what you will about sorting them into the two camps based on a handshake and small talk. Yes, it was a harsh and sudden judgment that had been acquired through long years of practice and honed by bitter lessons. In those days, I was still of the school of crisis management that said be as sharp as paper cut and twice as quick.

When the time came for the actual touring, I wasn't a bit surprised at how little the lists had changed from day one. I know of what I speak. Twenty years with traveling shows and strip clubs had taught me something about how to eyeball who'd be worth the day's pay.

6—Marcel

There was one guy I knew there from a previous gig working a medicine show on the county fair circuit about fifteen years past. Marcel was his name. Or it was the last time I worked with him. Thin shadow of a guy looking to weigh about the same as any horse jockey. Don't let that small size fool you. He was in the "working all day long" faction that I would take on any tour anywhere. He was also in the "partying all night" group, but that didn't seem to stop him from doing what needed to be done come sun up.

I was glad to see Marcel. He could be a wild ride on a loose mount, but he was another one of a dollar's worth of sweat for the buck guys. He was, as I said, thin as a knife's edge, with taped-together glasses and a thatch of straw-colored hair that looked like a five-year-old cut it with a pair of dull scissors. Always had a smile and a quick-witted comment, even when he didn't have a thing to say.

Doctore, is that you?

None other, Marcel, and glad to see you, I said, putting my arm around his shoulder. I see you're sporting some specs these days.

Yah, I got them for the driver's license.

Don't say. I reached over and straightened them as they began sliding down on his nose. Wear them to drive, do you?

I wear them all the time. Got in the habit of wearing them when I was going to college.

You've been going to college? Congratulations. What were you studying? I asked, trying to imagine him in a classroom. Not an easy task, mind you, though seeing him at any three-keg frat party was easy enough.

Theater. It required the fewest books. He laughed. Yup, I even graduated, and here I am…

In the same line of work you were in before you went to school. Quite a feat, I laughed, to have spent four or five years and a pile of cash you didn't have to get a diploma you don't need.

I got a scholarship from Uncle Sam, he said, because of my disability. He held up the left arm with the silver hook at the end and pushed his glasses back up the bridge of his nose. But I'll tell you, Doctore, you march into a theater class with this, and you wind up playing the pirate every time. I wanted to play Romeo, and sometimes sweet Juliet, so the typecasting got pretty boring after a while.

We both laughed as I pulled him in close to ask sotto voce: Are you in for the long haul?

I believe so. He shrugged. I've been here a few days looking after the stock, doing some stilt work and playing a little with the band. But if you're on board this one, Doc, it'll be a lot more interesting than what I was bracing myself for. I mean, they're good people, but most of them are actors. Not that there's anything wrong with theater people…

After all, you're one, I said. We both took a moment to let that sink in.

Marcel continued, so if you didn't bring the old RV with you, there's a bed waiting for you up there. He pointed toward the house. The men's rooms are mostly on the third floor, I think. I don't sleep in the house 'cause, as you know, I like to…. He stopped mid-sentence and stepped back to look me up and down. Holy Mother of all that's good, Doctore, I'm glad to see you in the flesh. It's always better when you're working a deal.

Yes, and this deal will be some wonder to behold…. I started to laugh myself but choked it off. If you don't mind, Spirit, let's keep this present circumstance between ourselves. No need to tell the actors that the director has arrived.

He looked at me and smiled. Oh no, Buzz, why ruin the surprise?

I wanted to savor the moment before I went up to the house to claim a bunk. Take in another breath of fresh air, feel the warm sun through the trees, the breeze bringing the smell of wildflowers across the meadow, the whole bucolic scene. Might as well add my oft-favored scent to the day. I pulled a cigar out of my coat pocket and fired it up.

Care for a smoke?

No, I gave that up in favor of booze, he said, inhaling the smoke that I had just exhaled. I can't afford two vices. He stopped, looking like a child that just been caught swallowing something they were not supposed to have. So, I chose the most expensive and immediately painful option.

I'll have to see if I can do something to make it easier for you, I said, handing him a cigar. If you don't want it now, put it away for an emergency. You never know when you'll have need of the transitory pleasure that follows the lighting up of a fine Dominican or Cuban when you can get one, or really any hand-rolled leaf.

Marcel took it and put it in his blue denim shirt pocket. I see you're driving a certified land yacht.

Yes, Spirit, a genuine '68 Lincoln with butter-tanned leather seats, I said as I opened the trunk.

What did this one cost?

Nowhere near as much as you'd expect to pay, but I will admit the maintenance for a relic such as this tends to stretch the budget in ways that make every shade tree mechanic who looks at it say, well, we'll have to send away for parts. They always have to send away for parts.

I pulled out my suitcase and the antique leather Doctor's bag that held my traveling office, which meant it held everything useful or that mattered to me. Then I said, Marcel, when position requires you to go big, you might as well go impressive.

And you still have a world of wonders in a carrying case.

Just like old times, Spirit. It is as it always was. I knocked the ash off my cigar and pinched the glowing tip. Might as well save the rest for the evening's ambulation. I'll have this sacred fire later with a small dose of the old medicinal I carry in this repository, I said, tapping the bag.

Still indulging that imported stuff?

As time and wallet allow, I say there is beauty in a twelve-year cask single malt as a norm. It is as consistent as the tick following the tock. You know the drill. Beer of necessity and for brushing the teeth, red wine for health, cognac to ward off the winter chill. Any of the Kentucky gentlemen when moonshine isn't at hand to be sociable, but Scotch remains my vice of choice, although martinis are an indulgence I've taken up in my dotage. A crap shoot, of course, until I meet a bartender that knows how to make a proper one. Then, worth sipping a second.

Shaken, not stirred?

Vermouth in and out again before the gin or vodka enter, stage left. Hell, just pass the green bottle over and let a single drop fall.

Marcel saluted me and turned to go his way. I circled the other direction toward the house, carrying my suitcase and the office bag. I nodded to the rag-tag crew fanned out along the porch. They were reading newspapers. The two women at sewing machines under the shade of the trees entered and headed up the plain wooden stairs.

On the third floor, I looked in each of the five oddly-sized and -shaped bedrooms to guess which were occupied by singles, couples or familial units. In the third room, two bunk beds stood on opposite walls with a single chair in the middle of the room. I surmised from the beer bottles, shaving kit on the chair and pants on the floor that it was single-guy territory. I put my suitcase on the top bunk of the farthest bed and lay on the thin mattress below. It reminded me of something— the army or jail came to mind, though I had been lucky enough to not actually spend any time in the former or serious time in the latter.

Then it hit me. This was like summer camp. The fragrant bouquet was familiar—unwashed socks, mildew and bodily fluids that had been absorbed by the mattress. The way the light came through the unwashed window, I saw newly budding trees as Van Gogh or Monet would have—as slabs of vibrating color. It was neither too comfortable nor too miserable to refuse. This would do for the two months we would be here building and rehearsing the show.

I lay down and closed my eyes, thinking that a catnap was what my inner doctor had ordered. When I got up, I would head to Junior's and call Frank to push the paperwork. I was here now, and, like Marcel, might as well see how the story ended.

7–Eggs and Bacon

The next morning, I came downstairs a little before seven to an awkward silence from the two brown-haired women drinking coffee in the kitchen. The small woman at the table, who I thought was named Rona, offered a few words: I take it that you're going to be the show's ringmaster.

News travels fast. Not that I had told anyone but Frank, but in service of knowing what's what, I made a note to find out how it had gotten back there so soon and to keep my wary eye on who brought it.

I believe that will be one of my functions, was my reply to the woman. I forced the friendliest smile I could muster before coffee and said, More to the point, I will also function as the tour manager, the keeper of the schedule and the purse, the arbiter of all contracts and the manifestation of the man, or men, or whoever the hell is owning and underwriting this traveling world of wonders from behind the velvet curtain.

Why didn't you tell us that yesterday? The woman asked. It feels like you're starting off on the wrong foot.

I hadn't decided yesterday whether this was worth the blood, sweat and tears that are sure to come. I responded, But you look capable of making what will be a long tour, and now that it is decided, let's be absolutely clear, young lady, that I do not start anything on the wrong foot.

Rona said nothing. Picking up her cup, she left the table and the room.

I might have to do some fence-mending with her later, but once said, my words hung in the air like dust mores in sunlight.

I recognized the blond at the stove was one of the Swede Girls I had met the day before, but at that point, I couldn't tell which was which as they were both about the same size, had identical haircuts and language skills.

Congratulations, she said in her charming accent, raising her coffee cup in a half toast before she brought it to her lips.

Thanks. I'm sure that in the days to come, we'll all get as cozy as bed bugs in a sawbuck motel.

I surprised her with that one as she had the look of someone trying to puzzle a meaning out of a riddle. Hell, I surprised myself as well, and rather than stumble further into a linguistic bramble of left-over Southernisms and old carnival colloquial, I walked over to the coffee pot and poured a cup.

It appeared the news was out. It didn't much matter how it had come out, the fact of it would make the rounds of the Rex crew faster than lightning to a golf club mid-swing, and they'd be looking at me differently now. For some, it would be the expectation of some kind of order amid the nascent chaos. For others, it would be a distanced disdain born of a mistrust of authority. Been there, done that on both counts. It made little difference. That first day I was going to continue observing who and what. I had no need to make any rash decisions or exert authority. I could afford to be the sphinx for another twenty-four hours. Let them guess whether my essential management style was Godzilla or Santa Claus.

I hardly knew myself what would be called for. What I knew was the coffee was hot and black, the day was sunny, and I wanted some bacon, eggs and crisp hash browns. When I opened the refrigerator door, I saw that I was going to be bitterly disappointed. That cavern did not know bacon—only fruit, vegetables, yogurt and what looked to be some kind of tofu.

I'll be back in an hour, I said to no one in particular.

I walked out the door, fired up the Lincoln and headed for Alma to find a decent breakfast. Once the bacon, eggs and a side of blueberry cakes had been ordered, I started making checklists in my little notebook. One list of who was doing what in and out of the show. I'd fill in the few names I already knew and spend the day adding names and functions as I walked the Rex grounds. Then a list of what would have to get put in place before the first performance. I had no idea if the show could be ready in three weeks, but if the schedule Flat Frank had relayed to me on the phone last night was accurate, the first outing would be at the headwaters of the Mississippi. I had told Frank he'd better mail me everything that he had if he expected to report to the Absent Owners that we were good to go because I'd need a little help identifying the specifics for this show and, more importantly, for the demands of the holy days of performing according to the schedule. What the assembled company's capacity to churn out product remained a mystery, but years of touring made the large strokes of what had to be done as clear as greasy fingerprints on the water glass.

There would be a third list of just what the hell I needed to do by the day, the week and for the entirety of the tour. I'd make that list in the smallest script I could manage, tear it out of the notebook, fold it twice and shove it in my wallet next to Ben Franklin. For more years than I can count, I've believed that it is good to have a hundred-dollar bill tucked away. It is a reminder that you are not poor. Not yet. The moment you spend it, you work to replace it with another. Keeps you sharp. Keeps you focused not on your wants but your wills. It is good to have a reality checklist next to Ben to remind you of the small steps taken every day that make the journey possible. It is double good to keep both within reach.

8–Central Organizing Committee

Two days in, I understood that the basic Rex building and rehearsal schedule had already settled into a weird variation of someone's summer camp experience—get up, eat what usually amounted to toasted bread with butter, honey or jam, black coffee from an industrial pot and oatmeal as thick as wet cement and about the same color. Then out for the morning exercise routines at nine o'clock—stretching and limbering up with a digression into yoga or martial arts, depending on who was leading them before getting to whatever else was on that day's agenda.

The agenda for each day was set at eight o'clock by an ad hoc central organizing committee consisting of Miss Red Boots, who was the big cat girl who seemed to be the de facto idea generator; Ben from the band; Sonja, the chief costumer; and freckle-faced Sissy, who did something I had not quite identified yet. They met at breakfast to determine each day's priority tasks and rehearsal schedule. I pointed out that as ringmaster and tour manager, I should be in that meeting. They agreed, but when I attended the next morning palaver, it seemed like a whole lot of nothing got decided, and neither my opinion nor Ben's was asked for or validated when offered. I might have the title, but at the moment, I did not have the control. That would change, but not before I confirmed who was the brains and who was the muscle on the de facto women's committee.

There wasn't much collective decision-making in the company except when they thought everyone needed to be "heard," and then all progress stopped as everyone gathered to speak at great length about any and every grievance, real or imagined, and the philosophical basis for doing whatever pro or con any company member posited as a solution to those very same complaints or problems.

The reciting of an action plan always fell to one of the central organizing committee women. What they said may or may not accord with what had just been proffered by the rabble. Hell, a couple of times, it was not clear that the summation of what would happen was even in the same universe as the rainbows and stardust-sprinkled conversation that proceeded it.

After my first experience with one of those confabs, I resolved to avoid having any group meetings if possible. My preference was that when I called people together, it would be to tell, not ask.

On the other hand, despite the easily conflicting emotions within the company, the decision-making mechanism was both more organic and more efficient than it appeared to be. As things needed to get done, someone would notice the fact of it and, like your busybody Aunt Martha, would just up and do it. Generally, the central organizing committee meetings boiled down to the same thing—each of them announcing this is what I'm doing today and then getting up to do it.

Every morning after the warm-ups, there was a merry-go-round of rehearsals for individual acts with whoever wanted to watch, then a session of commenting and suggesting changes. Acrobats, high wire walkers, clowns, stilts—they each had their turn in the meadow. The only act that everyone wanted to watch and had a fixed place in the day was Miss Red Boots and the tigers. It never got old watching her move them off their stands and then roll and leap, put their paws on her shoulders and jump through a hoop of fire. On most days, she'd skip the fire, and you'd be watching two hundred pounds of striped feline sail through a wire hoop like it was nothing. Of course, one of the reasons I couldn't take my eye off her was that while she treated her beasts like they were house cats, I knew that even a house cat would nip and swipe now and again. A nip or swipe from one of these tigers could be fatal. The last thing I wanted to do was deal with tigers gone bad or trainers entering emergency rooms, or worse yet, exiting this vale of tears.

9—Miss Red Boots

How Miss Red Boots came to the circus is an interesting story, but if I go into the whole of it now, we'll be derailed before we start. Besides, I don't know if I ever knew the whole of it. Suffice it to say that she was the circus or at least the heart of it. Whether it was a grandfather's inheritance or some ex-husband's divorce offering, Miss Red Boots, the big striped cats, her brother VX and the camel, all arrived with the circus tent on day one. Where she went, the rest followed.

She was not one to peel back her own story, so what little I got came from VX.

For starters, Miss Red Boots is clearly not her name but the familiar one I gave her due to the footwear she used in the ring. Victoria was her given handle. The same goes for VX, whose given name was Vincent. I came to call him VX because the peculiar slant of his left-handed penmanship created a large, stylized V at the front of his name and an equally large crossed t at the back that slanted like an X.

Miss Red Boots and VX were not twins, though it would have been easy to think so given the similarity of their traits—thin frames, curling hair, easy gaits, speech and mannerisms. She was the "knows better" older sister, and he was the "here, hold my beer" younger brother. Preacher's kids, they had grown up in a succession of prairie parsonages.

She had gone to Europe to study medicine and came back with tigers in hand. You and I both know there is a mystery in that sentence, but even VX didn't know how to unravel it in a way that would explain anything because he was fiercely protective of her and probably wouldn't share that secret if he knew it. She wouldn't cross that threshold of personal history no matter how many times we danced to the door. By the same token, she was totally uninterested in my story. We were simply working on a something that was bigger than us. We did not need the genealogy of how we came to learn our lessons. For her, the past was not prologue. For Miss Red Boots, even more than me, what was done was done.

Vincent was another matter. He had dropped out of high school to explore all things mechanical. He liked to know what went where and what happened when tab A was inserted into slot B. He liked to talk about his "sowing wild oats" past, the experiments gone wrong and the bones broken. When I didn't worry for his safety, it made him the kind of problem solver every circus needs.

10–Building the Beast

About noon each day, if anyone had bothered to cook, we'd eat a meal that generally consisted of some kind of soup and salad, cold cuts, cheese and bread washed down with lemonade or lukewarm beer. It was an even-odds bet as to what lunch was at that point in the adventure. No one was assigned to cooking, and no one consistently put their hand to the spatula.

The road rats didn't even bother coming to the kitchen. Instead, they fired up a battered grill next to the old pig shed most of them slept in. They lived on a diet of hot dogs, chips and beer. More than once, I found myself wandering in that direction at lunch to see what the news and gossip was from the "tote that barge, lift that bale" contingent. They always had wildly inaccurate gossip about everyone else and a wide selection of filthy jokes to pass the time.

Of all the Rex personnel that came and went, the road crew went the most. They were clearly living by a stealth schedule unknown to the central organizing committee, and that was just the way those boys wanted to keep it. How can I miss you if I don't know you're gone? There were always one or two guys present and working, but not always the same guys. Every time I went to Pig Heaven, I'd have to ask where so-and-so was or welcome what's-his-name back to the fold. In the end, the road rats that would be the beasts of burden for setting up and tearing down the Rex would have self-selected and made sure they could depend on each other to lift and fit, bolt and rig the mechanics that made the space for the sparkle to shine. It was the carny way. They knew it, I knew it, and I trusted them to hew true to the grain of it.

After lunch, there'd be some attempt at running a show from end to end with whatever acts the committee thought were ready to insert in whatever sequence felt right. Nothing was fixed except there had to be a grand entrance and, hopefully, an equally grand exit. Everything in between was trial and mostly error. All the time, Miss Red Boots and Ben were making notes. She was trying to arrive at some kind of grand theatrical theme for the show—something to unify and inspire, something that made sense with a camel and tigers but not an elephant in sight. Ben was trying to interpret her notes to arrive at writing or arranging the right kind of "jaunty" music to support this act or that transition from one act to another. Of the two, he seemed to be making more progress.

The remainder of the afternoon was like the morning, only more fragrant as the sweat rolled down necks and stained shirts. Everyone took a dollop of "free time" in the heat of the day, which generally meant doing whatever was unfinished from the morning, making leisurely trips to the river to swim or fish, more trips into town to buy this or that thing that had been forgotten or gone unnoticed the first time someone went. Some of the Rex crew took naps, some would read or write letters, but mostly folks worked without the bother of the buzzing hive. The unspoken rule of thumb was whatever was good for the individual was also in service of the whole. Building or repairing this or that was always a task for anyone who was around, assisted by whoever else was at hand. Every day, some build or repair got done. It was clear that the community would settle into building the beast in increments and that by luck or pluck, the Rex would be an actual company by the time we hit the road.

Using the notebook in my pocket, I'd repeatedly check the who's who list, charting who was on the farm doing what on any given day. It came in handy when I got to the singular moment everyone wanted my attention, the golden hour of handing out the pay envelopes. In theory, everyone was getting paid the same pauper's pittance, but the one power I did have that no one else did was the ability to add or subtract cash to the weekly stipend to match actual time served. When I subtracted, there was a plea and the requisite "But I did this or that, "followed by the promise to make up lost time or effort if I could just add the absent bucks back in. It usually took just two rounds of subtractions for folks to figure out that this was going to be the iron fist of capitalist exploitation of the workers. After that, they'd check in with me before they left and when they came back to keep me from dinging them a penny.

11–Bread and Water

Supper consisted of something healthy. It was the one meal that folks signed up for. They'd then cook what they thought was good for the rest of us. One night, there was a yellow lentil soup with wedges of sweet onion floating in it like so many tiny icebergs, cornbread with butter and honey, sliced raw vegetables (mostly tomatoes and carrots), several cheeses, more cold cuts, more lemonade and beer. Another night we had kabobs for the grill with lots of veggies and a few chunks of chicken clinging to a skewer for dear life. Other frequent offerings included three-bean salad and pasta noodles with a thin, spicy red sauce. Cheese was present at every meal, and meat was usually AWOL.

Bread was baked every other day, though I don't remember who did it. Maybe elves because every morning, there would be warm loaves on the table with a knife for slicing and a crock of butter waiting to be spread. It was good bread, with a substantial crust and a light, almost airy chew inside. It smelled of joy and was the perfect repository for local honey or creamery butter. I thought the regular appearance of such delight was a little bit of cruelty because once the tour began, there seldom would be time or facilities for anyone to make six loaves, or even one, for that matter.

Two weeks past my arrival, some folks were showing signs of borderline protein deprivation. We were getting thinner, and not just because heat and motion were taking it out of us. By then, the communal kitchen was suffering under the occupation of militant vegetarians who believed that tofu had the same nutritional profile as red meat. Their belief was not an altar that I genuflect at. It was, to my mind, a dubious distinction, but having already seen the budget, I knew of necessity it leaned away from red meat. Hell, it shied away from beef to chicken, and really, given how little was allocated for actually feeding a company of our size, slouched toward beans and rice. It might have just been my prejudice, but if I was losing weight—and I was—so was everyone else.

Every time a meal was late or missing, I reminded myself that I needed to hire a real cook, and the sooner, the better. Maybe not now while we were building this magnificent mousetrap, but once we were going to set the wheels of no return in motion, someone who knew how to feed the clamoring multitudes on the march with a budget the size of a titmouse would be a very helpful appendage. The days of too many or not enough cooks to spoil the soup would come back to haunt us as sure as the splinters on the wooden spoon sticking out of the gray mush I ate most mornings. The question was, where would I find the genius who could balance the interests of the carrot eaters with the "bring on the bacon" set?

Even if I had to pay a little more, it would be worth the effort of finding some old institutional cook who knew the joy of cheap cuts and the secret of making it go further than anyone imagined. It wouldn't matter if they were fresh out of the service or the state pen. If they could cook for forty, they'd be my man or woman.

At this point, you may be wondering why all this talk of food. That old saying, "An army travels on its stomach," is true of all large groups. Hunger has driven a wedge between a man and good sense more times than bad luck. Besides, I know what's coming a little further in this story.

If I had been hired before the Rex budget had been made, life's bitter lessons would have told me to fight tooth and nail for a lot more attention being given to the meals. But in that regard, I was Johnny come lately in learning that slow malnutrition would cost more in the end than anyone might guess when the powers that be took a red pencil to meat.

My goal of finding a cook got put aside when a more immediate problem of no water took center stage. Even though the well man twice had been out to look at the pump, it had not been fixed. What water there was had to be carried by someone from somewhere else. That water was reserved for making coffee or tea, for washing hands in the kitchen and for actually cooking. For drinking, there was bottled water bought in town over the objections of the conscientious, who declared their opposition to plastic bottles. These folks turned to glass jars refilled from the spigot at Junior's or the public park next to the river. As a consequence, a day came when no one seemed to be washing dishes or utensils beyond the pots and pans. It was an outright invitation to some kind of gastronomical disaster like typhoid. Paper plates were deemed to be the new norm until the budding environmentalists complained about wasting trees and also the smell of burning garbage at twilight. That's when the central organizing committee came up with a policy of having assigned plates and cups with your name written on them and silverware that you would wash yourself or bear the risk of food poisoning.

It was sheer dumb luck that no one was hospitalized.

Take a shower or bath? Are you kidding? No one wanted to use as much water as it took for that level of hygiene and tended to surface-wash with a wet cloth or bring a bar of soap along when they went swimming in the river. The Mississippi wasn't quite the Big Muddy in Alma. Besides, wet was wet, and lye soap was cheap.

Eventually, the well guy did get the missing part installed, and the water flowed again, but by then, we had gotten used to the stink of being human on a warm spring day. Just as well, because by the time the Rex rolled into New Orleans, we would be able to identify each other in the dark by scent alone.

12–Even or Odd

Following supper, if it was an even day, there was singing or music rehearsals and sometimes dancing. People would sit in a circle on the lawn singing shape note spirituals and '50s rock and roll while the eight-piece circus band banged out the tunes. It reminded me of the better part of church. There was something charming in the ease of it. On the odd nights, the women sewed or baked, and the men headed over to Junior's tap for yet another beer and some eight ball on the green felt table. No, that couldn't be right. Junior's might have been cheap, but on circus wages of seventy bucks cash per week, no one could afford Junior's three times a week.

Yes, that's right. Ten bucks a day was the per diem. Why anyone would work for a Hamilton a day was a mystery to me back then, and it still is. It went a long way to explaining the mix of naiveté and street survivor aesthetic that permeated the assembled multitude. But even at that cheap payout, once you got done handing thirty-some performers and roadies their pittance, we were burning through three thousand a week and hadn't done a single performance yet.

People were camped around the farm according to function. Four or five pickups used for hauling small items were clustered near the barn, and the six or seven cars on any given night parked along the gravel drive. It occurred to me that the proof of the ad hoc nature of this circus was manifest in that there were no new or even used RVs or three-quarter ton dual rear wheel rigs pulling trailers among the lot of them. Pickups with campers were seen, but the comfortable RVs that are the mark of modern circus and carnival culture were not. In the first class shows, folks would indenture themselves for a decade of wages to pay for the comfort of a thirty-foot Airstream hauled by a three-quarter-ton Chevy.

For the Rex, tents were closer to the norm, pitched in the spaces between trees or at the edge of a field. As I said, the old hog barn had been converted into a frat boy's dorm for the road rats. You could smell the ganja twenty feet from the door. Those who didn't have tents or campers slept in the house. It was a slumber party turned on its head and extended as far as you dared imagine.

The two dogs seemed to prefer sleeping beneath the hammock on the porch. Big Bearded Jim, who was responsible for Jack, the peg-legged canine, often slept in that hammock.

Farm life was improvisational. The performer's kids played with sticks, balls or makeshift toys in the shade of a willow tree. There was always a sewing machine or two next to the flowerbed with an extension cord leading back to the house where costumer Sue transformed bolts of blue spangled cloth into pantaloon pants for the band. The band would set up at the end of sixty feet of extension cords beside the ring for the daytime rehearsals and spend half the night jamming in the barn hay loft. They played hot and sweet, sounding twice as big as their few numbers.

Life was at once and always a race between improvisation and impending disaster.

13–Sharon

We woke up one morning with no electricity and no water. Scott the Dog, a big-bodied smile of a man with a full beard, who was certainly not a dog though he played Rover in one of the comedy acts, decided the proper response to the crisis was to look at all the fuses in the box, unscrew each one, spit on it, re-screw it with a penny at the base and then take a field trip to get some more. Not that he knew which were good or which were bad. It was the ritual of testing that mattered. And since he was going into Alma, he'd get just a few eggs and some bacon while he was at it.

The lack of electricity and Scott's breakfast suggestion turned out to be a popular crisis. It might have taken twenty minutes to organize who would drive what to which of Alma's three breakfast destinations, but fully half the Rex crew abandoned the pretext of that morning's schedule and headed to town. Pick a car. Get in. Drive. As Big Daddy used to say, when it is time to get on the bus, it is time to get on the bus, and when the circus bus left, our old bad habits needed to wave goodbye from the curb.

I climbed into the Lincoln to drive into town. I had actual errands that needed my attention at the post office and the bus station. Okay, I'll admit that I stopped at the little café by the railroad tracks where the waitress called everybody "Honey" and had a plate of ham, eggs over easy and rye toast with a decent strawberry jam. Slim Jim and his wife, Ruth, were in another booth eating pancakes. I nodded to them as I walked by and mumbled that I was waiting for Sharon, one of my old touring compadres, to get off the bus from Minneapolis.

They didn't need to know that, and they didn't care, but I said it anyway because waiting for the bus to arrive was the truth that justified the java stop. Flat Frank was having her stop by in his effort to get me a full complement of experienced touring performers to make this one-ring wonder profitable.

She's not keen on another tour, he said, but she wants to see you. God knows why, Buzz, but when I said you were at the helm, she allowed as how she'd be willing to make the stop. Must be sweet on you.

I think not, I said. We never went down the romance road. That would have been more trouble than a Georgia sheriff looking to fill a ticket quota. Jesus curing the blind, Frank, not with that girl. She's more Jezebel than I ever wanted and all the happier for never going there. Besides, you know as well as I do that I'm not likely to dip my pen in company ink even if she was sweet enough on me to sign for the duration of the Rex. Mixing business and knocking boots? I think not. Bad for business. And unless you're married to the act, bad for everyone trying to get along.

The Minneapolis to Chicago bus stopped at every town. When it arrived with a squeal of brakes and the wheeze of the door opening, the woman who got out looked not quite like the Sharon I knew. More like her older sister. She was still a tall, thin woman. Long brown hair and a big gap-tooth smile but looking more—let's call it… experienced. Half worn out, but still trying for pretty. She had often worked as a contortionist, but she could do any acrobatics, slack rope or ball act if there was any call for that.

She seemed to have aged ten years since I last toured her. And, of course, she had. But it was her walking with a limp that caught my attention. I wasn't going to ask, but right off, I understood why she might not want this kind of job anymore. What the hell, it was still good to see her, and it'd be good to have a conversation over a beer before she decided against the touring.

Hey, babe, got a kiss for a man who hasn't kissed you in years?

Look at you, she said, running her hand through the waterfall of thick brown tresses falling from crown to broad shoulders. You don't look a day older.

It was cheap flattery, but I took it the way butter takes to a warm biscuit.

She gave me a peck on the cheek, and I could smell the mix of patchouli oil and peppermint soap that was her unnatural fragrance. We drove out to the farm without saying much about the years since we had gone our separate ways. She asked about a couple of people we mutually knew, and I answered with as little as I could possibly say about people I had not seen since I had last seen her. On my side of the unspoken, I wasn't interested in talking about late-night radio in Madison, so there was little profit in why I had or had not kept in touch with the old gang of mine, hers... ours.

We listened to the kind of cloying country music that made me want to turn the dial but made her want to sing along, which she did. I did not ask about what's-his-name, the guy she ran off with when she quit the last gig we worked together, and she did not offer. I suspected that she'd left him somewhere on the sawdust trail, or maybe he'd left her. Hell, it's the way of every world where men and women are rash enough to fall in love. I've been in love enough to believe that nothing good can come of 90 percent of it but twenty miles of barbed wire heartbreak, and yet when that 10 percent of paradise by the dashboard light kicks in, it's magic enough to keep us all trying.

Sharon spent the first half hour getting introduced to as much of the company as crossed our path. Beginning with Mia and Maya, the Swede Girls who were doing the acrobat routines and a European-style clown act. Then she had a chat with Miss Red Boots and Miss Red Boots' tall, handsome brother, VX, who immediately got a little Sharon flirting action. A wink and a hand out to touch his muscled arm just inside the elbow, followed by a slow trailing of the fingers down the arm to the wrist. He shook his curly head like he had just got a jolt of electricity, smiled his gap toothy grin and blushed. She laughed and let it go. She met Elijah and his wife, Sonja, another costumer, followed by the two pairs of lovebirds—Tom and Claire, as well as Slim Jim and Ruth, now back from pancake time. Scott the Dog and his prettier half Rose and three kids were still in town, so they would be introduced when they returned or possibly not at all. It was just as well that I'd skip their introductions, because at that point, I wasn't sure I could put the right kid with the proper name. They were all blond, blue-eyed and rosy-cheeked cherubs somewhere under four years old.

She met chief tinkerer Loren Red Beard, the only member of the road rat crew that straddled the performing side as well. He was the Rex's constant and would be doing the whole river, though he too was obsessively involved in his own projects on his own time schedule. A nod to Big Beard Jim, who once had been a lawyer but now was better known as the guy who brought Jack, the three-legged dog, to see the circus. I was in the process of introducing her to Ben and his brother Danny when she saw Marcel. Sharon lost all interest in meeting the band and stared at Marcel.

Who's the guy with the hook? she said, pointing to Marcel as he crossed the field with a bucket of something on the way to the camel pen. He looks familiar. Do I know him?

Marcel, I said, trying to gauge how interested she was in meeting Marcel. Does she know him from some other gig? Has she some curiosity about how he lost the hand?

Then it hit me. Of course, she knew him, and she could tell the story of the hook better than I could. If she met him, she'd remember everything in the time it takes a fly to hit the windowpane—the whole terrible where and when of their history. It was legendary, at least in my orbit. I had heard at least three versions of that sad story over the years. One of them was Marcel's version, but since he didn't name names of amores, I had never quite fit the pieces into place so as to put him and her into the right chronology of crashing comets until just now. Once upon a time, they met, she flirted, then slept with him for twenty-five hundred miles across five states, then tossed him out like he was yesterday's popcorn oil.

Oh shit, I thought, this could be as hard as getting the mule to turn the plow at the end of a row. Maybe they will just acknowledge that was then and this isn't, or maybe it will be a fuckin' soap opera of painful recrimination and insufferable Diva the length of the Mississippi. Either way, I'm not telling her what I know—just hold it in my vest pocket until needed.

Let her claim her sorry story or let Marcel remind her of how "back in the day" she left him without a left hand when she broke his too-eager heart, stomped on it and went to the next affair. She was just doing what she did as naturally as a female praying mantis. He was doing what innocent men do. It was a simple disaster all around played out over multiple months and half as many states as were on that tour.

14—Innocent Man

Don't be afraid. I'm not.

Spirit Marcel says it and means it too.

The first time I saw that boy was maybe fifteen or more years before the Rex. He was just out of high school, working the odd carnival job. Had two good hands in those days. And what hands they were. Quick. Sure. I knew I had found the perfect shill. No one in a crowd in their right mind would think that his innocent face, with such a goofy grin, was there except by sheer chance. When you looked at that clear-eyed hopefulness, you could not imagine any nefarious purpose. He looked as unblemished as a newborn babe, even when he was in the middle of doing something stupid that would probably end in bodily harm and be best described in his own words as "Watch this…" or "What does this do?"

I probably saw in Marcel what my old mentor, Big Daddy, saw in me—raw potential waiting to be shaped and shined to a sparkly finish.

There were times where he'd be sleeping in the back of a van, curled up like a dog, twitching his way through some dream that left his mouth open and drool running down his chin. I'd look and say he'd be conserving his energy for when action was required. I loved that about Marcel. He learned fast, and what he didn't learn, he instinctively knew. He was the son of an industrial painter. His old man liked the big projects—factories, water towers, anything that required high scaffolds and color by the barrel. The boy learned a lot from his old man. He got a great eye for distance. Could tell you how big a wall was with one glance. Could tell you without hesitation how many gallons it would take to cover that wall. But his real talents were as a high wire guy or stilt walker. He wasn't afraid of heights and took to any act that required bird balance on a telephone line. The boy was a natural performer who moved as sure-footed and quick as a spider across a web.

Over the years, Marcel had more than his fair share of good luck and bad habits. What they might be, he couldn't remember because he was not cursed with memory. Maybe it was one concussion too many while losing his fear of heights. A moment arrived and departed without a regret. It is both his greatest flaw and my greatest advantage in our friendship. I remember what he can't. Can't say as I blame him. Why should he remember? Dead pets and lost keys. Troubles in school and the blows of bullies who thought he was easy prey. The accident that cost him his hand. Hospitals and surgeries coming along at regular intervals, if I'm to believe any of the dream-like multiple versions of the facts that he's told me. Why would you want to remember all that?

The boy can't seem to keep a girlfriend, so why keep *her* memory? Besides, another will come along soon enough. He is a genuine babe magnet. Maybe he pushes their "mother" or "nurse" button. Or maybe he's hung like a horse. Whatever it is, women want to take care of Marcel. Want to pamper and please him. And sweet Marcel, he's willing to let them or doesn't remember how that smothering care chafes him like a two-day-old diaper.

No matter his faults, as long as he was there when I was on the stage doing the "medicine show" pitch, we were good. When I looked out at the audience to ask if there was anyone that feels peaked or under the weather, Marcel would cough and timidly raise his hand, and we were off to the races.

Come on up here, son. You look a mess.

Yes, sir, I am. Feeling just awful. Got me pains in my back, neck, in my legs even.

Well, son, I got just the thing for you. Dr. Buzz's Genuine Tonic and Herbal Elixir. Here, let me open a fresh bottle for you. Take a spoonful.

Sure tastes good. Can I have another?

Well, son, I suppose you could have a second spoonful, but do be careful, this will do wonders for your aches and pains. Too much of a good thing is still too much.

Oh, Lordy, I do feel terrific. My pain is going away. Why, I feel like I could do a somersault. I could do a handstand.

Then, of course, he did a neat little back flip kicking his heels in the air as he went, or maybe he'd spring into a double somersault from a standing position ending with the splits. Yes! Did the kind of splits that would make the men in the crowd wince! Couple of them fellows automatically reached down low. If the crowd hadn't yet made him as a shill, this would cap it off for even the slowest-witted folks. No matter, the OOOHHHS and AAAHS just rolled out of their mouths when Marcel did it. The boy made it look so easy and fun. Not that it was, either. One bit of misjudged distance or bad timing, and even Marcel would be on crutches for a damned long time. But hey, I could get a good laugh out of the smart ones as they realized they'd been caught looking. That's when I pressed forward to the real "get the money" angle of the pitch. I played to their intelligence.

Yes, friends, as my assistant has so aptly demonstrated, this tonic can work wonders for anyone.

Now, you and I both know that the Food and Drug Administration, those watchdogs of everything bad for you, prevent me from giving away free samples of Dr. Buzz's Genuine Tonic and Herbal Elixir or from making unwarranted and unprovable medicinal claims.

I will make no such claim.

This Elixir is like the familiar healthy and hearty mother's chicken soup that very same FDA also says is unproven as to its health benefits.

*We all know how good that is for what ails you, but the FDA
says we can't talk about it as a miracle cure without testing and
licensing and piles of paperwork. No time for that. No need
either.*

*So, while little Spirit Marcel walks across this stage, which is
something the FDA will let us do, I'll tell you this—he drinks a
glass of Dr. Buzz's tonic each and every day.*

*It is composed of all natural ingredients, the purest herbs and
flower essences found in the great Smokey Mountains, picked at
the height of their potency and rushed to our modern distilling
laboratory where their health-giving essences are transferred
under the strictest of standards directly into the bottle.*

*Friends, what have you got to lose? For a very small fee, much
cheaper than medicines of lesser quality and potency which are
available by prescription at, I might add, a much higher cost
from your doctor or pharmacist, you can experience the vim,
vigor and vitality that comes from drinking Dr. Buzz's Genuine
Tonic and Herbal Elixir. I'll make you an absolute guaran-
tee—that if this doesn't taste better than water, or even wine,
and make you feel better after one week, after one small bottle's
use—I'll give you double your money back.*

I didn't reveal that the bottles were full of ordinary water flavored
with a little wintergreen and mint. Sometimes I'd add a little grain
alcohol to honor the old home traditions. Back when I first started
working with Spirit Marcel, we'd be three counties away doing the
same show for another set of entertainment-starved small-town folks
by the time the ones who thought they were too sophisticated to fall
for anything got around to thinking that maybe they had been taken
for fools. Well, yes, you can have your money back if you can find us.

Those PTA mothers' purses will snap open like it was a half-
price sale at the beauty parlor and the fivers would come flying out. If
it worked only half as well for them as it did for Marcel, they wanted
what was in the bottle. The real beauty of it was it couldn't do any

harm. It was entertainment. The FDA didn't give a hoot about water, and for all I knew, if you thought it would cure your aches and pains— if you really believed it could... The what do you call it? Placebo effect. That would kick in, and maybe it would cure you of boredom and constipation. Though I also know sure as a hound barking up a tree that there were plenty of times when it didn't stand a chance of curing you of anything.

It was too bad that the elixir couldn't replace Marcel's hand. Of course, we had stopped working the act a couple of years before his accident. Gone our separate ways for this or that unrecalled reason. But no matter, I loved working with him, and I was glad to have another chance.

He was still good with the stilting. Missing a hand was no problem when it came to standing on five-, eight- or even ten-foot sticks. As long as he could get up on them and down again, he was ready to dance. He was a true big top star whether he admitted it or not, so if one door closed, he'd open another. He willingly took up the care and feeding of animals, selling tickets, playing in the circus band, any of the quotidian things that had to be done to grease the wheels of progress behind the scenes.

The breeze had kicked little dust devils across the circus ring as I walked Sharon across the grounds. Turning her head to avoid the swirling sand, she saw Marcel sitting in the shade of the eighteen-wheeler parked next to the barn. Suddenly, she blushed, and I know that she'd got the whole it. It was as plain as the blood draining from that blush. The full and terrible who, what and when was front and center. She put her hand to her mouth as if to stop herself from crying out when she bit her hand.

Buzz, she said, I don't think I could do a tour with this show.

What's the problem?

I was toying with her now, because we both knew that the problem was five-foot-six of muscle and blood that had lost a hand at her instigation. I'm not sure that Marcel would say it that way. He might say that it was his lack of attention that was the proximate cause, but she was the reason his attention fled. She was the one who picked the hand from the sawdust and, not quite knowing what to do with it, placed it on the bloody band saw bed like a cat presenting a trophy.

You could say it was a long time ago as if the loss of cherished body parts is ever a long time ago. The memory is potent, but the looking to where a hand used to be is spur enough to remembering what was. He might say, as he often does, that it was his own carelessness, but whether he takes the blame or lays it at her beautiful feet, she was there. I can't remember if he lost it before or after she told him that what was between them was done. If it was before, the fact of it might have been causal, and if after, her ending it was merely cowardly. She'd know which, and she did.

You know, Babe, I could really use a girl with your talents in this show.

Yes. I'm sure you could. She leaned in to look at me with a curious mixture of affection and panic and then said, I don't have six months of hard knocks travel in me anymore. I just want to go back to Texas and work with horses.

I had to stifle a laugh because, in my world of wonders, no one wants to go back to Texas. Once gone, you stay gone.

She kissed me on the cheek—just like she did when she got off the bus with that infuriating hint that it should be something more intimate or affectionate—then turned without a word and headed to the car. Clearly, this was the end of the visit.

There would be no moment of recognition or sincere condolence, no begging for forgiveness or anything resembling reconciliation, confrontation or apology. For reasons that she now holds close as a poker player's all-in bluff, if Marcel is with the Rex, she can't be. That was as plain as the sound of me turning the key in the ignition to take her back to Alma. It was going to be one or the other. Yin or Yang. If the truth be known, I'd rather him than her. I knew what I could expect from Marcel. The iceberg had been spotted on the dark foaming sea and this time, the Titanic turned away.

As we turned onto the county highway, she said, Let sleeping dogs lie.

Right she is. Neither of us said anything more until I let her off at the bus stop barely two hours after her arrival. It'd be a good long while before the next bus came through. She'd need a book or knitting needles to pass the time. After she got out and started to cross the street, I leaned out the window and offered to buy her coffee or a beer to sip while she waited.

She stopped, turned and came back to put her hand on the door and keep me from opening it, then said that she'd prefer waiting by herself. She needed time to think.

Have a good tour, Buzz, she said. Get them there and get them back.

Stay well, Sharon, I said, and give my whatever to Texas. Maybe I'll come look you up when the tour is over.

That would be nice, she said, but we both know it wouldn't happen. I've been to Texas for all the funerals I needed to attend, and that was the only reason I'd ever had for going back to the Lone Star State.

On the way back, I stopped at the package store for a six-pack of Rolling Rock. I'm the kind of man who gives something to every bum who asks. What's a dollar or a dime between you and kindness? It'd be a consolation gift for Marcel from her through me, though I wouldn't tell either of them that. In fact, I won't even mention that she was there. Hold the news close so they won't feel reproached. He hadn't seen her, or at least I didn't think he had. Let sleeping dogs lie, indeed. Some dogs are happiest when they don't know what could have been.

15–Headwaters

Huzzah, huzzah, huzzah,
Step right up
Come closer
Don't be shy,
I have what your heart desires.
And if you're right, you will not fright,
If you believe, we cannot deceive…

The concept of the tour was simple enough. Make a circus with theatrical elements like the highly successful Montreal group Cirque du Soleil was doing across the border. Combine traditional circus acts with a story, add costumes, lights, maybe add a moral to the story to sweeten it up and drag it from one end of the Big Muddy to another, stopping in hamlets small and cities big. I'm sure whoever sold that idea to the guys that owned the circus made it sound like a good deal or at least an easy one. After all, it sounded like an interesting proposition when Frank laid it out for me.

The actuality of it was more like a one-legged man trying to kick himself. Trouble, coming and going. The story, such as it was, was the history of the Mississippi River from the beginning of time to the present moment with jugglers, acrobats, high-wire walkers, clowns and tigers. What the fuck tigers had to do with the Mississippi was anybody's guess, but they came with Miss Red Boots, who came with the tent, and no one had the good sense or guts to send them packing. I should have, but there were a few things concerning the Rex that were beyond my reach, and firing Miss Red Boots was one of them. If you wanted the tent, you got the girl. I'd just have to pretend that as far as the tigers went, they were pretty much 200-pound housecats. The Rex folks liked Miss Red Boots. She was talented enough to be five pounds of sugar in a three-pound bucket, though she had a bit more opinion about how everything should be done than I'd have liked. She came with the tent, and I wasn't going to take a chance on the tent leaving if she did.

Then there was the camel, but the camel didn't actually participate in the show except for the big ring parade around at the end. And even that was a really stupid idea because the camel, one of the tigers—Gertie, if I remember rightly—and when we could find them, a couple of dogs wearing tiaras were the only real animals in that big ring parade. It wasn't like a first-class circus where you had six elephants hulking around the ring with showgirls spangling on top. God bless, that is always a sight to behold, but not one the Rex could conjure. We didn't have any elephants, and Francis, the other big cat, was too young and too frisky to walk around the ring, even on a leash. The big ring parade at the end of the show sucked, at least as far as real animals went, but we made up for that with other distractions until I was finally able to nix the whole animal thing in favor of trying anything else.

A moment, if you will, about the camel as a generic feature of entertainment. The beast was nothing but a difficult sideline by any computational mathematics, barely paying its way by toting urchins around the outside of the tent at two or five bucks a pop if we could get away with the higher price. Most of what it earned went to food costs, and if I was the actual owner of the Rex as well as the boss onsite, I'd have sent the camel to the old humps home. I do surely hate camels. They're just not worth the trouble they cause, no matter how much money they can coax out of a pocket. But like everything else in this show, the money that made the decisions was some distance away talking to Flat Frank, who then relayed it to me by phone if he had a number or a telegram if he didn't.

God bless us all in those days when the cell phone hadn't been invented yet, and even then, I thought a telegram was more quaint than efficient as a communications device. During half the tour, I think Frank was the only thing keeping Western Union in business because I'd get one or two wires every day when we were not in a major city. On the other hand, I did appreciate it when money was attached to the wire. Big money or small, it all counted toward the care and feeding of the Rex.

Since it seems I got a hairball stuck in the craw, let me also say that I wouldn't have had a clue as to who the money guys were unless they came up and introduced themselves. For all I knew, the whole thing was a tax scam or a way to clean cash for some mob guy who had once gone to the big top as a boy and thought, oh yes, someday I'll own one of them. The Absent Owners were just that, off somewhere else, parsimoniously paying out what was needed in dribs and drabs to get us up and barely running. And after we were underway, Frank said they expected to taper off the support, and we'd pay for ourselves. Even the camel was supposed to make a buck.

When the sun rises in the west, that will be the day. I swear, that was the theory and about as likely as a rooster laying an egg and the hen crowing approval. Frank pointed it out more than once in telegrams as he complained about having to send another five hundred here and five hundred there. I laughed every time I went to claim the cash.

Later, I found out that the money actually came from a couple of trust fund philanthropy types whose family had made their fortune in defense contracting or something pharmaceutical they needed to do penance for. It went toward buying the last vestiges of a traditional one-ring traveling circus, with intentions—or maybe more accurately, pretensions—of reviving it as Art with a capital A.

Mine was not to reason why, mine was to take the cash and push this prototype of "art" down the length of Ol' Man River.

We were bound by a schedule I had not made to start performing in early May at the headwaters of the Mississippi River. It was item number one on a long list of performances. There was only one problem—we didn't actually have a contract for a national park performance. The headwaters of the great river is a little bitty stream at one end of Lake Itasca surrounded by towering pine and precisely laid out paths that take you to the so-called source. They've worked it out so you can cross the stream without getting your feet wet by stepping on carefully placed stones as it leaves the lake, where it begins its long journey to the Dead Zone. The safety and rules of keeping it pristine were defined along the trail, and the same mindset that ordained that path was everywhere to be seen. Nothing happens in the park without crossing an i and dotting a t in triplicate.

There was no performing lakeside because there was no room. Performing at the headwaters might mean doing a show in the parking lot if it were not for the fact that the Smokey the Bear hats were not keen on having us do any performing anywhere without the necessary paperwork, which we did not have because no one had thought to fill out the forms when they decided the headwaters was the place to start.

I drove up there on a Monday to see if I could work something out with the government representatives for a Saturday show. No way. Not the first weekend of May or the last week of Never. There were no permits to be had without being filed many months in advance. No contracts were in hand, and what was always the biggest stumbling block from my perspective, no reasonable amount of money under the table could grease the bureaucratic wheels to make those things appear in the time and place they were scheduled for.

At the moment in question, as I faced the disappointment of not being able to start at the tippy, tippy top of the great river, my immediate task seemed to be finding some other place to put a sixty-foot tent containing a thirty-foot ring where we could present an hour and a half of wholesome family entertainment consisting of a loose story, a half dozen more or less traditional circus acts and two tigers jumping through hoops of fire.

How does that all hang together? Don't bother. It didn't make much sense then, and it won't make much sense now. I really ought to say, though, that it got better, lots better, as we went along. Mosquitoes on stilts, steamboat races, even the Civil War got worked into the show, as did the old-school spectacle of the high wire and acrobatics, plus the always popular flaming hoops. We figured out a story day by day and worked every angle to make it good fun, or if not good, at least fun.

The fact of not actually performing at the source would be a disappointment for some in the Rex crew. I was not sure I could find another site nearby that was open on the start date. We could always take the crew to the river for some photo op of the "this begins here" variety or, if the spiritually inclined wanted, some kind of a blessing. Maybe we'd all take our shoes off and stand in the clear water wiggling our toes and singing "Kumbaya" or some such. Maybe we'd all pull down our zippers, lift our skirts and pee. I'd leave the what to do under the swaying pines to Marge, Claire or one of them folks that always seemed to have an "in touch with the earth" suggestion at the tip of their tongue about bringing us together to "heal 'n' help," as they put it.

For those of us not churched, or not churched anymore, the old-timey pagan rites are as off-putting as any sermon. Oh, I may quote the Bible as needs be, but I had more than my fill of religion before I left Texas and at surprisingly regular intervals after, as well.

16—Any Church Will Do

Redeemer Lutheran would be the one to redeem the Rex. That's the irony of a church in Bemidji, Minnesota, that wanted to do a fundraiser for something or other becoming the first to take a flyer on the circus, sight unseen. They even had a goodly sized lawn that they said we could set the tent on. Of course, what looked large when you're standing there with a middle-aged pastor thinking about fundraising with clowns and tigers didn't look quite as big when the first truck arrived, and Loren Red Beard got the measuring tape out of the toolbox.

We'll have about ten feet of the tent in the parking lot on this end, he said. The tension lines will have to be sunk into the blacktop about eight feet beyond that.

He looked at the pastor with the realization that the better part of an entire row of parking spaces closest to the lawn was going to go away, and a series of holes would be created, which would have to be filled in later. I could see the habitual Lutheran hesitation rising to the surface about making an actual decision now instead of sending it to a committee, so I intervened to ask the obvious.

Can we move it back far enough to not stake the lot? I asked Loren Red Beard.

No.

No, we can't? Or no, you don't want to?

No, we can't unless you want to collapse one end of the tent and lose at least a section of bleachers. And no, I don't want to because I'm not paid enough to work out the engineering of getting sixty feet of a three-pole tent with eight feet of support wiring all the way around into a fifty-foot plot of crabgrass.

Well, Pastor Lundquist, I said, it looks like we've got three choices. We can take out that first row of parking, we can leave the lawn as it is and just move the whole tent down to the softball field behind the grade school, or we can go without the tent—though that would also mean going without the high wire acts since they're strung from the center support poles.

As Lundquist was mulling over the choices, I was trying to figure out why had I said that. Just spitballing, I suppose. It would be a shitty way to perform our first show, open to all the elements. Who in their right mind would do an open-air circus? And as soon as I thought it, I realized that would be the option he'd pick.

And it was.

The semi rolled into the parking lot of the Lutheran church at a little after nine in the morning and began disgorging the circus. Showtime would be two o'clock or maybe three. VX, who was testing out the position of Chief Tech and Road Rat Wrangler, had the guys pulling the tent out when I got over to where the semi was idling.

The tent doesn't go up for this show, VX. Just set the ring in the middle of the lawn and bleachers in the sun around it. No lights. Don't rig any of the high wires, just hang some sound reinforcement.

I know, Buzz, VX said. The Red Beard said the same thing, but we can't get to the bleachers until the tent is out of the truck.

That's a shitty bit of extra work. How'd that happen?

That's the way it was packed. It's the old first and last rule.

VX grabbed the rolled canvas and shouted at a crew that waited for his command to give it another lift and heave. The entire assembly landed with a plop at his feet about a yard farther than it had been. It was section one of four that comprised the tent. Between grunts, he said that the tent was the first goddamn thing coming out of the truck and the last fuckin' thing we put back in every time, every single fuckin' time.

62

When the tent was extracted without having to be assembled, VX offered that the rest of it would go fast. In my line of work, you never said those famous last words, but I was hoping it could be a self-fulfilling prophecy. VX had already walked away, carrying the first section of bleacher support onto the far side of the lawn.

At three o'clock, the show did go on. It was not a clockwork operation but fits and starts were better than nothing. Having ditched the tent and any acts that depended on using the poles, there was an unfinished and unsure quality to the performance, at least from an inside-the-ring point of view. One performer after another came out of the ring and stopped to stare at the temporary act order that had been written onto a piece of cardboard in black crayon. The show was as rough as coarse sandpaper on cracked glass, and it sounded like it too. By the end, the company was split between those who were ashamed of having done what was done and those who were merely disgusted. No one wanted to small talk with the locals. Most wanted to put this one behind us—far behind. More than half the Rex crew wanted to pack and drive back to Alma immediately, while the pagan minority wanted to stay overnight and go to Itasca to see the headwaters in the morning for some kind of spiritual beginning. There was no point in voting because the results were already apparent.

In the end, the ones who wanted to stay reorganized themselves into as many cars or buses as would hold them. They would camp or pay for a motel out of their own pockets. They could go to Itasca and wash themselves in the water or whatever as long as they were back in Alma by Monday night. The rest of us would make the drive now.

I went over to where Pastor Lundquist was standing for the ritual shaking of hands and the thanking each other for the pleasure of doing business. While I did sincerely wish him well with the church's fundraising effort, I put out my hand and gladly took the thin envelope with the check in it. For us, at least, charity began at home, and we were going there post-haste.

When the semi began the six-hour drive back to Alma for a week of licking our wounds, I felt like a "Brer Rabbit scooting out of the briar patch" wave of relief.

17–Option C

In succeeding weeks, we repeated a drive from Alma to a destination du jour and back again. We went to paper milling Grand Rapids and then to Brainerd where Marcel spent every spare moment suggesting I should drive him to the amusement park where the figure of a giant Paul Bunyan would say your name when you walked up to him.

You got to pay someone to do that.

No, you don't, he said in a voice that was somewhere between amused and accusing me of denying him the truth of his last childhood dream. You don't have to pay anyone. He'll speak to you… really.

Who told you that?

My mother did, Marcel said. Then he looked at me to see if I was buying that one. I was not moved.

He revised his answer. Okay, maybe it was my Uncle Balthazar before he died.

It was still a no-sale proposition as I began to walk away.

Marcel called after me. What difference does it make whether you have to pay someone or whether it even speaks, Doctore? We should go and see it. It'll be a cultural heritage thing. You know how much you like the old and odd.

Not today, I said. This show is not righty-tighty. I've got no interest taking any extra time to go visit concrete statues of legendary lumberjacks. Come on, Spirit, focus on what needs to be done. We've got an Option C to run.

Then I relented for the sake of keeping him motivated. I said, Get your shit packed right away at the end of the show and then ask me. Since you're riding with me, maybe I'll stop on the way out of town. Then again, maybe I won't, but at least we'll have another show under our belts.

Marcel sulked until Scott the Dog and road rat Billy Bones spotted a bicycle that someone had left beside the big cat truck. Billy asked around about whose it was. Getting no response, he took it for a ride around the ring, raising the front wheel off the ground and rearing back to balance on the rear wheel like it was an unruly unicycle. Then Marcel wanted his turn, and before I could stop it, the three of them were having a bike trick competition. Around them, the bleachers went in, the wires and couplings got rigged, and finally, the space they were using for riding backward and doing flips became the prop dump filled with the barrels, hoops and stilts we would use.

Here's how it works. In most places, we have a sponsor, and that's all to the good. Sure money. They pay for the show, find us a location based on our specs, get the necessary municipal permits and do all the stuff that has to be done by a local guy with connections. I could do it, but it takes so much time, the tortoise could cross the finish line before all the paperwork was done. Leave that to the locals. Sometimes, favors have to be called in or given out. The locals are doing it to make money or boost civic pride or some other magnanimous shit that makes them look like the big dog. I usually don't care why they're doing it as long as they feel pressure to get it done.

As they used to say, don't insult the alligator if you have to cross the swamp again. If the space is right and the check clears, I'm good with whatever their reasons for booking us. I start to care when the eighteen-wheeler rolls into town and the rag-tag assembly of trucks, cars, and buses that is the Rex follow it in. I care that we'll have a place to set up and the necessary permits.

Usually, the local constabulary will come around to check us out. Heard there was something going on here. Yes, officer, a fundraising performance—did you talk with so and so? He's got it bought and paid for.

Sometimes various inspectors of health or fire will also pop up to make sure that everything is up to spec, but usually, they're not looking for a reason to shut us down. They just want to cover their ass in case something goes wrong or sometimes to cage a few free tickets. It always helps when the local sponsor has some clout or is the brother-in-law of the fire inspector or something like that.

It's Option A, B or C depending on what the sponsor deems family entertainment and how many shows are in the contract. Of course, the difference between A, B or C is how long we're staying and what they're willing to pay for.

Option A is show only, which usually means one performance a day for one or more days. Sometimes, if they pay a premium, we add a second show the same day. From my perspective, this is the best option because it usually means we get paid a fixed price regardless of how many butts are in the bleachers. When they pick Option A, I don't care how hot or cold it is, whether it's rain or shine. I get the cashier's check, or sometimes cash in hand, before we finish putting up the tent, and the show goes on.

Most of the crew hates it. It is, more often than not, a straight-arrow setup—perform and take down with no chance to rest, see the sights or make money on the side.

Option B adds in sideshows, which we don't really have. I hate option B for all the reasons I hate Texas—it is just too damned far to get from here to there.

Midways and sideshows are a whole operation unto itself that I know too well from the historical scars on my heart. They only make money if the crowd is free-spending or you cheat. When you run game tents, you need a minimum of two guys for every set-up. One to run the come-on and another to watch the guy running the come-on to make sure he isn't putting half the take into his pocket. It's best they do not know each other. It discourages theft. You also need a truck full of cheap dayglow stuffed animals you buy for four bits apiece and give out after a Lincoln or better of trying. Not just oversized bears, but arm-wrapping orange monkeys, blow-up sharks and superhero cartoon figures—whatever lame-assed bit of popular culture is currently in demand, or more likely, in wholesale supply at the time. It changes from season to season, and once you buy the stuff, the no-returns policy means you're stuck with it until you hand it across the counter or leave it behind.

Soon as I hear option B brought up, if there's any wiggle room, I suggest that they just get a second contract with an actual midway outfit. I start reeling off names and offering to make the call.

The Rex crew hates Option B more than they hate Option A, but not by much. They think it means extra work without making any extra money. They're right, of course. It is, at best, marginally profitable, but it does allow them to test acts that are not ready for the big ring or play at being traveling thespians. I mean, Scott the Dog is a great pitchman, almost as good as I am. He has a knack for the seemingly off-the-cuff talk that brings the crowd in close. The Swede Girls don't seem to mind getting a little extra exposure clowning, and one of the Toms is a juggling fool who can make five squishy balls going up and down look interesting. We can make a three-tent sideshow work well enough to make it worth the trouble by cranking out fifteen-minute performances repeated however many times for an extra 600 or 700 sponsor bucks per day.

Okay, then there's Option C, which replaces the sideshow with a parade. Usually, it means that we are part of a parade that they have already planned. We'll put the circus band in the back of a pickup and turn half the company into clowns. We're good for it. If push comes to shove, I'll even perch Sue or one of the younger girls in something with spangles, showing a little cleavage on the goddamn camel's hump and have Loren Red Beard or VX dressed in a striped stereotype of an Arabic gown and headdress leading the stinking beast down the street between the high school band and some float being pulled by a tractor. We can do join in, no problem.

Where it gets dicey is when they want us to BE the parade. With a crew of twenty-five or maybe thirty, including hangers on, we're thin on substance. Even if I throw in some kids performing something on a good day, we're not really a parade. We're a section at best. Can't put but one of the big cats on a leash and walk them down the street. Every time I think about that, I get hives. No old-timey Ringling Brothers steam calliope on wheels whistling a tune with this show. No line of elephants, tail to trunk. To make a real circus parade, you'd need two Rexes and at least one high school band.

When they want us to be the parade, we have to recruit locally, widely and improvise. We need a couple of days some place to work up interest in a Rex parade while talking the local high school band into formation and every VFW member or Boy Scout troop in town in uniform to carry flags. I'd happily lean on the sponsor to find at least a few dozen volunteers. Get a church choir singing, and while at it, give them banners of the state flowers of every state along the Mississippi on long sticks that they can proudly hoist. Reach into the theatrical education end of our traveling college of knowledge to organize a quick paper mâché workshop with school kids and then line them up in the garishly painted masks of lions and tigers they've made. Cut up strips of gold or silver sparkly cloth and pin them on the kids like sashes, and then line them up and send them down the street like a forest of shimmering foil leaves blowing in the wind while proud parents look on. Kids in the parade always equal parents on the curb watching and then coming to the show.

We'll make Option C work, but if the local sponsor really wants it, they better pay for the extra three days of residency it takes for the recruiting and the making and organizing of something that will stand in a line and move a block or two without looking like a mob scene from the French Revolution. Not many have chosen Option C, but those that did got their money's worth.

18–Now This is a Parade

Where was I? Somewhere north of Minneapolis in the merry month of May and still quite a ways up the river from the point of no return. Yes, that was it.

Brainard had opted for Option C and wanted us to build what they called a "blue" homage to the Father of the Waters. Okay. Good by me. We camped onsite for four days. On the first day, we set up the tent and hung the welcome banners. The Rex folks flooded the town with flyers announcing the workshops, which led to the parade, which led to the show.

On the second day, we had a workshop for the curious and what must have been every junior high school kid in town. They all made fish heads. Some wanted to wear them as masks, and others set them on top of their heads like finned hats. We had to tell them to come back the next day to finish whatever it was because if they wore the mask on the day they made it, they'd have nothing to show but a face full of wet paper and paint. You have to let stuff dry overnight before you paint it.

We'd usually let the kid who was the biggest pain in the ass ignore that advice. When it all went to mush, we'd point and laugh and say to the rest, okay, do you see what we mean? Come back tomorrow, and we'll make it last until your little brother sits on it.

Half the kids would come back excited to splash on the color. Some wouldn't, but the ones that did would always bring some other kid who wasn't there on the first day but wanted to make something as well. Sometimes we'd get them started on their own, but usually, Rona or sweet Claire, who seemed to like the mask-making workshops, could talk them into adopting one of the masks that were left by the nose pickers that didn't come back.

By the last day, the parade day, we'd make sure that every damn kid that showed up had something they could put on their head for the long march.

Ahhh, if you could only taste the buttermilk flapjacks with maple syrup joy that leaked through the Rex at parade time! That day was a dog that wanted to hunt. For all my bitching about the set up, it really was fun to do a parade.

The Rex Terrestrial, Celestial & Nautical Circus crew was all sparked out in their performance whites. White pants and shirts for the men. White skirts and blouses or dresses for the women who did not want to wear pants, though, in truth, pants made a lot more sense for everyone in parades. The Rex crew, probably twenty-six performers in Brainard that day, and maybe six willing road rats, would be interspersed with the other local elements of what was going to be a very small but excellent parade. It was the one time when I'd be happy to say that if the errant cousins or friends had come along for a day at the circus, thank God and give them something to carry down the street.

The ubiquitous police car was in front, followed by a contingent of American Legion members so ancient I was not sure they could carry flags the five-block distance from the schoolyard to the circus grounds. Behind them was a contingent of Boy Scouts carrying fishing poles like rifles. Fake fish, about half the size of each kid, hung from each pole. A couple of chubby beauty queens were sitting in the back of a black Chrysler convertible. Before the parade even started, one of them was practicing her wave while the others were checking their lipstick or rhinestone tiaras. There was a set of four women dressed in blue on horseback circling their steeds counterclockwise and waiting for the parade to begin. Behind the horses were the first of the two sets of fish head kids. These are the ones with masks and wearing old sheets cut up and fitted like ponchos painted with a blue wave or bubble designs. Then came the impressively large high school band in their orange and black uniforms. So much for the nautical blue theme, but this was their school colors. One of the local guys told me they were actually a competitive marching band and had the trophies to prove it.

That's wonderful, I said, wishing that I could have put the circus band in front of them. We will surely suffer in comparison. But what we lack in size, we would make up for in audacity.

The marching band was followed by a group of junior high pep club volunteers, mostly pre-teen girls and mothers with too much time on their hands. The girls, all carrying flower banners, had no interest in growing up to be the Junior League version of a pep club. Most of them will, of course, grow up to do exactly that, though right now, they were ignoring their mothers who kept waving at their kids between gossip exchanged with their ilk. The girls were interested in bubble gum and looking at the rest of the parade assembly.

Then came the second set of fish, this time the hat brigade who were straining in the wind to hold their painted cardboard fish in place. With every gust, one or two of the flat cardboard muskies or walleyes took flight, and the kid jumped out of line to retrieve it. There was a reason we put string ties on the fish hats, though it did no good if the kids didn't tie them under their chins.

Then came the pickup with as much of the circus band as we could spare in the bed around Elijah's drum set. It was mostly the horns since they could stand shoulder to shoulder facing the crowd.

Mia and Maya dressed as regular European-style clowns with swallowtail coats, red hats and noses supplemented by a couple of big shoe, bicycle horn tooting locals who were smoking cigarettes next to the swing set.

The rest of the Rex crew followed, carrying an odd mixture of tambourines, bells, whistles and handbills announcing the day's performance. Next to last was the camel with Loren Red Beard on one side and VX on the other to keep the grumpy beast from veering into the small crowd. We opted not to have Miss Red Boots walking Gertie, the better-behaved tiger, in favor of hazard duty on the back of the camel in a jerry-rigged mermaid outfit that is mostly blue cloth wrapped around her legs and a fake fish tail. Finally, bringing up the rear for no logical reason, was the mayor in the back of a white Chevy convertible with a couple of teen girls who threw to the crowd handfuls of candy and bubblegum they hadn't consumed.

Idling next to the curb was the city's street sweeper, the real last element of the parade, ready to whisk up and wash away any souvenirs the horses or camel left behind.

At the appointed time, the squad car turned on the lights, and we moved out. The first unit of the parade was in block two of five by the time the mayor left the assemble area. If he even would. The sky had been steadily darkening, and now, with the parade beginning, the sound of thunder could be heard above the drum cadences of the marching band.

A couple of fish hats sailed by. After another crack of thunder, the sky opened up like someone had flushed the celestial toilet. Cold black rain soaked everyone in the time it took to scream. The marching band fragmented into squawks and honks, breaking ranks. Black and orange figures ran in every direction, looking for shelter. I could see the top on the Chrysler going up as girls ducked under it. The masked fish kids, who couldn't see very well to begin with, collided willy-nilly as they tried to find their way to the curb where the comforting arms of mothers screaming their names awaited. At the intersection, road rat Billy gunned the pickup's engine, pulled out of line and headed east, trying make take the shortest route to the shelter of the Rex Terrestrial, Celestial & Nautical Circus tent. Through all this, Elijah sat at the drum kit, still pounding out a propulsive beat while the horns squatted down and held on for dear life as the pickup squealed away. I would have laughed if I had not been running for the circus grounds.

We delayed the show for a half hour, hoping the rain would stop as we ran a mandatory reality check. Was the tent structurally complete? Poles in place, lines all staked down, water coming off the canvas and not pooled and dripping into the ring or bleachers? Did we have everybody in the company? Did we have all the equipment and props in place? It was only then that I bothered to see if we had an audience.

We did, though they were wet and mostly standing beneath the canvas for safety. I doubt that half of them had bought a ticket. What the hell, let's give them something to think about other than the dismal sky and miserable rain. So, we ran the show or some semblance of it. The small audience got to see thirty-five confusing minutes of clowns acting out their circus version of "Waiting for Godot" and some lethargic tigers that were more interested in curling up and napping than standing on balls or leaping through hoops, flaming or otherwise. The locals applauded politely, and as soon as the rain stopped made their exit.

When it was all said and done, I saw Marcel coming toward me with a beer. Here, Doctore, you look like you need this, he said as he handed me the can.

Thanks. I leaned my head back, opened my mouth and poured in a third of the hoppy brew.

Marcel looked at me and said, Buzz, I know it's been a shit day, but you know we're going to drive by Paul Bunyan on the way back. He tilted his head so one eye was 45 degrees higher than the other. Can we stop? Please.

I thought, At least one of us deserves to get what he wants and nodded in the affirmative.

19—TV Girl

On Memorial Day weekend, the Rex was scheduled for five shows over three days in St. Cloud. Good money—all Option A shows. It was the heaviest performance load we had attempted to date and did not allow us to slink back to Alma to refine or repair between shows. We were there for the duration, and the fact of it necessitated camping. It would be a preview of the long exile to come when we did not have generous sponsors offering housing, kitchens or whatever. The company was split between those with pickup truck campers parking on the circus grounds and those with tents or sleeping in cars at a campground some thirty franchise eateries and two package liquor stores away. I was going to stay with the campground folks.

At about ten o'clock the night before our first show, the bugs and bug spray were out in force. Folks were sitting around a sputtering fire talking about the next day's first-ever endurance test of two shows in one day. They were drinking some cheap red wine and smoking a little Maui Wowie that Dan had scored from a surfer cousin. Suddenly, an unknown blond appeared at the edge of the clearing. She was about five foot four with a pixie haircut and a tight, curvy frame poured into tighter black jeans. She motioned to someone behind her, but I couldn't quite make out the shadowy figure.

Stepping into the light, she said, Who's in charge here?

Everyone looked around like they were trying to guess the answer and then, more or less in unison, pointed to me. Rona giggled. Dan palmed the joint and moved away from the fire.

I addressed the young lady. Indeed, I am in command or as close to it as anyone at this ring of fire.

I felt a little rush of blood headed for my feet when I stood, but once in motion, I stayed in motion and moved in the right direction, up and forward to meet her. Who wants to know? I asked.

Betty Mercer from something channel 7 news, she said, taking a step closer. I've come for the interview.

Interview? I said.

I had no recollection of an interview on my schedule. Did Lucy, Flat Frank's number one assistant and chief PR girl, schedule one that I did not hear about? She hadn't called Alma before we left or said anything when I called to tell Frank we were set up in St. Cloud. I was starting to think this was a fake. She didn't look like any TV reporter I'd ever dealt with. She looked to be about sixteen, if that, and dressed like she was heading to the dance floor at some Euro-disco. I figured the girl was pulling my leg but decided to humor her.

Right you are, Miss Mercer, I'm Dr. Buzz, ringmaster and tour manager. Always happy to talk to media representation of the local populace.

I did a half bow but realized I might be tipsy enough to fall over and bob back up. This was a too quick move, and it took all my concentration to remain upright.

As she stepped close enough to feel the heat of the fire, an equally skinny guy wearing khakis and a black T-shirt stepped out of the shadows lugging an industry-standard TV camera with station logos on the side. I guess this was a legit deal, after all.

Isn't it a little late for an interview? I asked. Can't this wait until tomorrow?

We had some difficulty finding you, Doctor... Buzz? Funny name, that. How did you get such a colorful stage name?

Long story but not for this interview. Let's talk about the Rex.

Anyway, Doctor Buzz, we went to the circus tent first, expecting to find you there. No one at the circus grounds wanted to talk on camera, and they were a little vague about directions to this location. We went to the other campground first.

In my developing marijuana munchies state, the first thought that loomed was, what other campground? I shook my head to clear that one away, and the next in line for cognitive recognition was—that's good news. Not that she had trouble finding me, but that no one at Rex central had talked to her. I never want the Rex crew talking to reporters. That kind of thing always results in awkward situations where something unfortunate gets said, or someone does something only a lawyer could appreciate. I'd have to find out who had the good sense not to talk to Betty Mercer and thank them. Yeah, maybe even slip a few extra bucks in their next pay envelope.

Okay, let's roll tape, I said. No, wait—that's your line. I laughed and tried again. What do you want to know about the circus?

Everything, of course.

She sat down in a lawn chair and gestured for me to do the same. I was still not entirely sure this was legit, and more importantly, I realized that doing an interview, in particular here and now, in lawn chairs by the fire would impinge on the well-deserved pleasures of the wine and smoke the Rex crew deserved. So, instead of sitting, I reached out and grabbed her hand.

Not here, I suggested.

But it would make such a nice background, she said, like a woman who always gets her way. Probably does, but not this time.

I pulled Betty to her feet and moved past the picnic table and bench, past the tents and toward the campsite's concrete shower house, where the overhead light was swarming with moths and various unidentified night flyers. The walk was good for me. It got the blood moving and cleared my head. She was half resisting but moving in parallel. She was complaining about something, but I didn't hear her, or if I did, I didn't care what it was. I was looking for the right place, one that was far enough away not to be interrupted by one of the crew puking and close enough for me to hear cries for help if bears should approach. Not that I could do much about bears, but if there was a problem, I wanted to be the first, or at least one of the first, to know.

We can do it here, I said.

The cameraman, who hadn't said a word, expressed his displeasure. Blank wall. There's nothing to look at. Too many bugs, they'll be attracted to the camera's light.

Okay, good point, I said, swatting at the first wave of banqueters on my arm. Where'd you park? We'll go there, or we can go to my car. It's a nice classic Lincoln, a real beauty, if I do say so.

I pulled her toward me with a single gesture, spinning her so that she wound up with my arm around the back of her waist. I let go of her wrist. She was close enough for me to smell the DEET in her bug spray. I started walking again, and the cameraman followed. When we got to the car, I released her and took a step back, bowing slightly.

She said, Roll it.

The on-camera light switched on.

I lit up my most sincere smile and said, Dr. Buzz, Ringmaster and Tour Manager of the Rex Terrestrial, Celestial & Nautical Circus, at your service.

The cameraman said, Screw it—the bugs are blocking the shot. He shut off the light and asked, What other choices do we have?

Perhaps inside the car is our last best option, I said and opened the door.

We set up with her in the passenger seat, me at the wheel. Rodney, the now-named camera guy in the backseat, bounced diffused light off the upholstered roof panel, and things settled down to a cozy roar. He was such a pro that there wasn't even a reflection of the light in the curve of the windshield, though the sound of the light-loving moths landing on it reminded me of the pitter-patter of rain. Since Betty Mercer and I were both wearing lapel mics plugged into the camera, moth lust was not transferring onto the soundtrack. Or so I hoped, because as sure as a great horned owl liked snacking on mice, I only wanted to do one Q&A to get this morsel swallowed and send her off to someplace that was not here.

I don't remember what she asked me. The usual stuff, I suppose. What it was like to be in the circus. How many people were in the show or how many shows we did or were going to do. I gave her the smile that came with my well-rehearsed answers and not much more. There was neither imagination nor real inquiry in her index card questions. She had a list and was going through them pro forma. That being the case, there was a minimum of wit but not one bit of redemption in my answers. I was not about to make her job any easier by giving her poetry.

Five minutes later, it was done. Hell, I'd have spent more time flirting—if I was inclined to that sort of thing—than she spent on the whole "wham bam, thank you - does my hair look right?" experience.

She did the interview and left. At least the camera jockey said thanks before he hauled the camera out of the car and followed her like a faithful retriever bringing back a shot bird.

Betty didn't know what she was missing. It was the essence of the interview that went off the rails. If she had just asked the right question, she could have gotten a Cracker Jack prize. Not that she'd have recognized it, but that's just my old-timey prejudice talking. She did not ask. Anything. Substantive. Anything that mattered.

The good Lord says, ask and you shall receive. Ask not the trite question trudging toward the dull expected answer, but the other one—the question that leads to the path less traveled. The way you find Aladdin's treasure is in the asking. "Open Sesame" is as much a question as a command. That's always the way it is. If you could just ask the right question, the world of wonders would open for you.

20—The Right Question

Nothing makes me want a good cigar like a good performance. I've seen it, heard it, and so have you. When the performance works, it contains every sort of receiving through an act of giving.

I don't care what you call it. Call it art, call it theater, call it enchantment, call it jazz or flimflam, call it preaching, politicking, shuck and jive. Call it by any name or no name at all—it works the same way. You can hear the little voice in your head saying, "Let's make the audience gasp with pleasure. Let's leave it all on stage. Make 'em weep for beauty and blush for truth. Make everyone glad they took the time and dropped the dime." In the blessed moment of a good performance, the cost is beside the point. Whatever works, works, and the only reason I've stayed in this line of work for as long as I have was for those rare and precious moments when it worked.

I know when it works. So does Marcel, Miss Red Boots, the Swede Girls, even VX, though he doesn't really perform so much as just be in a space. Now brother Elijah, nervous and agitated, is ready to puke from first entrance to last bow, always pushing himself to do more. It's all nerves and self-recrimination, but he's another that gives a dollar's worth of sweat for a buck. Maybe two. When he's on fire, he is a Roman candle. One glowing revelation after another. He's 110 percent wild man, possessed by the spirit of the divine inspiration. Icarus on waxed wings soaring toward the sun.

They've all felt the wild joy of what practice has made perfect and what some bestowed grace has made effortless. They all know of what I speak—always wanting to make it better but never satisfied. Even the road rats longed for the day the tent would go up like clockwork, and the ring would crackle with anticipation.

In those glorious moments when the whole Rex congregation was emotionally or psychically wired to each other, we were just like the preacher in the old Bible church with the voices in the crowd shouting "Amen" and "Yes sir, Brother," flying back up to him as he roared through the verses and lesson, making the rafters tremble before the word of GOD. That preacher's knowing of the right word to speak in the right moment with that old-time cadence prepared us, and then the Gospel choir came in. They hit the high harmony notes, and the entire congregation lifted up as one. Makes you want to be in Jesus's arms. Makes you feel the spirit stirring the waters.

Come on down to the river.
Lower yourself in.
Don't care if you're Ophelia.
Don't care if you're the creature from the Black Lagoon.
Let the water wash you in moonlight.
Let the waters carry you away.
The big river will take your sorrow to the salty sea.
Be made whole in the spirit of the waters.

Nowadays, the preacher class is more ephemeral—pretty good-looking and not hard to hear because they're all amplified and screen projected, so you can't miss them unless you close your eyes. Don't get much spirit there, just big money asks. Them old-timey guys, the Big Daddies of the world, didn't need that shit to make you want to testify or reach into the pocket and pull out your last dime for a blessing. They knew the power of the word and the rhythm of the build.

The modern circus is getting that way too. Feeling the push to get bigger and more electric. Big fucking projection screens and more lights, more smoke, less stink of animals and sweat. I hate it. The Rex performed "old school" surprisingly well without fancy effects. Not that we could afford that shit. Even if we could, there was a value in doing it with next to nothing. Cardboard and paint were the coin of our realm. At every turn, if I confess rightly, I wanted the audience to say that any performance of the Rex wasn't what they expected. The one they saw was worth more than the money.

If Betty Mercer had asked, "When is beauty transcended?" I would have said that it wouldn't be in St. Cloud because it was still too soon, but transcendence would happen somewhere between here and the mouth of the Mississippi. A perfect show. I could tell her with clear-eyed conviction what it would be when it arrived, but I did not know when that would be. Wait and see. Lights up, it's showtime.

21–Hot in Rochester

As June's heat began to load in, the tour was finally taking on its true pattern—arrive and unpack, then perform and pack again. Minneapolis, St. Paul, Hastings, and even a little tossed-in show in Red Wing were all behind us. The mechanics were not yet bred into the bone as an unthinking and instinctual process that would let us thrive in the soon-to-be nomadic, no turning back mode, but was at present an exhausting familiar muscle movement. A dance we sort of knew but could not yet enjoy. As the Rex crew got better at performing the basic functions of the circus, they also got better at complaining about the work of unloading, raising the tent and rigging it. Every road rat knew what didn't work the way it should. Some things could be corrected, but others couldn't and simply had to be muscled into place or jerry-rigged every time. Despite complaints, they managed to accomplish the very tasks they bitched about in shorter intervals and more ingeniously efficient ways. The clock was never our friend, and we knew it.

The work always needed more than my guys could get done. It was a given that at every stop, five or six local guys with muscle and a willingness to take direction were needed to get the circus set up within the three hours some fool other than me, who had obviously never done it, thought was sufficient for the task.

The "take direction" part was actually more important than the manly muscles. That's what physics was invented for—leverage—the fulcrum moving the reluctant poles or winching the cable into a place where the principle of dynamic tension will make it stay put. Assembly is a tricky proposition of sequences and parts. It was the best argument you could find for paying attention in high school physics. VX knew how it fit. So did Billy Bones and Loren Red Beard. Even Rona could call out the "what next" sequence from the opening of semi doors to opening the tent flaps fifteen minutes before show time.

The trick of getting it done was not knowing what to do but being willing to actually listen to those who did know. It was supposed to be part of my job to crack the metaphoric whip or to offer the carrot of reward—but Scott the Dog was so much better at it. He could smell the unwilling and unruly that would be more trouble than they were worth. He'd weed them out tout sweet. What do we offer a local boy (and 90 percent of the time they were marginally employed boys) for their sweat and toil? At five bucks an hour and a couple of beers along the way, they were earning more per hour than the Rex crew, but call me a three-toed sloth—I just never got around to pointing that out. Free tickets? Any fool who knew somebody could get free tickets without having to pull one box out of a truck. Do we take the first guys that come across the field to see what this is all about? Do we write it into the contract as one of the things the sponsor provides? The best help just wants to get the job done, and the worst help wants to run away and join the circus. May the good Lord save us from good intentions.

The Rochester sponsor had a couple of guys who owed him a favor or, more likely, had been sentenced by some judge to doing some hours of community service. The torn jeans boys were standing with the sponsor when we arrived, smoking the way you do when you can't drink. They looked able enough, and once I put them under Scott and Loren Red Beard's care, they stripped off their shirts to reveal impressive sets of muscles and tattoos. The next time I looked, they were assembling bleachers. The temperature in the tent was like the inside of a stuck oven. It was in the 90s outside with humidity somewhere this side of warm ground fog. The whole assembly process was slowed by the constant mopping of brows and stops for more water. Half the crew would trade this week's pay for a decent breeze.

The heat took its toll on all of us. I'd lost ten pounds in the last month, mostly sweating it out. I was drinking as much water and beer as I could manage, but half the time, I felt like I was on the verge of heatstroke bad enough to make me think I was back in fucking Louisiana. Too hot and wet to enjoy it if you were truthful. Makes for bad decision-making to be lightheaded and puking. I couldn't afford to be a disabled role model, so of necessity, I was taking salt and drinking water like I enjoyed it.

About an hour before showtime, the temperature had sneaked as close as a shadow to the three-digit mark, and the humidity was so thick that even the cicadas had given up their thrumming. This was jungle weather, and only the big cats were happy. Two days of shake and bake in a row made everyone hot and cranky. Rightly so, and if they weren't, I'd be worried. Night brought no relief because on the circus grounds there was no air conditioning. Tents, campers, the back of the car, it made no difference—it was stifling, and where there was a machine to produce cooling, it could barely keep functioning. What sleep there was to be had was with a glistening sheen of sweat. A couple of the kids pooled cash to rent a motel room. Not for lovemaking but for the air conditioning. Soon as word got out, they had company. It was so hot the prospect of having sex was repulsive. Touching another body? Why, you'd slip right off.

During each performance, I had a couple of tubs of water and ice sitting outside the performers' entrances next to the curtained changing area and prop dumps. The act would finish and take a soggy bow, then run out the door, plunge head, feet, arms, sometimes even a butt into the icy tub for a shock of cold and wet. Then they'd peel off the old costume and paste on the next costume, rushing to enter the broil with the next cue. For some reason, Rose had not been able to wash costumes after the first day's show, which made putting some of them on a sticky plunge into a smelly wonderland. It was not a good day to be the back end of a buffalo. Truth be told, it was never a good day to be the back end of a buffalo, but in Rochester, putting twenty pounds of burlap, fake fur and molded paper mâché over your head was the worst—'specially if you were the guy in the rear, with your head tucked between the hump and the sweaty back of whoever was working the head mechanism. I know of what I speak.

Summer hadn't begun in earnest, but I was already feeling lower than a railroad track penny after the highball freight with the thought that we might have week after week of high temps and high humidity all the way. I didn't know whether to increase my intake of aspirin, salt and water or just lay my head beneath the wheels of the next train. It wasn't so much that I hate the heat as I hate the unrelenting that seemed to be the heat's main feature. It was one of the reasons I left Texas. It was the reason I hated the South eight months of the year. It was what drove me to desperate drinking in air-conditioned bars.

For Miss Red Boots and a few of the others, the heat was a prompt to dress light and swim often. Unfortunately, I don't swim. I don't mind watching others swim, especially when the girls are skinny-dipping, but my experience of entering water where I can't see the bottom leaves me sitting on the shore with a baggie of ice on the top of my head. I've almost drowned three, maybe more times, but who counts? Once in a pool, once in a river, once in the damn Gulf of Mexico. I've got no taste for taking another chance in lakes or ponds, no matter how many times someone had dove in. Come in, they'd shout at me, the water's fine. It's fun, they'd say. Drowning is not my idea of fun, and I was not about to let any sizable body of water get another chance to take me under. I wasn't going to do that night pond swim thing, no matter how tempting it was.

Heat was a given. Performing was a necessity. To their credit, the Rex crew rose to the challenge and got through the two days in the oven without incident. No one died. No one suffered heatstroke sufficient to be hospitalized. Though we did not know it at the time, those shows were during the hottest temperatures of the entire tour. Having survived them made whatever followed seem bearable.

"Yes, this heat is bad, but this isn't Rochester" became a balm for our suffering.

22–What It Was

Huzzah, huzzah, huzzah,
Step right up
Come closer
Don't be shy,
I have whatever your heart desires.
Yes, friends,
The little birds fly seeking their nests
The weary sun sets over the golden lake
We call you to your rest as well
Here in the temple of Aphrodite
A world of delights under a canvas sky…

By the beginning of June, this was what the schedule had already dealt us:

> Bemidji
> Grand Rapids
> Brainerd
> St Cloud
> Minneapolis
> St Paul
> Hastings
> Red Wing

Rochester
Winona
La Crosse

...and that was all there would be of the Mississippi in proximity to the build. Alma had been good, but those days were about to end. What was still to come as we made our way down the long ditch of time included:

Dubuque
The Quad Cities
Quincy
Peoria
St. Louis
Columbia
St. Genevieve
Cape Gerardo
Louisville
Memphis
Greenville
Natchez
Vicksburg
Baton Rouge
New Orleans
And anything we could add on the way.

Dammit, twenty-six cities scheduled for visitation between May and October seemed like an invitation for an accident and delay, but with any luck, we'd get through the tour without a death or dismemberment. If we could manage that, I'd call it all to the good. I'm not picky about what a miracle looks like. You don't have to be a believer to appreciate the impossible made manifest. Big or small, I was all for as many miracles as we could get as often as they could be manifested.

Come inside my friends
With open hearts

With open minds
With open wallets
The small price we will extract
Will seem but a wink and a nod
As we say
If you're right, you will not fright,
If you believe, we cannot deceive…

What was the show, you ask? It's not that I'm trying to avoid answering. Well, maybe I am…. But here goes.

I don't rightly remember the exact order of the show, at least not at this point on the tour. There were so many versions that only the large strokes remain fixed in my perilous recall. Start with a parade and end with a parade. That beginning and end, really, hardly ever changed except for how many people we had in it, but the middle parts were rearranged on any given day. We'd note what seemed to please one audience and sour another and then adjust accordingly. We tried hard as a dog sniffing some dropped meat to get them smiling on their way out of the tent. After all, pleasing the audience was the name of the game.

The rule of thumb was always know where you'll start and where you'll finish, or at least when it's time to quit. In between, you give the best of whatever you've got on hand. In those between spaces, we looked to each other to fill in the blanks.

The fire eater is hot tonight
The sword swallower is sharp tonight
The girl that would be a mermaid
Combs her coral hair with an abalone shell
Monstro, the strong man, will chew bare metal
And spit out bullets for the marksmen's pleasure—
All before your unbelieving eyes!!

Every time the curtain went up, we got a little better. Tinkering with the look and feel and the how it runs until—how should I put it?—until there was just enough circus and enough theater to make a show.

23–Last Great Margarita Party

There was pretty much nothing left in Alma but love and blood the day before the Rex Terrestrial, Celestial & Nautical Circus left. I mean, really and finally left. Done and gone. We would not be returning to lick our wounds or attempt another desperate repair of any of the stuff that broke mid-performance or never worked to begin with. We would be in full "get 'em up, get 'em out and keep on going" mode from there to the Gulf. Whatever ties we had to this sentimentally hallowed vale of safety thick with summer's green bounty and repose were about to be severed. When the trucks pulled out on the morrow, there was no coming back.

It was commonly agreed that this occasion warranted a grand departure party. Something big. Everyone gladly took a chore and made a contribution. I offered to grill up a few yard birds using one of the six secret BBQ sauce formulas I had in my possession. Wily Elijah and Billy Bones volunteered to build a bonfire to rid us of the compounded scrap accumulated by the making of the show. Of course, it fell to Marcel and myself to arrange a suitable supply of alcoholic fireworks for the festivities.

Even a cursory examination showed our capital was limited. The treasury, which at that moment was at the wrong end of the pay cycle, had only $62.65 in spendable coin, suggesting meager provisions of about a buck and a half per person—sufficient for a small amount of medium-quality libations. Marcel offered to procure the necessary supplies.

To the astonishment of a greeting party consisting of VX and myself, when he came back from town, he revealed that rather than spend our savings on numerous cases of cheap beer as had been expected, he had bought a plethora of "margarita fixings." Upon closer inspection, it was also revealed that those fixings consisted of several gallons of no-name vodka, three bottles of equally suspect tequila sans worms, a dozen green plastic limes, six twenty-pound blocks of ice and one can of frozen margarita mix, which Marcel claimed he had purchased for the recipe on the back. Even for a man of unbounded faith, or perhaps especially for such a man, it looked like a miracle would be in order.

Despite VX's motion to immediately impeach him from whatever office he held, Spirit Marcel assured us that he would prepare a concoction that would be the epitome of drinks, the Mount Everest of pleasure, the likes of which we had never tasted before and would likely never taste again. I gave him my blessing, and he retreated to the barn to produce that outcome.

While I was laying the seven halved chickens on a length of chain link fence set on concrete blocks that served as the grill, I could hear the Swede Girls—those tumbling, big-boned blondes—laughing in the kitchen at some private joke as they made potato salad by the pound. Marcel materialized at my side to ask if the oil from the chain saw he was using to slush ice might affect the taste of the margaritas. I answered in the affirmative and heard him muttering about some people's pansy-assed taste buds as he drifted back toward the inner sanctum of what he called his "sensory laboratory."

He wasn't seen again until the bountiful feast—a true culinary celebration—was laid out. There were piles of succulent, moist meat, crisp golden-skinned chicken slathered with a delicate patina of char-basted sweet and hot sauces, mounds of creamy white potato salad, plates of sliced oranges and onions arranged alternately with red Maraschino and dark fresh cherries sprinkled over the top like so many like Dippity Dots. There were hard-boiled eggs and the usual array of bland cheeses, piles of garden-grown carrots, thick-crusted wheat and rye breads fresh from the oven, big black pots of baked beans, vats of the omnipresent brown rice and more. Just as the milling throng was lining up to fill their plates, the barn doors opened and Marcel gave three blasts on a trumpet before he emerged pulling a red wagon carrying two tin washtubs. Each held a heaped mountain of shaved ice— one a delightful snow cone red with bits of crushed strawberries stuck like trapped climbers here and there on icy ledges, the other an evil glowing green.

Twilight might have well called the forest fairies into the empty rings of enchantment as Marcel ladled out his carnival-colored concoctions to as many of the company as were willing to try it. He often convinced them of its safety by imbibing a small sample of his own handiwork. To my amazement, it didn't seem to have much of an oily taste, but by the anticipated grace of a forgiving God, had a substantial cumulative and very potent effect. By dark's descent, the company was in a decidedly celebratory if not fully inebriated state, with even the sanest and most dour of the tour's participants pounding spoons on the bottoms of pans and calling out for peace, love, free sex and joyful sacrifices. Babies stood open-mouthed at the sight of their parent's communal playfulness.

The entire Rex seemed to move as one from the picnic tables on the lawn toward the field where for so many weeks, the ring had stood. They danced with still nimble feet rising and falling to a single primitive beat from those pots and pans, twirling and snaking away from the empty plates and chicken bones toward a mammoth pile of scrap wood, paper and discarded furniture set before them.

Brother Elijah hushed the company, called down a rough blessing from the four winds, from the sacred Trinities of the eternal and essential Male (Father, Son and Holy Ghost) and Female (Virgin, Mother and Crone), from the duality of Yin and Yang, from the singularity of the Self creating the Universe within Consciousness and the Big Bang that gave rise to all that we know and are. I don't remember if his invocation touched on any particular religion, but the nod seemed to be to all and none.

Looking upon the assembled congregation like a man in love, he prepared himself to set Prometheus's sacred gift upon the pile. This is what he said:

What shall you offer the spirit world for our coming prosperity? Come, friends, family, lovers, members of this wandering company. Let us make a solemn promise under the cloak of night that while Dawn's crimson brow will be here soon enough and with it our new beginning, we are marking the dark now with that which we would leave behind. What sacrifice from thee to we shall assure us the blessings of the morrow? A trinket? A gift? Your most precious art or some cast-off rubbish? No matter, offer it up, brethren. Make sacrifice and thus be blessed. Each and every one, now is the time to make an offering of your good will and for the grace of our life together in this center ring!

With that, he produced a match, lit a crude torch made from a rolled section of newspaper and placed it upon the kerosene-soaked pyre. In an instant, the flames shot into the starry night, accompanied by an owl hoot that could not have been better timed. It evoked something so communal, so primitive, it was answered with a ringing voice of awe from deep within the animal body of each of us. It gave me the willies because I really wasn't much for that feel-good sort of spirituality. But no matter, it was a genuinely spiritual moment, and I was not immune. What began as a collective exhale of breath turned into a low moan released from the back of the throat and turned again to a soaring trill as it left the mouth to echo off the eighteen-wheelers packed and ready. From young to old, a cacophony broke out of great heart-felt whoops and shouts.

What followed was a kind of Dionysian madness. In an instant, the field was nearly empty as every adult member of the Rex Terrestrial, Celestial & Nautical Circus dashed to their rooms and campsites, to costume trunks and toy boxes, tool kits and libraries to find something to feed the roaring fire. In the next instant, they were back and racing around the now-imagined circus ring with its silk banners fluttering, all of them laughing, banging those well sounded pots, pans, and wood blocks, beating out distinct, separate, but danceable rhythms. Then it coalesced into a collective heartbeat, unbroken and unabated, growing ever louder and faster as performers and road rats, lovers and hangers-on darted out of the drumming circle to add a bit of cloth, a well-read paperback, a stained work shirt, a piece of sheet music or whatever to the bonfire. Returning to our place in line, we danced a common step, unrehearsed but seemingly known in blood and bone over the months of living with each other, and sang a lyric that had first risen from Rose's lips to be learned by everyone at once and repeated in variations of volume and harmonies with giddy delight:

Come, you bright fools and dancers,
We travel the world without answers,
Letting laughter make sorrows yield,
Letting laughter make sorrows yield.

Instruments appeared. The circus band picked up the beat and began to improvise on it. Scott the Dog on the big baritone sax was paving the bottom with Dan and Loren Red Beard's honking alto saxes like Chicago traffic at rush hour an octave above him. Ben was tearing up the electric guitar, which had suddenly reappeared with amps plugged in and turned all the way up. The two Toms were on trumpets blasting the ghosts of James Brown's Kingdom of Funk. Stand back Phil Spector—this was a real wall of sound. The drums and percussion of old pots pounding out a rock-steady backbone, then a marching band double time, followed by bump and grind cadences. My God, that's when Elijah showed himself to be a veritable drumming demon, the left-hand alternating double four-four beats on two different drumheads overlaid with the right hand's syncopated flourishes on a snare. He was a man possessed of a trembling spirit, dancing in place and drumming the arrival of our collective Judgment Day.

And on repeat, now with harmonies above and below the verse:

Come, you bright fools and dancers,
We travel the world without answers,
Letting laughter make sorrows yield,
Letting laughter make sorrows yield.

At that very moment, one of the Swede Girls somersaulted over, or was it through the flames? A shout of joy went up. A shout that was one great huzzah! Sparks leaped into the night like a thousand fireflies declaring our being at home in the natural world and embracing the starry night. It felt as close as I'd ever been to a witch's Sabbath until I actually was at one, but that was years later—another story for a later time.

It wasn't, of course, a witch's Sabbath because, as near as I knew, we didn't have any witches in the circus or perhaps too many to count. But the moment was something I recognized as elemental. Our Dionysian revels. Whether named or not, it was the right thing at the right moment to say goodbye to one world and hello to another. None of us knew what that next world would be, but all of us knew that this world, the world of building the Rex on the farm, was finished.

I swear, for once in my life, I had seen happiness visibly manifested. Men, women, children dancing hand in hand, feeling the energy pass from one to another, the sheer joy of Bacchus loose amid the Nymphs, with bare feet flying up from the grass to kick at the stars and fall back to the firmament with a stomp of the ground, declaring this ground solid. I thought I might get sick from too much happiness, swoon from the power of the emotion and worry that it might stay. After all, I was reared in Texas by people who knew that no good deed went unpunished. They made sure I never forgot the terrible truth of it. It scared me to think how rare and fleeting happiness was. Here was the utter repudiation of sorrow, a beautiful communal entwining that made me shudder in anticipation that tomorrow we would be on the road where every sort of undeserved pain awaited.

Eventually, parents carried sleepy children off to bed. Young lovers, who had arrived at this encampment holding hands with giddy hopes for the start of an adventure, or who had met in the circumstance of becoming a one-ring spectacle, left to kindle more personal fires. Those humbled members of the Rex that could still walk staggered by to congratulate Marcel on his unqualified success. It was certainly high-octane, 100 percent drinking material. What secrets were held in the icy folds of those twin peaks of washtub wonder? Tapping a ladle against the pot he was wearing, he declared everything he had bought and whatever he had found—rubbing alcohol, mouthwash, and peppermint candy. I saluted my junior partner and retired to the living room couch to embrace Somnus, the King of Sleep. I knew that when morning came, it would be too soon.

24–Shotgun

Let me tell you something else about the wonder that is Marcel. That boy knows what he likes and likes what he knows. He works the crossword puzzles with a goddamn pen. No changing your mind this time, Baby. Got a brain that can recognize the obvious and just as easily deny it in favor of possibility. There are a lot of, well... *maybes* in that boy's world. Got a brain that has been seriously damaged and can't retain the obvious beyond those first few moments of recognition, but he gives it an effort.

The morning after the night before, he recognized that he was in no shape to drive. He had collapsed beneath a truck, and when I dragged him out, his mouth moved, but no sounds emerged. He just reached into his pocket and gave me the keys to his pickup. That boy knows pain when he feels it.

Before I loaded him on the blue bus, he broke away from my grip and half-trotted on unsteady legs into the house, re-emerging with a Mason jar. He carefully poured into the jar the remains of the two tubs still in the wagon. In morning light, this liquid looked like a bad urine sample. He carefully cradled the jar like it was a Faberge egg and climbed on board the waiting bus.

Pitiful sight, it was, looking at that poor Spirit once he shrunk into the seat in a fetal position, substituting a pair of undershorts with the waistband pulled down over his face for the pot he had worn last night. No amount of Dr. Buzz's Tonic would affect a quick cure for that boy. I was not sure if even the hair of the dog would make a dent in his pain. I offered him some aspirin, but he whimpered and waved away the tablets.

Around the farmyard, the sound of the diesel engine's roar announced the moment. As VX walked by, I held out the keys to Marcel's pickup.

Drive it to Iowa.

He took the keys, made a right turn toward the old red Ford, threw his pack on the passenger side, started it up and pulled into line behind Scott the Dog at the wheel of the blue bus and the truck carrying the big cats. One by one, the Rex Terrestrial, Celestial & Nautical Circus's haphazard collection of trucks, buses and bailing wire pulled out of the yard until I was the only one left.

I closed the front door of the house, went to lock it but realized I didn't have a key. Did anyone? So be it. I took a quick walk around the grounds to see what might have been left. A pile of scrap lumber here, some empty paint cans there, the matted grasses where the big ring had been with the still smoldering ashes of the bonfire in the center. I would have buried the ashes, but the shovels were on their way to Dubuque, Iowa. I opted to pee on the embers with little consequence other than to darken the ashes and send a bit of steam into the morning light.

The time had come to climb into my own chariot and, like Apollo, chart my course from dawn till far waiting night.

Not quite an hour after we'd left Alma, the blue bus pulled over beside the big river. Marcel's truck stopped behind it. Coming on the scene, I immediately wondered if this was the first of the frequent and always inconvenient breakdowns that plagued every traveling show I'd ever worked with. I pulled over to see if I could be of help.

VX was leaning over the hood of the pickup, laughing so hard he was holding his sides. Scott the Dog was sitting at the wheel of the blue bus, tears running down his cheeks. Marcel was sitting on a guardrail by the side of the road loading his shotgun, the underpants still on top of his head. The jar of special margarita mix shone brightly on top of a guardrail post about thirty feet from where Marcel sat.

An eye for an eye, a tooth for a tooth, Spirit Marcel declared to no one in particular. Cradling the shotgun barrel in the stainless-steel curve of his hook, he waved the shotgun in the general direction of the Mason jar and fired. Missed. Whether by an inch or a mile, I hadn't a clue.

Stand still, you son of a bitch, Marcel shouted.

He fired again. Buckshot, margarita mix and glass flew into the bushes. He smiled like a man who at last was fully satisfied and said, Now Mr. Drink-me-down, you damn teeth-chattering, good to the last drop destroyer of livers, you can feel my... oh God, what have I done to deserve this? You can feel my pain!

Then Marcel handed the shotgun back to VX and climbed on board the blue bus. Scott watched him settle into the seat and pull the underpants back over his eyes. Scott shrugged, pulled his own sunglasses into place and gave me a thumbs-up. He put the bus into gear. It protested with a sound of the clutch not quite fitting, but when he hit the gas, the bus lurched forward and back onto the road.

VX said, I'll be telling this story when I'm an old man. Took him three tries to hit it.

Yes, you will, I replied. Put the shells for the shotgun somewhere he won't be able to find them without a bit of a search. I don't want it to be that easy for him to settle an argument.

Right you are, VX said, though I never think of Marcel as the arguing type.

Nor I, but if it's all the same, a bit of hesitation before loading a shotgun offers a moment to consider whether it is the best course of action. I don't want that boy dead or in jail.

I got back into the Lincoln. Now we would all feel our pain. We were truly on our way.

25—Get Better or Die!

We had hardly started, and we already needed a miracle. I still do, I suppose. Every day in every way, we're looking for a panacea for all that troubles us. Sometimes we are so deep in alligators that we don't hear the prayer leaving our lips, just feel the nip of teeth at our ass. Why did we think we could drain the swamp? Well, I've got some advice to share—hard-won words that carry more than their weight in clarity, profundity and panache. Something short and sweet, conveying the essence of what matters most in relation to trouble and miracles.

Get better or die!

I'll say it again. Do you need a genuine, certified cure for the blues, depression, abject poverty or the common cold? Do you want that one sure thing, words of wisdom that can change attitudes, prompt action, make the sad happy and the happy ecstatic? I've got four little words that ring the bell of truth and serve as infallible good advice.

Get better or die!

Call it motivation. Call it an invitation for the improbable—no, the impossible. Whether it arrived as the central canard of the Rex's organizing principle by the fickle hand of Fate, those simple words have reverberated through the years as the truest words ever spoke on the Rex tour. Plato would have recognized the truth of those words and been jealous that he did not say them first. They manifest both our working philosophy and our essential existential condition, worthy of a Camus or Sartre.

Get better or die!

The first time I uttered those words was in a field sprinkled with week-old elephant dung buzzing with flies. We were at post-Alma stop number uno: Dubuque, Iowa, stuck between the railroad tracks and the river levee. We had been consigned by the city fathers to the same patch of no man's land that the Carson & Barnes Circus had occupied the week before. Who the hell scheduled this tour anyhow? You can't have one circus follow another the same month, much less successive weeks. It does a disservice to the art—more to the point, to the cash box of the one that follows. Did no one check the local civic calendar? Did one sponsor bother to talk to another in this picturesque purgatory? Did the local sponsor not want to make money? I did, but clearly, I was not there to ask the essential question of what came before or after the arrangements were made and now was living with the messy consequences of a failure to communicate.

I was living with flies! By the tens of thousands, though it might as well have been millions.

Flies, goddamnit, are the natural accompaniment of elephant turds! Both turds and flies were manifest from one end of the field to the other, dotted like green lily pads on a backwater pond as evidence of the casual disregard for health and sanitation that only a big-assed circus with big-assed elephants can have. I'm not disparaging Carson & Barnes, they were always good to go, but for some reason, had neglected to properly clean up before their departure.

When Miss Red Boots complained that the flies were irritating the tigers, I told her that we would have to make the best of it.

No—shit, she said, perhaps unaware of the irony of the phrase. The flies were the irritating discomfort we all shared, but she wanted to remind me that it was not her, me, or any of the Rex crew she was concerned about, but rather the tigers who were not so good to work with when irritated. So, what did "making the best of it" mean now? It meant no solution to the fly problem, which meant no tigers in the ring.

I said, Well then, we will have to make more than the best of it. We'll have to rise up to embrace the essential philosophical conundrum of living. We'll have to get better or die!

Or words to that effect.

She turned and went to cover the cage with mesh cloth that kept in the flies that were already in where the tigers swatted and ate them, and more importantly, kept the larger horde of the irritating winged nuisances out.

We began shoveling the evidence of *Elephas maximus* into a borrowed wheelbarrow and ended up sweeping the field from one side to the other with a mixture of water softener salt and surplus school compound. Yes, the very same stuff you used to create fake vomit in fourth grade. I had no idea where it had come from or how much it cost, but when Loren Red Beard brought it to me, I wanted as much as we could get because it worked wonders on calming the lingering insult of the olfactory atmosphere.

Marcel mixed the elephant excrement with hay and a few bags of garden potting soil, painted a sign that said, "PREMIUM GARDEN FERTILIZER," and sold it for a buck a pound. Sold forty bucks worth the first day. By the second, he was asking me where Carson & Barnes had gone because he needed another fifty pounds of pachyderm to meet the demand.

After we put up the tent, as many of the band members that could fit climbed into the back of a pickup and went around town to play bright, jaunty tunes while the best-looking girls in the Rex crew passed out flyers and discount coupons for the show. This worked up a crowd for the first show. The smell of industrial-strength insecticide we had fogged the tent with—suggested by a note somebody scribbled to us on the back of a flyer— was heavy in the air, but we put on a show with no gas masks and a minimum of coughing. Then, at the end of the day, we swept the ring again, went to bed, and in the morning, plotted what we would do to bring that day's crowd through the door for the next one.

Marcel suggested that I should take those words—Get better or die!—to heart as the only true and appropriate motto of the Rex.

He talked Sonja into making a flag from a design he arrived at while reading a Classic Comics version of Treasure Island. She agreed to sew the motto around a tippy crown atop a skull and crossbones. By osmosis, it seemed that the Rex Terrestrial, Celestial & Nautical Circus took those four words into its collective heart.

26–The Big River

The great ditch of time is what I like to call it. An apt description, factual evidence of the geological process at work, especially between St. Anthony Falls and the junction of the Missouri. When you are on those waters, you are really in the scenic middle section of the 2,552 miles it takes the Mississippi to make the 1,475-foot descent to sea level. Look it up if you don't trust my numbers.

On each side of the valley, those are some big-assed bluffs the river has carved over many centuries of flood and freeze. It is easy to forget that the top of those bluffs is where the states of Minnesota, Wisconsin, Iowa and a bit of Illinois reside. It is harder to forget the thousands of gallons of water evaporation rising off the ever-moving current trapped between the bluffs, intensifying the humidity to jungle proportions. Wet 'n' hot. A summer heat that clings day and night. A breeze will not dispel it. While building the circus in Alma, the river was always a few miles downhill, but even when you didn't see it, you felt the effect.

Red Wing, Alma, Wabasha, Fountain City, Winona, La Crosse— every one of those towns was built because the river was there. Lumber or steamboats needing fixings or a guide who could get you a few miles up or downstream in the olden days when the channel changed course with every moonrise or rainstorm. Between each town, a shifting puzzle of backwaters and deadfall sandbars. Best to have a pilot or regret not having one.

It was twenty-nine locks and dams between Minneapoli
St. Louis that served making money. Twelve barge tows and dredged
channels made the river reliable. Profitable even. Think of it—twelve
barges harnessed three across, each carrying 1,500 or more tons of
wheat, corn, coal, chemicals, what have you. Moving night and day.
Think twenty or more tows up and down the channel between St. Paul
and St. Louis or between St. Louis and New Orleans on any given day.
Then add the number of tows and barges up and down the Ohio and
Missouri, and you begin to get some sense of how big the machine that
this industrial river was. Whoo, that's some money there. That's what
the Corps of Engineers is for.

Maybe I'm getting ahead of myself here. The river takes 650
miles to get from Itasca to St. Anthony Falls. Most of it is pleasant
enough, actually flowing north from the national park stepping stones.
It's a slow-moving stream like so much spilled thread before it reaches
Bemidji, then turns toward Grand Rapids, and afterward picks up some
width as it slides toward the Gulf. Still tame. Fish, paddle a canoe,
swim in it if you don't mind a little pesticide or fertilizer runoff from
the adjacent farm fields. Not much to look at most of the way, each
stream and pothole lake adding its bit till you arrive at St. Anthony
Falls.

These days, the falls themselves aren't much more than a lot of
water spilling over a low concrete wall, but in the 1830s, they were
a good half-mile downstream and had a spectacular sixty-foot drop
before the limestone gave way in the river's quest to make itself a
rapids. Long after the natives called it whatever they called it and
that sanctimonious prick, Father Hennepin, renamed it after the saint
whose feast day it was when he stopped there, the falls were worth
a visit. Some wag built a tower at the bend where the University of
Minnesota now sits and charged tourists, who had taken the steamboat
to St. Paul and the excursion carriage from there, a "dime to climb" to
get a better view.

James J. Hill built a stone arch bridge over the river just south
of the falls to get his Great Northern trains headed west toward wheat
and timber lands. Charles Pillsbury and James Ford Bell built flour

milling plants alongside the river, using the power of water to mill the wheat to make the bread. The city of Minneapolis became, in the words of somebody, "the First City of the West," meaning on the west side of the river. Saying this ignored St. Louis, which was making its own wealth on getting folks and goods up and down the mighty Mississippi, but civic pride and the hustle for spending money being what it was, they said it anyway.

Humm, I seem to have digressed a bit. But you ought to study up on the history of the river because it's a good one. Anyway, my point was, or should have been, that when you talk that ol' Miss-iss-ipp-I, there are three geographical rivers to consider. The itty-bitty beginning, the blessed middle of twelve barge tows where the landscape bulks up in the prettiest way, and the river after St. Louis, which is more an industrial sewer than a picture postcard.

The Rex made stops along each of them, and while the show didn't change much after Alma, the dark and rhetorical themes of danger implied in the high wire or trapeze became more pronounced as we continued our descent.

27–Marcel and Miss Red Boots

Frank sent me a telegram saying that by way of a friend of a friend, there were a couple of shows to be added in Macomb, Illinois. It was a college town, he said. They'll dig it.

It was there that I almost lost Marcel to flesh and the devil.

Marcel was this far from leaving—or more truthfully, being carried off by a love-struck princess. On the next stop, Peoria, we did lose the camel but got him back—the camel, that is. That was easy, but I'm getting ahead of myself. I should be telling one story at a time. Before I get too far afield, I'll say that Marcel is smarter than the camel and almost as thirsty, but it took more than a case of beer to get him back in harness after that night in Macomb.

It was sweet Miss Red Boots who started the trouble. Her and her simple white dress with the supposed blue polka dots. They were actually little cut-out holes with blue threaded trim. They only looked like polka dots. Beneath them was nothing but suggestion.

It was late, the show was run and the gear packed for the next day's performance when most of the imbibing company retreated to a den of inebriation down the street from the circus grounds. Classic place. Pressed tin ceilings, though you could barely see them with the dark and the smoke. A long bar with twenty feet of mirror and ornate carved cupids holding the bottle shelves. Nice pool table. Scott the Dog was there sipping local beer with VX, Billy Bones, Slim Jim and Big Bearded Jim. Rona and one or maybe both the Swede Girls were there too. If I remember rightly, always smiling Rose, the mother of two towheads, had left her kids in somebody else's care, and was nursing a couple cold ones with the full-grown girls.

I was shooting eight ball with Marcel and the two Toms when Miss Red Boots came into that little oasis of hedonistic pleasure wearing that simple white dress with the tiny blue polka dots and nothing underneath. This was a compromise between a prim and proper dress designed for comfort in warm weather and a little bit of a tease. The dress looked good on her. She kissed both of the Toms and sat down to have a double something, a departure for her since she usually was more of a wine sipper than a seven and seven bumper.

It had been a so-so show night with the big cats. They were lethargic, and she had to work her ass off to make it look exciting, so she was entitled to have a good time. More than entitled—she deserved some kind of reward for her valiant effort to make uncooperative tigers look entertaining. She deserved every round put in front of her and had one and another. After a third, when the talk got trashy, I offered to buy.

It was the same thing all around, if I remember correctly. Truth is, I don't remember much about that night except that the assembled company had decided ex officio, and as a committee of the whole, to get skunk drunk. About the witching hour, Marcel went to piss and was gone for a good long time. He came back wearing a white dress with tiny blue polka dots. Looked pretty good in the dress, too, except his legs were way too hairy to be attractive. Had a nice shade of lipstick on. Had the pale blue eyeliner that was favored by the circus girls who bought most of their beauty supplies from Rose, who bought them from stores in the bigger stops.

What is this? VX asked. You've changed somehow.

Tom said, Hey, take a walk on the wild side. Any boy can swing a ding-a-ling, but not every boy has the stuff to be flung fashion forward.

Miss Red Boots followed him out of the restroom wearing his cheap blue suit and white shirt. She had wiped off her lipstick and pulled her brown tresses up into a tight bun on top of her head before she jammed on Marcel's favorite gray porkpie. Damn, he was lucky the hat was too big for her, or she would have ruined it for sure the way she tugged it down around her ears.

Marcel picked up the pool cue and began singing, Just me and my shadow strolling down the avenue.

Tom said, Your shadow wears your clothes better than you do.

Miss Red Boots came to the table and began stroking Marcel's cue in a most suggestive manner. Then she took it out of his hand, leaned over the table, gave the ball a long squint as she tried to gauge the just right angle.

Six ball, corner, she said with confidence.

Her movement was a smooth back-and-forth gesture propelling the cue. Click. The green orb obediently exited the table.

Doctor, have you got a fag? she asked me, then scrunched up her face and added, Err, perhaps that was a poor choice of words. A cigarette, if you please.

I replied, Here, go for broke. I handed her a cigar and said, Sorry, no fabled Cubans tonight, but this smokes well enough.

Miss Red Boots leaned forward, and I lit it up. Marcel was fluttering around the table like a nervous moth, turning little pirouettes and jetties for the amusement of VX and the Toms.

I looked at Marcel and said, How about you? Want a big one?

Sure, Doc. Just stick it between my lips the next time I swing by. He turned to Miss Red Boots and said, Merciful God, don't your legs get cold in a dress?

Miss Red Boots took a good hit on the cigar and blew a cloud his way. Of course, she said. But you get used to it. Sit down, Marcel, you're making me nervous.

Marcel sat down, saying, You're just being cruel because I have better legs than you do.

Miss Red Books chuckled and said, Half the men in this company have better legs than I do, but you're the only one wearing my dress, and I do not want it ruined.

I'm the only one who can fit into it, Marcel said, laying across the pool table, one foot reaching towards the floor and the other crossed over his knee, his back arched and his arms tucked under his head in a crude approximation of the classic Marilyn Monroe centerfold pose.

Flirtatiously, Marcel said, Don't hate me because I'm beautiful.

Get off the table, one of the Toms said. Your messin' wit' the balls.

The larger Tom grabbed Marcel's foot and began to turn him like a lazy Susan, walking around the table from left to right. Marcel's arms shot out, sending the pool balls flying.

Oops! Marcel kicked Tom's hand away and sprang to his feet, landing upright on the green felt field. Sorry boys, he said. But this game has been canceled due to the stage show. He began dancing in place, kicking his foot out with each quarter turn as he hummed "The Stripper." One of the black pumps he was wearing left his foot and sailed over the bar, and he muttered, Oops again, gents.

As the pump flew over the bar and landed on a stack of empty beer cases, several of the locals noticed something unusual going on. They moved from mild amusement to muttered threats and vocal insults in the space of a single turn of the head. The bartender put down his rag and picked up the black pump.

Cut that shit out, you freakin' homo, the bartender shouted. And get off my pool table before your rip the felt.

The two Toms grabbed Marcel by the legs, lifted him into the air like a child on a playground swing and placed him on a neighboring chair. He lost his balance and fell, sending the chair crashing into a table, spilling several drinks in the process. At the same moment, the music stopped and the only sound that could be heard was breaking glass and Marcel's unceremonious thump as he hit the floor.

Shit! He said. I think I popped a button.

My dress! Miss Red Boots exclaimed. Have you ripped it?

The bartender began cursing incoherently. The entire Rex Terrestrial, Celestial & Nautical Circus company froze and then turned to give the bartender a look that was somewhere between contempt and warning. As a single entity, every member put down their glasses, pool cues, buffalo wings, celery, whatever they were holding, and rose to their feet, moving to form a circle around Spirit Marcel.

No harm done, I said, running my hand across the green tabletop. Just having too much fun. But if you don't want our patronage or our money, we'll take our business elsewhere. We always go where we are welcome, and we have certainly felt welcome here with the splendid hospitality that your double shots have provided up to now. Thank you, sir. If you take offense at our foibles, we will take our leave. No foul meant. Yes, I see there is no harm done.

That's when Billy Bones shouted to everyone and no one, Or we'll kick your ass if you want a fight.

I gave him a look meant to convey a sense of urgency about the inappropriateness of that unhelpful statement.

It was not more than a few seconds, but each tick of the proverbial clock felt like long hours. The silence remained charged with menace. A half-dozen rough-looking locals in various states of inebriation looked back and forth between the circus and the bartender. On both sides, muscles flexed, fists opened and closed. Around the pool table, two or three cues rose to combat readiness in Rex hands.

I stepped away from the table and gestured toward it. In my hand, a trio of Andrew Jacksons peeked out at the bartender. Fact is, I've always thought that a fistful of dollars was a better solution to conflict than spilt blood and broken bones. If I could pay our way out of a brawl, it would be money well spent.

For the inconvenience, and the chair, I said, laying on the bar that legal tender's homage of a grateful nation to its most racist president.

Just keep him off the table, the bartender said as he picked up the cash, slipped it in his shirt pocket and turned his back to start drying glasses again.

The tension broke, leaving in its wake the smell of sweat, booze and cigar smoke. The big-haired waitress came over to scoop empty glasses off the tables. As she did, she gave me a wink. I asked for another Jack Daniels. Dammit, that was a moment where I would have appreciated a premium single malt, but that was not to be had in this bar or maybe in this town. There was nothing to do but return to the cigar that Miss Red Boots offered back to me. The residual electricity in the room reminded me of the first air after a spring storm, thick with ozone and the echo of departing thunder.

A Swede Girl took Marcel's hand and led him out the side door for a breath of fresh air. VX and I traded glances. He rubbed his long equine nose, laughed a silent one meant only for my eyes, then called the waitress over to order another round for the locals, telling her that I'd gladly pay for it.

The good Doctor's made of money, he said, so give yourself a generous tip while you're at it.

I made a little mental note to dock this round from his pay.

Miss Red Boots picked a quarter off the pool table and dropped it in the slot. The pool balls crashed into the bay. She began racking them. Billy Bones, he of the wild hair and intemperate tongue, chalked his cue. Normalcy returned—or at least the illusion of normalcy, such as it is, when the circus is in town.

Billy Bones whispered to me, Buzz, what should we do? Marcel is…

Take the boy out for a ride, I said, as I watched Miss Red Boots nudge the cue ball into position. Take the boy out to the moonlight fields where he can dance amidst clover and fairy dust. Where he can run naked if he has a mind to. This town is too small to be forgiving, and rumor is faster than news, faster than the telephone and so slippery that by tomorrow half the town will want to run us out on a rail and the other half will curse themselves for having missed the spectacle. But either way, it might be a good bounce for attendance.

I glanced at Miss Red Boots, who was now sinking the third ball in a row. To Billy Bones, I added this request: And take this girl as well. She's too hot for her own good, and before she cools, she'll cost me a lot of money.

What happened next? I really ought to have Marcel tell me that story again because the details are very fuzzy. Let's see. They did go out for a ride, him and VX and Miss Red Boots in a car with some sympathetic locals who offered to give them a tour of something or to take them to some party somewhere. Must of been very sympathetic because the way I heard it, one of the locals took a real liking to

Marcel. Six or eight people crammed into a car looking for a party in the middle of the night. Driving through Illinois with cornfields on the left, cornfields on the right and Marcel sitting on some guy's lap singing, I'm going to wash that man right out of my hair.

Miss Red Boots was next to him in the back seat with her feet out the window, sucking back warm beer until she puked. Seems like the scenario I heard her tell, anyways. Maybe the driver pulled over, but she didn't quite make it out the door before she sprayed the car. Stunk it up pretty bad. The driver wanted to leave her in a ditch, but VX came to his sister's defense and convinced him otherwise. The evening ended with windows open and the driver swearing at the top of his lungs.

Meanwhile, the guy under Marcel must have liked show tunes because he was drooling into Marcel's cleavage and playing patty cake with him. Was that it?

Don't remember how they got home or when, but I remember Mr. Drool sent Marcel flowers the next day and came to every performance, sitting in the first row waiting for Marcel to come into the ring. He'd whoop and cheer as if Marcel were the brightest star in the firmament and then hang around the back of the tent after the show wanting to make small talk with the boy. Marcel was flattered for about two minutes, then started looking for a way to sneak out. Made it hard to get any work done, looking over his shoulder half the day to see if Mr. Lovesick Puppy was nearby. He didn't want to hurt anybody's feelings, but Marcel was just not a settle-down-in-Illinois kind of guy.

28–The Camel Escapes

The next stop was Peoria. Not exactly on the Mississippi, but close enough and more to the point, a decent-sized city with a Kiwanis Club that was willing to pay for two nights and a matinee. We set up in a baseball field behind the junior high, thanks to the weight of a school board member who was also the vice-president of the aforementioned fraternal group.

In the middle of a matinee on a lazy summer afternoon, I was standing by the back entrance watching Rose and Ruth doing the trapeze act, which always amazed me because Ruth was short and curvaceous. You know, heft up front and heft in the trunk, which I suppose helped her balance—but she had more than what you'd expect from the run-of-the-mill trapeze artist. After one unfortunate incident in La Crosse where her tits popped out, I told her she needed to tape them in. Double stick or duct tape, I didn't care, but free-swinging boobs and grade school kids were not a good combination.

Anyhow, I'm watching the act when VX comes up and whispers in my ear that the camel is gone.

What do you mean *gone*? I asked.

Escaped, he said, then physically turned me around to look out the tent in time to see the camel taking a right turn off the field and head up the street. Oh, bless me—what have I done to deserve this?

Like I said, camels are trouble. Trouble with a long memory. They say an elephant never forgets. Well, a camel doesn't forget, but more

112

to their essential evil selves, they don't forgive. They carry grudges. A camel gets it into its head that you did something to offend it—looked at it cross-eyed, didn't give it enough water or too much, whatever the slight—and the son of a hump will want to get even. They'll bite, kick, spit, stand on your foot, fart or shit on you while feigning complete innocence. And I don't mean quick revenge. No, they'll nurse that grudge for months, and long after you've forgotten what you did to offend them, they will up and let you have it.

Like I also said, the only reason to have a camel in a circus is money. For reasons that have always escaped me, parents think it's cute to have their kids ride a camel. That being the case, you put a saddle on a stinking bag of hair on stilts, disguise a stepladder as stairs, hoist the kid up, and for five dollars a pop, put a kid or two in the saddle for a walk around the tent. Then the parents take a picture, or you take a picture and charge them another couple of bucks for a copy. The kids always have a mix of horror and excitement that is amplified the moment you lead the camel away from the steps, and they experience the sway of the beast plodding, plodding, leaning this way and then that with each step. Some kids get sick and throw up. Jesus, now you've got to hose the puke off the camel, which just pisses the camel off. Some kids want to go faster, but that's not going to happen. A camel at full gallop is way too fast, and we don't strap the kids in. No one with the sense God gave a doorknob would let a kid ride a camel at full gallop. Adults with the sense God gave a turnip don't ride a camel at full gallop. A camel that bolted into a gallop would toss a kid to the ground in three steps.

Which was what this one had done. I could see the kid lying on the ground, crying. I could see the parents rushing over to check for damages, looking up lawyers in pocket address books. But most of all, I could see the camel running away. Though I often wished the camel would disappear, this was not good for anyone. Certainly not for me or the Rex. Fuck a wet mop, not even for the camel.

I motioned for Scott the Dog, who had just come out of the prop dump to come over. Here, take the top hat and coat. You're going to announce the next act, and I'm going to catch the damn camel.

113

He looked confused but took the coat and hat.

Outside the tent, it was still a beautiful day. The sun continued to shine. The white clouds floated like marshmallows in an aquamarine blue sky. VX drove up in Marcel's pickup with Marcel leaning out the passenger window to keep his eye on the camel's progress. He opened the door, stepped out to let me slide between them with the gearshift between my legs.

He's headed south, Marcel said. But then he added the last thing I wanted to hear. Oh, shitty shit—there's a police car behind him.

It was true. The camel was heading south at something less than a gallop. It had slowed down to a walk when a black and white pulled up behind it. The camel ignored the cops. The squad car turned on its lights. The camel paid no attention, of course, just continued resolutely toward some unknown destination. We accelerated out of the schoolyard and over the curb. In less than a block, we fell into line behind the squad car.

Pull over, came the slightly distorted voice from the squad car. Pull over now.

As if the camel would listen.

The second announcement pissed off the camel, causing him (and yes, the camel was definitely a him) to pick up the pace and angle off from the street through one of Peoria's parks. I was praying that these guys wouldn't use the siren. Instead, they just repeated their demand that the camel stop, which the camel clearly had no intention of doing. At least not until he came to the tennis court, where he darted around the net and positioned himself four feet behind the foul line along the chain link fence.

It was at this point that the squad car, having driven to the end of the block and onto the sidewalk via the handicap easement, came racing back, lights still flashing, and pulled to a stop at an angle to the camel and the fence. There was room for the camel to get past the cops, but it didn't move. Whether it was confused or frightened, I don't know. The cops got out of the car and pulled their guns, moved to the side of the squad farthest from the camel. We were on the verge of a standoff with the camel pressed against the chain link fence and spitting at the cops and the police waving their guns at the camel while shouting orders the camel obviously could not understand.

We were past ready for a big-time circus intervention. The three of us got out of the truck and walked up to the cops.

I said, Officers, please, let us handle this.

Who are you? a beefy black cop said, turning his head toward me. This is a dangerous beast.

Well, I might agree with you that this camel is a danger, but mostly to himself as you are armed, and he is not. We should know, sir, as this is our son-of-a-bitch camel.

I leaned in so there would be no mistaking my next words, which were: This is also an expensive beast and, if you shoot him, there is the problem of the body, its removal, its disposal, and of course, a long, tedious bit of paperwork required to explain what happened. As I said, I'm with the circus encamped down the road, as are these gentlemen.

The cops just looked at me, confused about what to do next.

Pointing to Marcel, I explained, This man is a certified camel expert and will be able to resolve this situation without resorting to anyone needing to shoot the aforementioned camel, much as you might like to.

The beefy cop looked at me, then at his partner. He seemed dubious, though I could not tell if it was based on what I said or his intense desire to shoot a camel. I pressed in a little closer for one more try before my hand would be forced to reach for the wallet.

I said, It's not just your paperwork, officer, but a barrage of insurance company inquiries and a trial that will surely follow as their lawyers will seek someone to blame for an animal cruelty claim and the parallel willful destruction of property inquiry that will have to be determined. Face the facts—no insurance company is going to want to pay the cost of a dead camel and will bring the entire machinery of substitution for economic loss to bear on the City of Peoria.

The other cop asked me, What do we need to do?

I answered matter-of-factly, First, please, put your guns away. I waved Marcel, who had been spitting back at the camel for the fun of it over - Marcel, will you inform these officers as to what is needed to subdue this errant dromedary?

Dromedary? The second officer was processing that word.

Camel, I explained. Dromedary is the actual name for this species of camel.

Marcel looked them up and down. He looked at the camel, which was now rubbing his back against the chain link fence, perhaps scratching out fleas. The camel groaned with pleasure at the scope of the scratch.

Marcel turned to the cops with his instruction: We'll need two cases of warm beer. Cheap is fine, this is not a premium situation.

Beer? The first cop seemed skeptical.

Rolling Rock if you've got it. Marcel said. Definitely warm, not chilled. Cold beer is of absolutely no use.

To my surprise, the cop radioed in the request. There was a bit of back and forth with the dispatcher about the camel, about the request, about our intervention, but in the end, a positive affirmation came over the speaker, and ten minutes later, a second squad arrived with two cases of warm Rolling Rock. The officers delivering this cargo got out of the car, carried the case over and placed it at Marcel's feet. They looked at the camel, which turned his head to hiss at them. One cop started to go around the front of the squad for a closer look.

I wouldn't do that, I said. He'll spit, and if you're close enough, he'll take a bite. It will require stitches.

The cop stopped in his tracks and came back to the fold. Marcel, on the other hand, opened the case of Rolling Rock, picked up a bottle and walked toward the camel shaking it as he walked. When he was close enough for the camel to focus its attention on him, Marcel popped the cap off the beer bottle with his hook. Beer spray hit the camel square in the face. The camel reared back and instinctively licked the beer dripping off his nose.

Marcel turned to me and said, I need another one, Buzz. He reaches back expectantly. I handed him another beer. He vigorously shook it, popped the cap and sprayed it on the camel, then tossed the empty toward the net. Another if you would. Keep them coming.

After the first five bottles had been emptied, the camel was anticipating the next one and started opening its mouth as soon as Marcel began shaking the bottle. By bottle number ten, the camel was leaning forward, allowing Marcel to move within an arm's reach.

VX had now replaced me in the bottle transfer chain. I'd stepped back to huddle with the four cops and was trying to discern whether this situation required a bribe—excuse me, a contribution to the policeman's benevolent fund—or maybe passes to the show or something else that would minimize the paperwork and time-wasting delay that an "incident" like this might require. They beat around the metaphorical bush while Marcel fed the camel bottles twelve through eighteen. Finally, a twenty each for the local cop charity and eight passes to tonight's show put the cops into the squads and backing away.

At least they'll have something to talk about in the squad room. Fucking alcoholic camel!

Sweet Blessed Mother, that was close, I tell Marcel, who is now finishing off the first case of Rolling Rock. He is literally standing a foot from the camel. He is not shaking the bottles now, just popping them open and pouring the beer into the camel's mouth. The camel is swaying rhythmically from foot to foot but otherwise seems quite calm.

VX comes alongside the camel and attaches a new lead to its bridle. Marcel reaches out and takes the original lead that had been yanked out of whoever's hand that had been guiding the camel when it got the notion to leave.

Marcel said, Yes, right on, Doctore. That was great…

I had to interrupt, saying, I think this qualifies as one of the most bizarre hours of my life spent, how do I put this—trying to keep a camel that I hate alive long enough for me to kill it. The only positive I see is that I don't have a dead camel on my hands.

I noticed Marcel grinning at me. Then he said, Oh, Doctore, it's so much better than that. We've got an entire case of Rolling Rock left. Man, once we chill them up, it'll be golden.

Marcel turned the camel around and began the trek back to the circus grounds. I had to admit, he was right. We did have a free case of

117

beer to show for our effort. I picked it up, put it in the pickup and drove back to the marshmallow white tent with the Rex Terrestrial, Celestial & Nautical Circus banner flying beneath an aquamarine sky. I was so glad to get the camel back alive, I didn't think about selling or trading it for something sensible for at least two hours.

Even though we had another show that night, I was ready to check out of Peoria. I'd had enough, and leaving seemed like the easiest thing to do.

29–Peanuts, goddammit

In St. Louis, I met a guy, old as dirt with wrinkles on top of his wrinkles. Had a face that looked like a wheezing prune. He could have been Tommy the Wino in old age, or Tommy's poorer cousin. Could have been me if I had taken another path.

Tommy was the first real bum I knew, but that's another sad story. He did tell me one thing that was as true then as it is now. As true for my life as for his. You can take to drink, drugs and fast women, but it does you no good. Drinks, drugs and especially fast women are only as good as money will buy, and when the money's gone, so are they. What satisfies is being able to look at your naked self in the mirror and not turn away.

The peanut guy was Elijah's story of the day. He sold them down by the Arch. Dressed the same every day—black suit, black shoes held together with duct tape, no socks, faded shirt more stained than white, and a little red bow tie. Carried a paper grocery store bag. He always said the same thing:

Peanuts, goddammit. peeeeenuts, peeeeenuts, goddammit!!

No one would buy a thing from him. He just was too scary. Looked bad. Smelled dead skunk in the roadway worse, and if you could get past that, there was plenty more to offend you. Even the black suit couldn't hide the fact he pissed his pants and didn't even notice. Naturally, the guy spent the whole day walking from one end of the levy to the other, muttering and shaking the grocery bag at whoever came within spitting distance. Hell, he'd have to sneak up on people just to get close enough to ask the question. If they saw him coming, parents would send their children running for cover or cross the sidewalk like he was bad luck personified.

Elijah decided to buy some peanuts. Christian charity? I think not. Curiosity about what the guy would do if he had to make change was more like it. Walked right up to the guy and said, Can I have some of those peanuts?

The old guy looked at him, started muttering all kinds of shit under his breath. Elijah couldn't understand a word of it except for the price. One dollar.

Seemed kind of expensive for my tastes, but Elijah smiled a big gold tooth grin and slipped the guy a couple of Washingtons. The old guy looks at the pair, then looks at Elijah again and says,

Thank you, young man.

I'll tell you the truth about that. Those peanuts were so old they could have passed for relics of Ra dug out of the great pyramid by Napoleon. Man, those nuts had forgotten the meaning of plump, done shriveled in their shells like spinster sisters afraid to come out of the house and made lonely little knocking sounds when you shook them. Open one of them up and they looked like little rat turds. The absolutely worst peanuts I ever saw, much less tasted.

For the sake of the experience, I tasted one.

30–Under the Arch

St. Louis was where my tour went off the rails, and it wasn't just the thought of leaving that stuck in my craw. I felt like I was this close, this dammed close to winding up like the peanut guy if the coin toss came up anything other than the bet I had placed on this tour. What was heads or tails was unimagined, but I could feel the air waiting for the flutter and the surety that would follow. I could feel my fingers turning the weight of chance before it was sent airborne.

Yes, yes, as sure as the future contained in the dregs of a teacup for the reading, it was one of those moments when life could change and did. As it often is in such cases, there was a woman right in the middle of it all.

Not one of the circus babes. I learned long ago that you can't be the boss and the lover at the same time. Even if they were inclined, I'd have to say not while we're on tour. That was my ironclad rule, and I was sticking to it.

What knocked me off my pegs was a big-boned, long-legged, ex-Texas tease who also just happened to be working for the chamber of commerce sponsor.

Athena was her name. Might have well as been Godzilla, because she just roared through my heart like it was Tokyo ripe for the stomping. Saw her and felt the dam of good intentions burst. She was one of those women who, when you look at them, you see possibilities. You think to yourself, why yes, I do believe in miracles and forgiveness.

121

We did a show in the shadow of the Arch. God bless, that arch is one beautiful piece of work. Fine by any standard, soaring up, a curve of stainless steel glinting in the sun looming over everything. When you stood with the circus tent pitched on green grass between the concrete slabs at the base and the muddy Mississippi, the Rex looked tiny. Inside, knowing the mass of the thing was above you made me feel smaller than the mouse in the corner.

The shadow of the Arch crossed over the tent. The roof was glowing white before the dark line of the shadow arrived. It grew like the tide coming in until finally, for a few moments, it covered the canvas sky. Real special, it was. I stared as it continued across until the other edge of the Arch shadow slipped off the canvas leaving the white glow of sunlight on the roof complete. The arrival and departure sure and uncaring. Yes, it was beautiful in the way an eclipse is beautiful. Surprisingly quick, if you looked at a fixed point, and I had.

After the show, Athena asked me if I wanted to have a drink. Why wouldn't I? We had met a few days earlier and exchanged some small talk. Mostly I just felt myself wanting to not get too close because, at first glance, she was everything that I said I wanted in a woman. Good looking, sure, but more to the point, whip-smart and quick to get down to brass tacks. Probably smarter than me, but I didn't need the trouble of finding out how much smarter she might be. I'd see her once or twice in the sponsor role and be on my way. Then she asked if I wanted a drink, and me not being one to turn down a drink with a good-looking woman, and certainly not when the sponsor is paying, I agreed.

I gave VX and Loren Red Beard the lowdown on the last of the post-show packing up—where to take the load and where to park it in, which lot by the church we had commandeered as our temporary headquarters. I didn't need to do that because they knew what I knew, but it was habit or pride. I wanted to remind someone, maybe myself, that I was important enough to be able to leave for a little sponsor hospitality and not be thought of as shirking the work. Or maybe I wanted to show Athena that I really was Johnny on the spot. I figured I would be gone an hour or two. I picked up my leather doctor's kit as always, which, if you remember right, functioned as the Rex's essential management office and left them to the tear down. I threw the bag into the back seat of Athena's sporty little car and settled in for the ride.

We drove to a newly gentrified neighborhood on the edge of downtown. Doesn't matter which one, they're all expensive propositions of hope against better judgment amid rundown buildings and vacant lots. But if you must know, I could see the smokestacks of the Budweiser brewery in the distance. She was playing Muddy Waters on the sound system, and to my mind, it was the right soundtrack for a neighborhood that looked more South Chicago in the early '60s than St. Louis in some supposed post-integration glory.

As we were getting out of the car, she asked me if I really needed the bag with me.

I answered, It's my office. I usually don't let it out of my sight.

Well, she said, this is a quiet, dark bar and we're not here to work. Leave it in the car, please.

There was something about the way she said please that rubbed me wrong. Not wrong enough to argue, but it felt not quite right. I hesitated, but wanting to be accommodating, I did leave it on the floor of the car.

You know what's coming, don't you? In that moment, as she put her arm around my waist, I didn't say this is a bad idea, but I should have. Common sense should have said leaving anything in the car was a very bad idea. Common sense was gone, and all I could see was the pleasure of her arm around my waist and the prospect of her company. I was already smitten and soon to be proved a fool.

After a couple of drinks and some small, mildly flirty conversation, I forgot everything except the martini buzz and the smell of her perfume, when she said, It's time to go.

We walked out to see the car window broken and the bag gone. Gone— oh, so very gone.

123

31–The World Turned Upside Down

In an instant, the well-made martini buzz was also gone. Panic took center stage. If my heart stopped or pulse raced, I didn't notice because I was entirely focused on the mental list of what was in that old leather bag, What I needed, what I would regret losing or could not replace. Contracts. Address book of personal and touring contacts. A Polaroid camera plus two fresh packs of film. There was certainly a half-dozen Polaroid images of the circus crew and quaint St. Louis landmarks that I had shot in the last two days. Miscellaneous postcards I had collected from local flea markets, including a rare set of St. Louis Exposition hand-colored linens. Dammit, they were worth money to a collector, but the breaker of car windows and snatcher of bags was probably not that collector. Various pieces of mail, including one plain 6 x 9 envelope with a $1,200 check, the last payment for last week's performances. The standard "always be prepared" stuff—razor, shaving cream and toothbrush. Was that everything?

Oh, there was one more thing, the only item I could not list on a police report—nearly two ounces of primo marijuana—enough serious munchie fuel to roll joints for the entire company. Not even mine. I was holding it for Slim Jim because Ruth was on a tear about him smoking too much weed.

Sure as pig shit on the meat-packing floor, I was somewhere between, or simultaneously, wanting to throw up and snapping into crisis containment mode. As one of the old boys I used to know said, whether the nail hits the hammer or the hammer hits the nail, it was bad for the nail. And in the twilight of a gone bag, I was sure I was the nail.

Now was not the time for panic. Now was the time to do something. I had better be the hammer.

She felt bad. I felt much worse. She went back into the bar to call the cops. I immediately headed for the nearest alley to look in the first dumpster I found to see if there was anything that might have been tossed out of the bag as useless. And then I looked in the next one and the one after that, working the distance, I figured it would take a kid to run before he stopped to look at what might be in the bag. I was still banging through dumpsters when I saw the squad pull up with lights flashing. I reluctantly dropped the lid and went back to the car to go through the standard questions. They were punctuated repeatedly with the essential "look" I knew was coming every time the cop stopped writing, glanced up from his clipboard to give one or the other or both of us the "How stupid are you people, this is St. Louis…" stink eye.

There wasn't enough sympathy from the boys in blue to fill a shot glass.

As the cops left, Athena said she needed to make it up to me. How she'd do that was a mystery I put aside at the time, even as she put her arm around my waist and steered me back to the car. I was still primed for finding what had been lost. It was one thing to lose my personal stuff, but it was quite another to lose the elemental pieces of the tour in that bag.

Suddenly the adrenaline rush was gone. Drained like old bath water leaving a wet empty space. All I wanted was a good night's sleep. First thing in the morning, I would get VX, Marcel, Scott the Dog and anyone else with a little spare time back to the scene of the crime to do a proper grid search of every alley, stairwell and dumpster in a four-block radius.

Come on, Athena told me. I'm taking you to my place.

I didn't try to talk her out of it. The prospect of a night on a couch seemed preferable to going back to the forlorn church school rooms we were calling circus central, where half the company was encamped. I did not relish drinking cheap beer and eating more rice and beans to compensate for my having lost next week's food, gas and per diem money. It was only during the drive to her place, when I went to roll up the missing window that I recognized that she had suffered a loss as well.

Her place was above a union hall, the kind of "who'd think to live here" place a hipster artist would have. She pulled the car into the alley and parked it with the broken window so close to the worn brick wall that I couldn't open the door. I climbed out the driver's side and leaned against the graffiti-decorated wall as she unlocked the door. We went up metal stairs, a hollow clank sounding with each footstep, and then encountered another anonymous double-locked metal door.

When Athena turned on the light, I could see that it was a good-sized open loft with a view of the Arch beyond anonymous brick buildings. White walls with bolts of tie-dyed silk looped between the joists and beams caught the light. They hung dreamlike, more a suggestion of room dividers than actual walls. There was a gossamer flutter of fabric constantly moving as the ceiling fans attempted to dispel the heat. She lit a dozen candles of various sizes, then shut the lights off. It improved the effect, casting softly hued shadows dancing on white walls. She went over to what I supposed was a kitchen, basically just a sink and refrigerator against one wall, opened the fridge, pulled out a bottle of champagne and handed it to me.

Open it, she said, and pour two glasses.

It was not a request as much as a command. While I did that, she went to the far side of the room and began filling a gigantic claw-foot tub that sat on a raised dais. I figured I would just take my champagne and settle into a chair while she did whatever she was going to do.

She said, Come here. Take off your clothes and get in this tub. You need to relax.

It was easier than thinking about what I hadn't done or needed to do. But that would be half a truth. I hadn't been treated this well in a long time, and I wanted to have a moment when someone cared for me in any way. I wanted to immerse my suddenly aching joints in the warm, welcoming tub.

I took off clothes infused with a day's sheen of sweat and panic. Got in the smooth white lagoon. Leaned back in warm water and sipped champagne. I closed my eyes and was on the verge of falling asleep when I felt her get in the tub, displacing a few inches of sudsy water and slipping her long, smooth legs past my waist. She leaned forward and kissed me. It began as soft as a butterfly grazing a petal, but as she pressed in, the feeling grew more intense, then it subsided again. Call me Odysseus, she might as well have been Circe.

She leaned back, picked up her glass and studied me over the rim. You are thinner than the clothes you wear, she said as she ran her foot from my chest to stomach and along my thigh.

I have broad shoulders, I said. I suppose I buy my shirts to fit my shoulders, not my waist.

Oy, this had certainly turned into another kind of day. Three hours ago, I was finishing a performance when one of the sponsors asked if I wanted a drink. One hour ago, I was searching a dumpster in a panic for a stolen future. Now I was sitting in a bathtub with a woman who grew more beautiful by the sip. I couldn't tell whether she pitied me or was playing some kind of game. It did not matter. I did not consider the possibility that she might be attracted to me. Like most misadventures and great discoveries in my life, by the time I came to the answer as to which of those statements was true, it was too late to change the outcome.

I did not need to consider the possibility that I was attracted to her. That was obvious to me, though obscured by soapy water.

I'll skip the details of the lovemaking that followed us from tub to bed. One kiss led to another, to rising out of the warm water in a twirling embrace that was half dance, half wrestling for a hold on wet skin. Never mind the covers, those would be turned back later. A tangle of arms, legs, fumbling, thrusting, the sharp exhale of breath. It was all good or as good as it could be, given my distracted state of mind. She did everything she could to focus me on physical pleasures in the present tense, and while I tried, I found myself repeatedly imagining what happened while we sat exchanging pleasantries in the bar.

Someone was walking along the row of cars looking for something of value, maybe trying a door here or there to see if some fool had left it unlocked. Then the first view of the jackpot, a leather bag on the floor between the seats. A not-so-casual look around to see if anyone was coming. There was no one to interfere or care. A hammer, a tire iron—hell, even a well-placed kick of a steel-toed boot—something capable of smashing glass in a single blow. Glass sprays the dashboard. The reaching in and then what? Would it have been running or a deliberate walk away with the bag in plain sight? Stepping into shadow to open the bag. Score. One of those quicky, snap-a-picture kind of cameras and some film. That can be used or sold. What's the rest of this shit? Paper, and more paper? Fuck that. Postcards? Who needs them? Or maybe I'll give them to my aunty to use for decoration. Then, if they reached all the way to the bottom, double score. Weed. Mothafucker, forget the rest, just drop it along the way, I'll take the weed, the camera and the bag.

32–The Morning After

I woke up in her bed and should have been happy. Athena had a goddess name with a correspondingly classic form. Not so much muscular but toned, the curve of hips and belly suggesting a woman at ease with herself. I looked at her in the half-light of the loft, smiled at the thought of kissing her, and then the panic returned. I sat up to see where I had left my pants.

I couldn't stay there. Couldn't really. The need to find the missing pieces of the office was stronger than the feel of her arm around my shoulder. She was so beautiful in her nakedness that I swear if it weren't for the urgency of my upset, I would have jumped her bones there and there. But that would have to wait for another day if such a day would ever come.

Athena, wake up, I said. You've got to drive me back.

She glanced at the clock and replied, It's not even seven in the morning. You've got time.

I haven't got time. I've got to get back over there because every minute I'm not looking for the office, the chances of someone else finding something I desperately need grows. Those garbage trucks start emptying dumpsters early.

She knew where "there" was and got out of bed without complaint. She started the coffee, then got dressed and drove to circus central.

After my arrival, I laid out the essence of the story but skipped the champagne and sex. The dependable ones went with me back to the starting point and fanned out along a four-block search grid based on where the car had been parked and what I conjectured the escape route to have been. I started where I had ended last night. In the third dumpster I opened, I found all the correspondence still bound with a rubber band and, to my amazement, the plain brown envelope with the check still inside. For a moment, nothing else mattered. Next week's groceries were paid for. Resurrection is hope manifested. Finding that was the stone rolling away from the tomb.

Searching one block to the west, VX found my address book lying next to an abandoned car. When he handed it to me, I declared the search over. I did not expect to reclaim this much, but even a blind squirrel finds a nut now and then. We waited for the rest of the crew to report their failure to find anything more.

That's it, boys, I said. We've done what we can. I have enough of the essentials to reconstruct the tour.

Loren Red Beard said, Time for a beer.

It's nine fuckin' o'clock in the morning, VX responded. I want some bacon.

So? Loren Red Beard looks VX's lean frame up and down and said, Beer is a breakfast beverage where I come from and a fine complement to bacon. Didn't you hear? The Doctor is buying!

Yes, I was. On the way to the nearest open bar, which wasn't but half a block away, the guys didn't say anything other than to repeat mumbled sympathy. After the first beer, the mood changed. They let me know with small jokes that for a smart man, I was pretty damn stupid, and even more to the point, one lucky fool at that. I couldn't disagree. For a smart man, leaving a bag in a car was an obviously stupid thing to do, so over the second beer, I tamped down any desire to defend myself and stayed as quiet as a treed opossum. Let them scratch the lesson into my hide so I wouldn't forget it.

I was as surprised as I was pleased when Athena came by that afternoon. I felt the smile light my face like a hundred-watt bulb. Now that I had recovered the two items that would have cost the tour dearly, I found myself looking at her with an interest that would never see professional courtesy again. I recognized that she had taken care to ease my panic even if it meant being willing to make Plato's two-backed beast.

I was curious as to what was what. Momentary kindness or something more elemental? Watching her walk into the circus tent, I saw both the woman wearing the black jeans and crisp white blouse and the naked woman beneath with the appendix scar on her belly.

She asked, How are you doing, Buzz?

Better, I said. I leaned in to create some sense of intimacy. I want to thank you for what you did last night. It was very generous.

And I'll do it again tonight, she said and laughed a short ascending note. No excuses. I'll pick you up after the show. I want you to appreciate the city for the good people that dwell here.

Clearly, she was one of them, and I was fully prepared to appreciate her. And I did.

The next day, the tent came down for the last time in the shadow of the gateway to the west. We were headed to Columbia to do a couple of university shows, or so I thought until I called Frank to check in. He was out, but Lucy was in. She told me that those University of Missouri shows had been canceled. Not what I wanted to hear. We needed the money, and we needed the momentum. We had been sitting in St. Louis for nearly two weeks—three shows each in two different locations. Everything had slowed to a crawl. Everyone was out of the rhythm of arrive, set up, perform, tear down, pack and move on.

What were we going to do with a five-day hole in the schedule? A quick consult of the map and conference with the central organizing committee led to a decision to take the company to the Hawn State Park campgrounds outside of St. Genevieve for the duration of our suddenly open days. The company could rest, relax and rehearse.

Athena came by as I was checking off the departure list and simply said, Why don't you stay here? I'll take you down to St. Genevieve at the end of the week.

I explained that I had a car so I could drive myself. Yes, I had missed the point of that offer. She was not asking if I needed transportation, and a beat later, when I got it, I flushed.

She tried again. Don't you have to do an evaluation with your sponsors? She asked. I'd much rather do it now than over the phone two months from now. Then she whispered, I am not ready to let you go.

Those words focused my attention as surely as the broken window and missing bag.

I made a poor and certainly hasty excuse for my sudden impending absence, then sent the Rex crew on their way. I'd be at the campground in four days or meet them in St. Genevieve in five. No one believed I had any business more urgent than Athena, but no one was going to point that out. Why should they—we were too obvious. They looked at me, they looked at her leaning on my shoulder and saved their considered judgment for the campfire I would not be sitting at that evening. In the firelight, they would say whatever they would say, and by the time I did arrive, whatever was said would be smoke and ashes. Gone from guess to gossip to story to fact.

Right then, I didn't care. For the first time in a long time, someone was not ready to let me go. It had been years since anyone had said that to me. I was the old alley cat looking at a bowl of sweet cream.

That was the moment I began to spin the web of wishing I could live in a loft with white walls and find some suitable work for a man of my age and skills in the shadow of the arch. I still had plenty of mojo and enough street cred, despite my recent lapse, to make a mark. Maybe produce some theater or music in some joint frequented by local hipsters and well-heeled tourists. I thought about being half of a couple hosting dinner parties for the fashionable folks in her orbit. Not my people, but then again, I've been so far out of it for so long that some folks actually thought that I was ahead of the curve. You know, cool—or that I once was chill.

The Rex crew got in the cars and buses. The semi squeaked onto the street, followed by the big cat truck and the camel's trailer, a half dozen pickups, and the sea foam blue bus, all headed in caravan toward the state park campgrounds. I followed Athena back to her place. Everything was in motion, including my emotions.

33–Stinkbait

How do you spell trouble? Marcel put it so succinctly:

You found me on your doorstep, a basket case with chips,
You took me in the house and joined me at the hips.
You chased away the boy in me and now you hate the man.
Your intentions were as false as the essence of your tan.
I know that you are bad for me, I know that you are bad for me,
I know that you are bad for me, but I'm not in Junior High.

34—My First Wife

I know that you are bad for me, but I'm not in junior high. I felt the same way about my first wife, at least for a couple of months at the beginning or maybe at the end.

Last I heard, my first wife was a psychic advisor steeped in New Age hoodoo in Houston, Texas. Serves her right to end up there. She used to mock me for being from Texas, and dammit, no one mocks me for being from Texas better than myself. As far as the New Age thing went, she always believed that the department store of life had more to offer than her Episcopal upbringing and was happy to buy whatever new or old spiritual items were on sale at any given moment.

My first wife always had a blind eye for her own indiscretions and twenty-twenty vision for mine—and everyone else's. She was like my mother in that regard, but with more than my mother's Bible-based judgments of where you'd end up. She had the gift of actually seeing the future. Well, maybe not THE future, but a highly probable unfolding. Prophecy. Foresight. The writing on the wall. Call it what you will, she'd tell you not only if there was a train coming round the bend but when it would arrive.

My first wife would have taken one look at Athena and said, you're burnt toast. Well canoodled toast, but boy Howdy, you're going to get burnt just the same.

She hadn't mentioned this gift while I was courting her. Of course, she was just eighteen when we met, a lanky, dark-haired girl with a toothy smile wearing short shorts and a peasant blouse. She knew how to flirt, and I knew how to reciprocate. I was so low to the ground the fast ones went right over my head, and she was as fast as they came.

We were made for each other, hot to trot, an accident looking for a place to happen. I had just left Big Daddy's employ and wanted her the moment I saw her. I put the hook in myself and handed her the line. It was a miracle that she wasn't pregnant within forty-eight hours of our first diddle.

I was her ticket out of utterly predictable domesticity with her ma and pa in a Chicago suburb.

She'd have never gotten me within a hundred feet of the altar if I knew before the fact that she could see the future clear as moonshine in a store-bought glass. Hell, when I found out, the first thing I did was try talking her into cashing in on that rare gift. I mean, what if she could pick the ponies? Bet the trifecta every day while sitting in a luxury box sipping cold ones. Know what was dealt with any hand of cards? If that's possible, book us a suite in Vegas and buy me an eyeshade.

She looked at me like I had just tortured her puppy and gave me some mumbo jumbo about how it would be unethical to use God's given talent for easy gain, and besides, it didn't work that way. I skipped the unethical and focused in on the "it didn't work that way." Why not?

Her gift was not something we could bet on. If there was a bird in the bush, she'd know it, though she couldn't say what direction it would fly when it was flushed out. Her vision was outlined but not detailed. The best she could hope for, she often said, was to not be on the street when the piano dropped. And I don't really blame her. She saw my stumbles long before I did and told me in a hundred different ways not to walk under ladders.

One time she took me down to the local pawn shop to help her shop for a gun. When I asked her what she needed me for since she could pick out a gun on her own, she said she wanted me to see what she'd use on me when I did what I did.

Did? A moment of transposing, and it became: what I was going to do.

I don't know her name, she told me, but I can see the color of her hair, smell her perfume. So, I just want to know whether you'd rather get ventilated with a lady's .38 or this swell .45?

That spooked me. Yes, sir, I was so skittish I minded my p's and q's for a good long time. By the time our marriage had about run its course, I had my heart set on doing something foolish just for the hell of it. I had tried to be so good for so long that doing something that would have justified her using a gun seemed inevitable. I wanted to find me a stripper named Bambi or Sissy and go for broke.

35–Bubbles

In those days, I was pretending to be a daytime manager of a not-quite upscale tits 'n' ass club in Chicago. It was not in the Playboy class, but didn't smell like porno theater seats either. It was a job meant for putting food on the table, and I was doing my best to not get beat like a drum by the over-stimulated patrons or the money-laundering mob guys who arrived with paper bags my boss was happy to deposit. It was what it was until Bubbles came on the scene. One look and all my hope of being saved for something better had her name on it. She was just the kind of girl I'd be willing to get shot for.

She was a tall, thin blond with boyish hips that moved as smooth as well-greased ball bearings. Just right in the front and back for my taste, not too curvy, with a face that I wanted to cradle in my hands like it was my grandma's heirloom China cup. She was a few years younger than me by the look of her and maybe more experienced in some ways of the world. Not likely a rebellious college girl out for misadventure, but still not hardened. Though she said she was taking classes—as is almost always the case for a certain kind of girl by choice or chance, street smarts or bad luck—her education was not entirely academic. She gave off a very strong "been there, done that, moved on" vibe. I'd done the carnival and Big Daddy's apprenticeship and gone to marrying. I recognized the graffiti…

Every time I saw Bubbles—I never was sure if that was only her stage name or a carried-over nickname—I wanted to take care of her. I don't mean every time I saw her on the Commodore stage, though she danced well enough. I mean that every time I saw her sitting on a bar stool between shifts or walking across the parking lot to the beat-up Buick she drove, I could feel me wanting to make sure she was all right. That girl deserved better than this.

For all her tough girl bounce, it seemed to me she needed more than a teacup of tenderness. Somewhere along the line she had been bruised so deep it left me wanting to kiss the purple and make it better. From her filling out the employment application to the last she walked out the door, I had a case of Sugar Daddy, though I didn't have the dough-re-me for me to be one. I didn't even know what taking care of her would be, but I wanted to be her big brother, father confessor and Sam Spade all rolled into one big "here let me do that for you."

I wasn't objective, which put me on the verge of being a terrible boss with nothing to show for my overt sentimentality. I didn't know a whit of why or what for, but she was the magnet, and I was steel. Her looks and sweet smile offered reason enough for any man to spend bucks on the overpriced drinks to watch her work the stage. As a manager, I didn't have to spend the bucks, but I got the urge same as every other dog that was sniffing her leg. I wanted her something fierce. Oh, doggies, that was an itch that I wanted to scratch, though that didn't happen. It would be unprofessional and shit... Why kid myself or you? Wanting is easier than doing.

She had a two-hundred-something-pound biker boyfriend who she wasn't likely to leave even though he took her for granted and smacked her around now and then. I had a clairvoyant wife with a .38.

We had a lot of sincere conversations about going to school and making some better life for herself while holding hands over Old Fashions and a short denouement of whatever electrical charge seemed to rise up between us when we looked each other in the eye for more than a glance. She knew I had it bad. There was nothing ever more physical than holding hands or a hug at the door as she left work. I never even kissed her. Well, that's not quite true. I never kissed her in that way, though my lips grazed her cheek or the back of her hand more than once. She'd laugh and call me an old-fashioned gentleman. Me? A gentleman? If that wasn't an indictment of how little she thought of me, nothing was.

In the end, she needed a little help with a… let's call it, a medical thing and couldn't or wouldn't ask the boyfriend for some reason neither of us wanted to discuss. She came to me in tears, and that was all she wrote. I was willing to give her help, though I had no part in making the problem. She said she'd pay me back, but that was less important than the idea that she had come to ask me.

At the clinic, they asked if I was the husband or the father. Yeah, it was one of those problems. I said I was the guy who's paying the bill, and that's all they needed to know. I did what I did because I was in love with her without an expectation that she'd do anything in return, and she thanked me by disappearing afterward.

I don't mean took a couple of days off the runway. I mean, she got out of the car, went through the front door and poof! She wasn't seen or heard from again. When she didn't come back to the Commodore or even to pick up the week's check, I went over to her place to see what was what. A ten spot got the super to open the apartment door. Place looked hard lived in. There were dishes with crusted bits and the start of a green mold in the sink. There were clothes still hanging in the closet, but no real evidence that she was there and none that she was gone.

I looked around, but with the super standing at the door, I couldn't open the drawers to see if the underwear was still folded or look in the jewelry box on the dresser or in a hatbox in the closet to see if there was cash or just the smell of money gone missing. I wanted to wait and see if she'd come back in an hour or so, but the super began tapping his foot, humming a "get along little doggies, it's your misfortune and none of my own" tune.

A day or two later, the biker boyfriend made a point of stopping by the club to ask for me. He wanted to know where she was. All I could say was your guess is better than mine, she's your girlfriend. I had already crossed her name off the payment book and reconciled myself to her being my first lost love. I wondered if it would set a pattern, and if it did, I was in for a long rough ride.

Maybe the first wife, knowing how it would end, chose not to say or do anything. Maybe near the end, she knew I was just another cut-rate King David working on Bathsheba's case. Since she could see the future, she could see that for all my hot 'n' bothered wanting Bubbles, it meant less than kernels at the bottom of the popcorn bag. I wasn't going to get anything more than a peck on the cheek and the satisfaction of my hand stroking the fantasy.

You'd think I would have learned something in the years of carnivals and such before and since then. Maybe I forgot the lessons of the first wife, but here I was leaping to "happily ever after" with Athena before I even knew what story was being told. If I had an ounce of self-knowledge beyond the thrill of punching out of my weight class, I would have shown the thought of "until death do us part" out the door as soon as it announced itself. She deserved a better man than me.

Everything that was right with Athena was predicated on being able to end my affair with the Rex. Much as I might say that was possible, for all her faults, the Rex would be hard to leave.

36–Is You or Is You Not?

Even with little to do in St. Louis, the next three days passed too quickly and soured steadily. The weather mirrored my disposition—sunny for the better part of the first day, cloudy and becoming a thickening drizzle the second, and a steady black rain falling all day on the third. Athena was everything I had thought I wanted, and yet as soon as she left to go to work, I wondered why I was there. It was not that I didn't enjoy her company. I did— far more than I'd care to admit.

Even now, all these years later, I can conjure the faint smell of Chanel that nestled where her neck joined the collarbone. Even now, my fingertips could recognize the curve of Athena's breasts, my bones would feel the way her weight settled on my hips when she straddled me, or my tongue recognized the taste of rye whiskey and lipstick when she kissed me at night. I tattooed a hundred details of the tilt-a-whirl that her moving in time and space made on my frontal cortex— the way the arch of her feet fit in my hand when I went to massage them, the way the morning sun shone on her hair, reminding me of a wild fox, the slickness of sweat and smell of sex on our bodies as we lay side by side in the double bed. Those particular realizations came in retrospect rather than in the present of then.

What my antenna was receiving was how the rhythm that had dominated every day of the Rex had made me uneasy with what was replacing it. I'd sit in a chair staring at nothing but wondering what the Rex crew was doing now. Who was screwing what up? Who was stepping up to take care of the punch list of things between chaos and confusion? I wanted to call them or be called, but I didn't know if there was even a phone at the campground. I hadn't given Athena's number to anyone who might be inclined to call me because I hadn't asked for it, and she hadn't offered. When the phone rang, it would always be for her. As far as the Rex was concerned, I was surely long gone and probably on the verge of best-forgotten.

We were in a cone of silken silence in a 1200-square-foot cocoon. Athena pretended the Rex was history and offered me every invitation to consider this moment as the only one that mattered. Call me Odysseus, she was a Siren calling me to shore, and I was still half lashed to the mast of the Rex. Maybe she knew I was already slipping away. I certainly did. I should have been thankful to ever see her kindness. I wanted to create something grateful out of whole cloth, but like the woodpile that's waiting for the axe, I feared good wine, good sex, and good conversation would cut me down to size, and I felt awful about it.

Things had to be sorted out. Someone had to call Flat Frank and tell him what was what, and it had to be me if only it was to say that I'd quit. I had fallen out of the circus world as sudden as Alice down the rabbit hole, and each day that I was gone, I grew steadily more morose and irritable. Nothing seemed to fit. I had pledged to get the Rex from one end of the Big Muddy to the other. Did I really mean to abandon that promise? If I did, would Athena be my safe harbor or the rocky shore of my shipwrecked emotions?

Athena had noticed my distraction from the beginning and redoubled her effort to ease my confusion or perhaps make me forget. The physical pleasure was intense. We ate well, drank well, smoked a little weed and tried to replicate as much of the Kama Sutra as we could without injuring ourselves. Then she gave up trying to hold my attention and told me to leave. Well, not leave so much as to make a real decision. Is you or is you not my baby? Was I staying or was I going?

I tried to tether myself to my desire, though I could not conceive of how to satisfy that impulse and my sense of duty to the Rex.

If I go, when will I see you again?

I'm not sure you're seeing me now. She ran her fingers through the short stubble of my hair, creating a small electric charge. You talk about us, she said, but you think about them. She leaned in close enough for me to feel her body heat. My Pavlovian dangle stirred to attention. My desire was obvious to both of us.

You want me, she said, placing her hand on my erect member, but you don't know how to be with me. Stay with me, and we'll find our way. I can make you that promise, Buzz, but you have to be here with me. Really. Here. Not on tour. She ran her hand across my chest, tapping the breastbone above the heart. You should learn, Buzz, how to give yourself to something other than work, though I don't think it is work for you. It is something else, something bigger and deeper rooted that I can't get you to let go of.

I started to say, you're wrong. But she wasn't.

There was no mistaking it. She was a Texas girl and knew the look, the walk, the way you can take any of us out of Texas, but you can't take the stubborn out of us. She was Austin-bred all the way. Professional parents, liberal politics and college at one of the East Coast schools—Smith or Radcliffe, because her parents couldn't afford the pretension of Vassar. She was the kind of girl I would have killed for when I was growing up, clearly out of my league and proud that she was even willing to be seen with me. She was smart and sexy, everything I should have wanted. And I did, but not enough to know how to let go of the road and the Rex.

Look, I'll finish the tour and be done with it, I said. Contract complete, ready to start a new chapter. I'll come back here, and the Rex won't be a distraction. I said it like I meant it because, to my thinking, it actually made sense. I had done it before—finished a tour, finished a good long run of this or that and shook off the dust to find something different. I mean, I had reinvented myself so many times that if I had a certificate for every completion, I'd have had a history wall like Big Daddy's, each one a testimony to been there, done that, and gone on to the next.

Just like that? She said. Promise? Another six weeks and then… Do you really mean it, Buzz?

Of course, Athena. You should come down to New Orleans for the finish. We'll wave the crew off and take a cruise. The Virgin Islands or Cuba by way of Mexico.

She kissed me and said, I'll hold you to that.

I packed my bag, got my jacket, kissed her a quick one on the cheek, like I was going out for a pack of cigarettes and would be back in a jiffy even as I felt the Lincoln's keys jingle in my pocket. *Maybe* I would be back. It had been a long time since I felt so confused about what to do next. It felt unnatural, and that had to end.

She stopped me as I turned toward the door, her hand holding the jacket's collar as she whispered, I want you to think hard and long about what you have to look forward to after the tour is over. Is there anything that you will hold onto that is not "us?" If there is, can you let go of it? Think about us, Buzz, because I will. Forget about the fucking crisis that brought us together. It did bring us together. Focus on what we can be together. Do you hear what I'm saying?

Yes. That was all I could say, all she wanted to hear.

With that, she turned me around one more time and kissed me like she did the first time, soft and fluttery, shifting to passionate and wanting and then slowly fading away again. Then she pushed me toward the door and turned her back to me. Maybe she was crying. She certainly moved her shoulders like she was, but I couldn't hear her choking back tears. I know I was surprised—not that she might cry, but at how close to waterworks I was myself.

I hoped that wasn't the case because if tears were flowing, I'd have to go back into the room. If I did, I might as well pull the barbed wire out and build the fence. Truth to tell, I wanted to go back into the room, wipe away her tears and tell her that I was a fool. Her fool. For as long as she'd have me.

Instead, I carried my bag down to the Lincoln, not knowing if I would ever see her again. I shouldn't have a blind pig's chance to find that kind of truffle a second time. That was the stuff of movies. Boy meets girl, boy loses girl, boy gets girl again. The real world didn't work that way, especially when the boy walks out on the girl. There was no reason on God's green earth that she should want me now or ever again.

This would probably not be one of those "once upon a time in the land of make-believe" stories with a happy ending that my ma used to like. She'd read them to me, and I'd think that something doesn't make sense here. Now I knew if I was in one of those stories, I'd be the man who had to wear out his iron shoes before the end of the story. I suspected that at the end of this story, all I would have was worn-out shoes and no girl.

37—Burning His Stuff

Just shy of two hours later, I pulled into the campground. It looked miserable in the rain. Buckets of rain—enough to make me think of Noah. Puddles threatening to become ponds and the rutted mud of the red dirt road did not bode well for a driver who was not used to slip sliding or didn't have four-wheel drive and big ass tires. I was not about to get the car stuck and pulled the Lincoln off the road, easing it onto a little rise where the water could run downhill in every direction. There was no ark in this campground, but if we didn't get the circus out of the mire, we might as well turn our attention to building one.

I cursed the weather and myself for not having a raincoat or even a poncho in the pride of Ford. I used to have one, but where it went was a mystery. I got out and headed toward the first Rex-identified camper in the line in hopes of finding a towel and a cup of coffee.

Buzz, you look like shit! Tom told me.

Thanks—you don't look so hot yourself. Where's Claire?

She's doing some tea with Ruth and the kids. Here, take this. He poured me a cup of hot black asphalt that he passed off as Turkish coffee, fresh brewed. I was more than happy to take a sip.

Did you see him on your way in? Tom asked.

Who?

Loren Red Beard. He burned his stuff and walked away.

He what?

Okay, Buzz, here's the rewind—it's been raining cats and dogs for two days here. We can't do anything except hunker down and wait. Then this morning, when we looked out the camper, there's Loren piling wet wood in a fire pit. I wanted to laugh because it wasn't going to be much of a fire with the sky pissing like this. He stacks up a neat little pile, then goes into his camper and comes out with a bunch of stuff—clothes, books, his old guitar—and lays them on top of the pile. Then he gets a can of gasoline out of the truck, pours it on everything and lights it up. Kaboom! It shakes the windows, and there's a fucking fireball rising a hundred feet in an angry red cloud. Everyone is looking at him now. Some of us even go out to see what the hell is going down. He goes back into the camper and comes out with another load. VX tries to talk to him. Scott goes to reason with him. They're asking him what he's doing, or maybe Scott just tried to grab the guitar off the fire before it was totally ruined. Loren is having none of it. He takes the burning guitar out of Scott's hands and puts it back on the fire.

And what did Loren say? I asked.

Nothing. Tom picked up his coffee cup and poured it back into the little metal pot he had sitting on the stovetop burner. He lifted the pot and swirled the contents. Want another cup? Tom asked.

No, I'm good.

Anyway, Loren pretty much stripped his camper of everything he had inside that wasn't bolted down and burned it. At one point, he poured more gas, another fireball went up… I swear it singed his beard. Loren was standing there just watching as his stuff burned, glassy-eyed and smiling. Least that's what VX said he looked like… Like a man possessed. Me, I wasn't going to get into it. Not with Loren.

No shit.

Finally, Tom said, Loren said he needed to go for a walk. He handed VX the keys to his truck and headed down the road toward the highway. I'm surprised you didn't see him. It couldn't have been more than ten or fifteen minutes before you got here. What are you going to do?

What can I do? I asked. I suppose I could drive around, see if I can find him. But then what? Would he even get in the car? Maybe it's better to let him take a little walk and sort whatever out. If he doesn't come back by the time we leave St. Genevieve, I'll have to hire someone else. Crap, I'm not keen to do that. Maybe I'll give him to Memphis to come to his senses. If he hasn't come back by showtime, Memphis, he's fired, and I'll hire a new guy.

Sure you will.

Damn straight, I will. I don't know what put a tick up his butt, but if he doesn't come back when it's done sucking, he's gone.

I heard myself say that and had to laugh. Of course, he'd be gone if he didn't come back. Of course, I'd have to hire someone to do his work. The fact of it was as plain as a field that had to be plowed by a stubborn mule. What a pain in the ass this was going to be. Where would I look for someone who knew how to rig a tent or someone who could repair broken machines with duct tape and bailing wire? In an effort to spare myself the pain of having to hire anyone, I hoped he would come to his senses or what was left of them and return post haste so I wouldn't have to deal with him not being there for the last six or ten or how many getting-ever-stranger weeks were left of the tour.

If he did come back, what would I say or do then? I'd have to burn that bridge when I crossed it, and there was already one pile of smoking debris hissing in the rain.

Hell, if I had thought about it for another five minutes, I'd have realized how valuable Loren really was to making the Rex run and gone looking for him like he had gone looking for the office bag when I needed help in St. Louis. But I didn't. And I didn't have a clue as to which way he went.

The rain was coming down like it was aiming for a hundred-year flood, and all I could do was hope that it would drive Loren to shelter somewhere close. When it stopped, I'd get in the car and drive ten miles in every direction looking for him. Then he might realize what he'd done and come back just as I'd realized what I had done and come back to the Rex. Loren Red Beard had at least as much sense as I did.

As far as I could tell, my luck had changed. For the worse, it seemed. The fact was I had left Athena, and Loren Red Beard had left me. The day was lower than a tadpole in a mud hole, and the losses were starting to mount up.

38–Meeting and Parting

St. Genevieve was one of those towns that had lived by the river and pretty much died by it as well. It wasn't that there were a lot of vacant stores, except, of course, there were. It was more like the town oozed an aura of worn-out, peeling paint and dusty shelves in every one of the stores that were still open. Maybe they had decided it was easier selling year-old goods. Maybe no one cared what was for sale anymore. The local chamber of commerce had hired the Rex to bring a little gaiety to the proceedings, and after that spell of sitting on our ass, we were ready for some of that ourselves.

The rain had finally stopped. That was a gift. Since a good portion of the Rex tent or gear had not come out of the trucks to begin with, there was no loading of wet canvas to be done. We simply ran a checklist of everything and everybody. The only item missing was Loren Red Beard. I'd already said to anyone and everyone, especially Marcel and VX, all I needed say about that, so we turned the keys and drove to St. Genny, hoping to greet a miracle.

Right out of the chute, one of the miracles of meeting and greeting happened. For the second time since we had bought the boat, the Collapso had arrived at the same place at the same time as the rest of the Circus Rex.

Have I not told you about the Collapso?

Don't get me started.

Well, do, because I have to tell you something to make sense out of the circumstance. Maybe just enough so you could understand how rare and precious this event was. The boat was a half-baked dream proposed in the giddy days of building the beast as a recreational alternative to the rigors of the tour, but was really nothing more than a rat hole on water that was sucking money out of our pocket.

Humm, if I didn't know me, I'd say that sounded a tad on the bitter side. But I do know me. And believe me, when it came to anything and everything touching upon that boat, I was as bitter about it as I was about the camel, and for plenty of the same good reasons.

Before we left Alma, someone—and mercifully, I've forgotten who—suggested that we should have a boat accompany us on the journey. The idea was that it would sail down the river, and when we were not doing shows, the Circus Rex crew could spend their free time relaxing on the boat. There were only two things wrong with this idea. The first is that there was precious little free time on this or any tour. Twenty-four, twenty-five or whatever the number of cities stretched from one end of the Mississippi to the other in six months meant the rule of thumb would always be arrive, set up, perform, take down, pack up and move. Even in places like Minneapolis, St. Louis, Memphis or New Orleans, where we would be in residence for a week or two, there was still a show every night and matinees on the weekend. The second thing wrong was that I only had one big cat girl or one pair of performers who could do a high-wire act. If Miss Red Boots took a day off to lounge on the boat, I had no act.

I had argued this at the time, but the argument fell on deaf ears around the tribal table. Every one of the Rex performers thought a boat on the river was a swell idea. None of them had ever done it before. I took my objections upstairs through Flat Frank to the distant ownership. For reasons that remain a mystery to this very day, I was overruled by them behind the curtain as one or more of them actually approved the boat scheme, but then, when they saw the prices of available boats, they were too cheap to pay top dollar for a reliable nautical conveyance. They said we could get one if we could find one for under 30K and sold it once we got to New Orleans.

Thirty thousand? That was barely enough to buy a bathtub on the riverboat market.

Those members of the Rex crew most anticipating the dream of Huck Finn on the river were beyond reach. Those who didn't care about a boat didn't care. I didn't need my first wife to see the future through a glass darkly at the time of purchase. The fiction that this would be fun was yet to be disproven, but the truth of the matter was that breakdowns and extended bouts of repair would soon overstay their welcome. Once we had the boat, the necessity of delays to fix this or wait for that part to be delivered became more frequent and the cost more expensive as everything and everyone headed south. It seemed not to have settled in anyone's mind but my own that you could not put people on the boat and have them sail from one stop to the next and arrive at the same time as the eighteen-wheeler.

Let me put it this way—the only people who could afford to take time on the boat were those who didn't perform, set up or take down, which by my calculations meant the useless hangers-on—those disabled by accident, children under the age of six and the boat's captain, Bobby Johansen.

Even now, when I think about the cost of repairs, the time needed to get that boat within a hundred miles, within three days travel of where the circus was at any given point, it is enough to make me weep. Not that Captain Bobby cared whether he was ever anywhere approximating the location of the Rex. He was working off a vastly different calendar than I was. His was cosmic and personal. Mine was terrestrial and quite pedestrian. This was his final gig as a man before he had enough money tucked away in his piggy-wiggly bank to pay for the sex change that would make a new and improved lesbian out of Bobbie Johansen. I was trying to get a small circus from point A to point B.

I had to give Bobby credit, though, after having heard his story in dribs and dabs when I would get him to talking during the long and frequent hours spent waiting for boat repairs to be finished. He'd been a combat pilot in Nam. After getting shot down one too many times, after three years of bad rice as a POW, after a threatened court martial for insubordination upon his return, he came to realize that the only thing he hated worse than the military was being a man. Yes, sir, you can salute that patriotic flag of God and Country morning, noon and night, but that don't make it right. He had done the "man up" thing long enough.

The fact was, Bobby thought being a man was so fucked up that he figured he would lose nothing by jumping the fence. His girlfriend agreed that Nam had taken a terrible toll and was, he proudly reported to me, looking forward to having Bobbie be a happy girl girlfriend. From Bobby's perspective, the thing standing between him becoming a her was a six-month drift down the mighty Mississippi providing recreational asides for a group of stressed-out circus performers who never knew where the boat was when they were on shore and where the circus was when they were on the boat. It sounded like a double-down jackpot to him and hell on troubled waters to me.

39–What Can You Say?

The Collapso. The name said it all. Of course, it didn't start out with that name, but it certainly wound up being every bit the Collapso.

That was the year Jacques Cousteau was doing a documentary on the Mississippi River. You might remember him as a famous French explorer, documentary filmmaker and celebrity, with a magnificent international crew manning his equally magnificent yacht, the Calypso. It was still anchored in St. Louis when our pitiful little accident on the water under Captain Bobby's command limped into St. Genevieve.

While we were in St. Louis, some of the Rex crew had rubbed shoulders, and in the case of the Swede Girls, perhaps a bit more, with the visiting Frogs. From that moment on, we knew that our worlds stood in absolute contrast. If the French were eating cold caviar on water crackers aboard the Calypso, the crew of the Rex Terrestrial, Celestial & Nautical Circus were eating canned tuna on three-day-old sourdough aboard the Collapso. If the French were sipping vintage champagne aboard the Calypso, the Rex Terrestrial, Celestial & Nautical Circus folk were sucking a lukewarm Blatz on board the Collapso.

Yes, giving credit where credit is due—the Collapso had arrived in St. Louis while we were there—but we had been there for nearly two weeks when it appeared. And here it was again. If that didn't qualify as a miracle, I was prepared to eat my top hat.

The first thing I heard from Dan is, now that the boat's here, who's going to get to take a cruise?

Today? Anyone who wants to, for all I care, *after* the show.

No, not today, he said, this next week, between here and Memphis.

I looked at him wondering how it could be possible he doesn't know what the schedule is. No, it's not possible. Everyone knows what the schedule is. We go over the schedule every day. What happens today, what happens tomorrow, what happens the day after that. We've got shows between here and Memphis. Louisville is the biggest, remember that one? Besides, no one gets to ride the boat if they're in the show. By my back-of-the-envelope calculations, that meant Captain Bobby and Lance, the wandering musician who had arrived in Peoria and hadn't left yet, would be on board between here and Memphis.

Come on, Buzz, Dan said, how about if we just take one day and go down to meet the show in Cairo?

What makes you think that will only take a day? The boat hasn't been—oh, how shall I put this?—*reliable* about arriving when and where I need performers to be. Yes, I do believe reliable is exactly the word in question. If anything, this boat has been spectacularly unreliable. No, let me put that another way, I can count on one hand the days the boat hasn't broken down.

Dan turned to look at the boat bobbing in the prop wash of a twelve-barge town heading upriver. Come on, Buzz, he said. Don't be such a spoilsport.

Spoilsport? I broke out laughing at the thought. Let me tell you what I am, Dan. I'm the goddamned ringmaster and tour manager, that's what I am. My volume was creeping up, and I was holding on for liftoff. I'm the keeper of the clocks and the signer of the checks, the first, last and only word of the Almighty Absent Owners. Those same Absent Owners who are expecting their investment to pay off for reasons that we cannot guess. Hell, even I, or especially I, can't see how that is going to happen. But supposing we could see a return on their investment. How would we do that? How does this one ring wonder make a dime's worth of profit on the dollar? By staying on fucking schedule without getting anyone killed or left behind, that's how.

But, Buzz…

Get out of my sight and get out now. Go down to the river and take a swim. Loll about the deck of the Collapso with a beer in hand if that pleases you. Play cards, shoot craps, or rub your man root raw for all I care. Do whatever you want to do for the next two hours and thirty-five minutes—for *precisely* two hours and thirty-five minutes. Not a second more. Because in two hours and thirty-six minutes, I'll step into the tent, and ten seconds later, it will be showtime! The show is the only reason we should be here, and with every passing day, the very reason I'm getting, ummm, more and more cranky.

Do you believe that? I'm starting to get irritated at the amount of pissing up a rope that has to happen to get anything done around here.

Let me be clear, Dan, I am not happy that Loren Red Beard left and that you are now suggesting that you will do the same because that's what being on the boat at showtime will mean. If you are not in the ring at show time, you'll be as done and gone as our absent, lamented friend.

Don't tell me that a week or a day on the boat isn't leaving. It damn well is, and as the Catholics would say, it is a near occasion of sin. You, sir, are tempting me to anger. You can work or you can leave. If you want to work, if you want to get paid again, the moment I step into the ring, you will be standing at attention at the tent entrance ready, set, and go, go, go—running in carrying a big ass puppet with a smile on your face to make those showbiz wheels turn and churn under the bright canvas sky. And when I see that, I will be the happy camper you dream of me being. Then, and only then….

Dan started to say something, but I held up my hand with the index finger extended in the universal gesture of silence.

Now I am done talking, so done that I do not need or intend to say another word. Neither should you. Just nod your ascent and get to doing that job of yours, the whatever it is that needs be done, as long as it is out of my presence.

Not five minutes later, Marcel had me sitting on a folding chair beneath the shade of an Oak dripping Spanish Moss with a cold beer in hand to lower my boiling point. His only comment on the entire exchange was that my restraint had been admirable, considering that I was bluffing.

Oh, but Spirit, I wasn't, I informed Marcel. I've had it up to my armpits with complainers and slackers. There's nothing for it. I'm getting meaner than a cornered porcupine and rightly so. I'm not righty-tighty… this show is souring in my mouth. I don't know why I came back.

You can't say that, Marcel replied. You're the man with the plan, the guy with more history of how to get it done than this whole company, except maybe Red Boots. Folks may bitch, but they are looking to you to be the driving wheel that gets us gone to the end. I know the girl threw you for a loop. She was a looker and razor-sharp, just the way you like them, but you shouldn't let your leaning her way keep you from seeing that you're needed here.

I nodded, This tour hasn't been easy, Spirit, and is likely to get harder as we go. If anyone, including you and me, isn't going to pull their weight, I'd rather they get the hell out now and be replaced by someone more willing or more gullible.

Marcel held up his beer in a half salute and clinked the bottle to mine before saying, Hang on, Doctore, there are bigger fish to fry down river.

Two hours and ten minutes after I finished my beer, I stepped into the ring with my top hat and white tails to begin that day's prestidigitation. When I looked at the entrance, Dan was ready to enter the tent with a smile. It was showtime!

40–Waiting for the Collapso

Sometimes you have to take desperate measures to get rid of that what won't go away. That's not so much a piece of wisdom or good advice as a simple, sad reality.

I felt that way about the Collapso. I wanted it gone, but I had no easy way of getting it done. No matter what happened. Halfway down the Big River and two-thirds of the way through what was fast becoming a benighted tour, the boat came fully into focus, and I was not happy about what I saw. One bad turn after another.

After the ugly incident when the camel escaped in Peoria; after St. Louis and the troubles with barefoot street kids climbing every fence, going over, under and through the buses, trucks and circus tents looking for money or something to steal; after the accident in the shadow of the Arch when the brakes on the blue bus supposedly failed and it rolled backward off the retaining wall far enough to get caught on the lip and requiring a tow truck to lift it back over the precipice; it was just one bad karmic moment after another. I had about reached my limit of accidents waiting to happen.

The Collapso was exhibit number uno of the principle that what could go wrong would go wrong.

Come to think of it, it was not St. Genevieve, but Cape Girardeau, our next stop, that might have been the last time the Collapso was where it should have been when it should have been anywhere. It was easy to forget because I was all for forgetting Cape Girardeau. I wish I could say it was another version of "been there, done that," but though it was a performance that went without incident, it was also without spark.

There were too damn many "what ifs" coming to pass between St. Louis and the next forced hiatus at Fort Defiance to even begin to think about. There was the cancellation of the Colombia show when the Rex sat for the better part of a week in the rain on the state park campground floodplain. Six inches of standing water meant the semi was in mud up to the axles and had to be winched out. Loren Red Beard burned his stuff and walked into the wet. In St. Genevieve, the poor folks paid admission with nickels and dimes because it was the end of the month, and the welfare checks hadn't arrived yet. That was a sign of the times come around again. Then there was Cape Girardeau.

What should I say? We did a show. A center pole wire came loose or snapped or wasn't fixed properly to begin with. Half the tent sagged. No one got hurt. We were lucky.

Lucky accidents are no different than unlucky accidents. Every accident has a cause, an effect and a cost. Luck has more to do with whether you bear the brunt of all three or some combination of them. If there was anything I wanted from luck it was to simply hold us steady until we got to Memphis.

After passing through half-pint towns in Illinois and Missouri with more abandoned hope than money in anyone's pocket, we had arrived at the confluence of the Ohio and Mississippi Rivers. We were sitting once again in a stubble field of a so-called park outside of Cairo, a town that is definitely not Egyptian, and waiting for the Collapso, or more precisely waiting for the Rex crew that was on the boat. After St. Genevieve, I'd felt bad about how I had chewed Dan a new one, and by Cape Girardeau, I'd had just enough of a lapse in judgment to agree that some of the Rex crew could take the boat as far as Fort Defiance, about sixty nautical miles.

Fort Defiance was well-named. The wind never stopped once in the two days we were at the conjunction of the Ohio and the Mississippi. An old grove of trees stood along the edge of the two rivers marking the forest that had once occupied the land for a hundred miles in every direction. Beyond the point, the swift currents of history mixed that which was the East—the produce and effluence of Pittsburgh, Cincinnati, Louisville on the Ohio River—with that of St. Paul, Dubuque and the Quad Cities along the Mississippi plus Bismarck, Pierre, Omaha and Kansas City on the Missouri.

Meeting just north of St. Louis, the Mighty Misery and Ol' Man Miss joined to become a true highway of commerce, a virtual industrial strength sewer that drained sediment and chemical runoff from half the national landscape into the Gulf of Mexico. But here at Fort Defiance, with the depressed economies of Illinois farm towns on one side of the river and the not yet harvested fields of Missouri corn on the other, I did not think about implications of history and ecology. I was focused on a more mundane problem—why was the Rex Terrestrial, Celestial & Nautical Circus always and eternally waiting for the arrival of this folly we so aptly called the Collapso?

While sitting on a folding chair, the meaning of a day late and a dollar short came to mind. Also, the approaching autumnal equinox and whether the world was out of balance. We had been on the road long enough to feel what was right and what was in need of correction. I did not want to be concerned about corrections beyond cleaning Marcel's shotgun, which I had started without knowing why. Somewhere in the back of my mind, I knew I was going to have to use it sooner or later, so I'd better clean it first.

A beat-up pickup stopped at the edge of camp and let George, one of the dependable road rats, get out. Since he was supposed to be on the boat, I figured the boat had landed upriver a bit. Wrong. Oh, it was upriver all right, but landed was not the word George used to describe its condition. Grounded. Grounded on a goddamn sand bar without a working fuel pump. Stuck close to the channel but not close enough to be in it. Waiting for Godot or his nautical doppelganger to raise it up and carry it away.

That time had finally come, and everyone who heard George's woeful tale knew it. Time for decisive action. I loaded George and Marcel's shotgun in the Lincoln and headed along the floodwall road looking for the scene of the accident. George gushed on with details. They might as well have been so many gnats splatting on the windshield for all I cared. The decision I was about to execute was as certain as a squashed gnat. It was past time to pull the plug on the Collapso.

If you didn't know where it was, you could have found it by the sound. Sitting forty feet from the shore and perhaps half that distance outside the channel marker, it was like a frat house on the water. You couldn't hear the frogs singing their evening love songs for the sound of rock and roll pumping out of the speakers someone had set on the deck. No matter, I'd fix it soon enough.

I left George on shore to be the welcoming party and took the shotgun into the waiting canoe. Paddled like a silent avenger across water that gave meaning to the phrase, too thick to drink, too thin to plow.

From a deck chair, Rona shouted, Hey, the Doctor's here. Come on board, have a beer.

Rona, get up and turn the stereo off.

What? Shouted over the roar of Talking Heads.

Turn the stereo off. Fuck it, I'll do it myself.

I tied the canoe to the rail, hoisted the shotgun onto the deck and followed it onboard. Rona looked up from her chair with an air of vague indifference as I opened the sliding glass door and brought the gun into position.

Clear!

The first round went straight into the stereo. The shot actually went through the console and the particleboard wall behind it, splattering chunks of plastic and cassette tape across the room. Heads turned, bodies appeared at every door and window.

Now that I have your attention, I've come to tell you that this is the end of the line for the Collapso. In case you have forgotten while riding this slow boat to nowhere, we have a circus tour in progress that needs your attention.

Lance stood in the door with a guitar in hand and said, Buzz, can you put that shotgun down? It's making me nervous.

I looked through him but put the gun on the table next to me before telling them, I will now say to all assembled on this floating den of indolence what I said privately to Dan, to VX, to any number of you previously—that if you wish to remain on the tour, if you wish to remain employed with the Rex Terrestrial, Celestial & Nautical Circus, you'll pack whatever is useful, get off this boat and never look back. Do I make myself clear?

Dan shook his head and said, Doctore, no need to be so harsh.

Harsh? Dan, you seem to be stuck on that word. Harsh? Me? Harsh? Harsh would be my setting this cursed box of trouble on fire. Harsh is leaving Fort Defiance without bothering to come out here and then hiring replacements for every sorry mother of you on this freshwater Flying Dutchman in Louisville, in Memphis, on the byways and waysides of every rest stop along the interstate between here and the next show if I need to. That would be harsh. Extremely satisfying, but a little over the top.

Getting no response, I continued with: Let me repeat myself. I, Dr. Buzz, do solemnly declare as tour manager of the Rex, as the eternal collector and dispenser of the money, as the keeper of the schedule and the giver of the orders by the power vested in me by the Absent Owners and this shotgun, that we have come to the end of the boat. Bobby can stay on board until I can arrange for this sucker to be towed away, or Bobby can pack his duffel and get on the next canoe with the rest of you. Bobby's the only one with a choice that does not constitute mutiny. As far as the proverbial rest of you are concerned, there is no party hearty on the water while the work doesn't get done. We're long past fish or cut bait. It was cut fucking bait yesterday when the Collapso failed to arrive at the confluence. Never mind that we don't have a show today. That is your salvation. But we will have one tomorrow, and since I cannot afford for you to not be present and accounted for when that show happens, get packed and get off now.

There was a fair amount of grumbling, but the Rex crew gathered their stuff. Bobby opened the cooler and took out a beer. He offered it to me, but when I waved it off, he popped the top, took a long sip and said, You ought to at least leave someone to help me get this thing put away. Lance is good. He's not crucial to the show. Hell, he's not even crucial to the band.

Hell yeah, I agreed. Lance is not even in the show except to hang around backstage getting in the way of the costume changes when he wants to be helpful. He can stay. You understand, Bobby, it's nothing personal.

No, nothing personal, Buzz. Just another good idea gone south. There should be a boatyard in Covington, Kentucky. You can make arrangements for the tow, and I'll take care of the rest.

Don't bother asking about repairing it. Sell the sucker if you can. Leave it if you can't, and we'll let Flat Frank work out the gruesome details and exorbitant costs with the Absent Owners.

I think I'll go with you as far as Memphis and fly home.

I said, Call Frank when you get the boat secured and give him your departure plan. He or Lucy will buy you a one-way ticket and prorate your fee. I'll confirm arrangements when I speak to him from Louisville.

Bobby scrunched up his face and said, I want my full fee, Buzz. It's not my fault that you folks didn't know what to look for in a boat.

Don't do me like that, Bobby. You can argue the fine print with Flat Frank as representative of the Absent Owners. You might get what you want if you talk to Lucy first because she's a big-hearted girl who can sweet-talk Frank. She might even have a line to the backers I never met. You argue fees here and now, I'll go full skunk on you. I'll give you two weeks' pay and call it done. Talk to Lucy if you want the whole pie with ice cream on top.

I plucked the shotgun from the table, shook Bobby's hand and said, Good Luck with everything.

Bobby's parting words were, Are you sure you don't want a beer?

After the first four came off the Collapso, George piled them into the Lincoln and turned back to Fort Defiance with instructions to drop them and bring back a pickup. The remaining three ferried whatever useful equipment, extra food and beer we could carry off the boat. I had to admit a moment of sadness as I looked at that forlorn little boat listing on the sand bar. Captain Bobby lit a Coleman lantern to conserve electricity. Lance was sitting on deck playing his guitar. I could barely make out the words to some sad, sappy love song. When

George and VX arrived with two pickups, we loaded up the gear in silence and drove the sullen ones back to the waiting Rex Terrestrial, Celestial & Nautical.

Sorrow was short-lived in that company. An autumnal equinox celebration about to begin. While I was gone, the central organizing committee had reconvened and made a decision. Miss Red Boots said they had sat in the circle and talked it through. We would go on, the whole company, as one organic whole.

As if that needed to be decided, I thought. What other realistic options did we have? And boy Howdy, what made them think a talking circle was needed in the first place? But Doctore, get a grip, put down the shotgun and don't say a word.

For once, I listened to my own good advice, thanked them for their decision and opined that we would finish this tour in style. Yes, all as one, all the way to the Gulf. Then I surprised myself when I said, Now's the time for some pagan dancing around the fire and we best be getting to it.

The moon rose, a plump tomato red over the horizon, sliding toward lighter pumpkin orange as it floated free of the fields. Successively shifting colors, it turned gold, butter yellow, cream cheese white and finally, a dark mother of pearl as it crossed the heavens. On the windswept shore, the sparks flew up as the company whirled around a roaring fire. Happy feet sent puffs of dust upward that the wind carried over the waters.

About midnight, we saw Cousteau's mighty Calypso with the well-dressed, well-fed, well-paid crew motor by, lights shining brightly as they made their way downstream. They hoisted their glasses to the dancers as they passed and gave a blast of their horn. The band, now back in harness, raised their own horns and returned a long B# that echoed off the water and landed somewhere in Missouri.

In that passing, I had witnessed a miracle, though I did not know it.

In the morning, the Collapso came into view. I could hear the strained chugging of its ten-horse outboard as it turned out of the mist-shrouded channel and headed for the park's single landing slip. Behind the wheel, Captain Bobby was a happy man.

How in the name of Schrödinger's cat can this have happened?

Bobby filled me in, saying, Maybe the French don't know which side to drive on, or maybe they were having a little sport with us, but when the Calypso passed by, they were on the near side of the channel. Shot right past, not more than twenty feet away. As they went by, their wake lifted us off the sandbar and we slid back into the channel. We were free and they were, as you would say, Doctor, the proximate cause.

Piece of cake after that, Lance chimed in. We just fired up the outboard and came on down.

Piece of cake, Bobby? I asked.

Hardly. But by luck or God's grace, here we are.

Yes, by luck or somebody's grace. I was not fooled into thinking that anything had changed. It had not. This was not enough time or money to keep that impossible dream on the water. When nine o'clock came, the circus packed and left the confluence of the two rivers. Cairo waited. We would continue along the Mighty Mississippi, always moving closer to the Gulf and the end of the tour. I did not turn to look back at the forlorn Collapso tied to a tree or at Captain Bobby sipping coffee beside the embers of last night's fire. That chapter was done, and I had already turned the page.

The Collapso sat at the Fort Defiance landing for two days until Captain Bobby was able to get a tow to come up from Covington to take it to its final and long overdue rest. There it was moored in the care of some old river pirate by the name of Love, Captain Love. At least, I think that was his name. Sat there for two or three years. Heard that it had been sold. Heard that it had been given to the good Captain in exchange for back rent due on mooring fees. Heard that it burned mysteriously one night. Heard all kinds of things, but I just don't know. I didn't want to know then, and I certainly don't need to know now. Better not to know the fate of the damned but to believe that it was as it must be and was deserved.

41—Better Not Said

Are you getting as tired of this travelogue as I am, Pilgrim? Are you thinking to yourself, Jesus, nothing much happens in this narrative. No car chases. No murders. Not enough sex to justify a proper bodice-ripper cover. Okay, maybe the end of the Collapso was interesting, but is there any excitement after that?

The fact is, you're wondering if there is anything tying it all together. Well, friend, this is testimony, which is never as convenient as fiction. The further fact is I'm telling you the story, or at least as much of the story as makes sense. Hell, I'm trying to leave out most of the boring stuff. That's the terrible reality of my life. There is a lot of boring stuff.

Of necessity, I've been skipping some of it to avoid the dull repetition that reality offers. I mean, what do you think circus life really is? Plenty of nothing, my friend.

Okay, maybe I've skipped a few details of the tour that I should fill in. Ben, the good-looking guitar-playing leader of the band, hooked up with a girl named Amelia or Orlando or something in St. Louis, and now she's tagging along. The Swede Girls, when they weren't in the ring, continued to knit and trade recipes with Sue or Marg and whatever volunteers showed up to help with the show, then stayed around for dinner. No drama there. When Scott the Dog or Mark aren't working, they're playing with their kids tossing the baseball back and forth over an imaginary first base and riding bicycles. If I loaded this tale with that sort of everyday happy home life, you'd think it was even duller than it was.

There is some good stuff yet to tell. A couple of decent jokes, a sudden appearance, and an international incident are yet to come. There will be a little more romance and the blessed Lord's second coming, but for everything I include, there are ten things I have to exclude.

We left Fort Defiance, did Cairo, and crossed into Kentucky. Nothing happened. Pulled into Louisville, did a weekend of Option A shows for the Optimist Club. No one fell, cut themselves on sharp edges bad enough to require stitches or broke anything that could not be fixed with duct tape. No one quit. The volunteers showed up and actually worked. The sponsor paid us. We pulled out again and headed to Memphis. No trucks or buses broke down. Bear with me, and I swear by Athena's red hair that since I'm telling you about the days when things do not go right, this story will get interesting again.

42–Payne's

Oh, I see that I've gone a bit off course here. You came to hear about the Rex, and so I should return to the narrative in progress.

Most often, the story I tell about Memphis is about the quest for bar-b-que. If there was one thing that I knew, Memphis was the bar-b-que crossroads of the South. Texas brisket, Carolina pork, St. Louis baby backs, every style of slow-smoked cooking was represented by one or more establishments. Even before we arrived, the road rats began making lists of places to check out. Any bar-b-que joint that was appreciatively mentioned more than once to anyone in the Rex crew or among the local sponsors or volunteers would get put on the list.

As it happened, a mere block from where the Rex settled in Memphis, there was an unassuming bar-b-que place called Payne's. It'd been a former gas station or some such—very tiny place. Painted black on the outside and black inside. No tables, just a counter, and behind it, the smoker. It was strictly takeout run by two ancient African American women, Miss Bessie and her sister, Miss Effie. No nonsense women. The menu was also no nonsense—pork ribs, rib tips and pulled pork sandwiches. Jo-jos and slaw on the side. You wanted something to drink, you head on over to the 7-11 across the street. You want some beef brisket, chicken or dessert, you can go to one of those fancy places down the street. They did what they did, and that was straight up all they did.

Boy Howdy, what they did was fabulous. Charged $3.65 for a pulled pork sandwich that started with a square of wax paper, then a soft white bread bun. On top of that was pork with a bark charred almost black, leading to a moist and nearly pink inside. On top of that, a dollop of creamy coleslaw, not too sweet and definitely crunchy, then mild or hot sauce lavished on the other half of the bun. Miss Effie would open the smoker doors, reach in bare-handed, pull out a good five or six-pound slow-smoked pork shoulder, slap it on the table, tear off chunks of warm flesh and pile them on.

It didn't take long for the news to spread through the Rex crew. If you said you were going to Payne's, you'd have a lot of friends pressing money into your hand with their requests for this and that. I was pretty much addicted to the pulled pork and went for one every day we were in Memphis. It didn't stop us from checking off other places on the list, but the truth was that for the Rex crew, nothing beat the taste and convenience of Payne's. It became the cornerstone all others were measured against.

I remember standing in the ring announcing the high wire act, looking at the tent entrance and seeing VX with a stain running down his pants leg. I was sure that he had a Payne's in his pocket. Just about forgot what I was doing, the hunger for one of my own was so powerful.

Still, there were other places that needed checking out. One of them was a place called Craig's in Eads. I don't recall who suggested it, but no one seemed to know how to actually find the place. Not that Eads was that big, but we had been going to most places with a "local guide" just to make sure we didn't go into the wrong place at the wrong time. No one wanted to take us to Eads, which should have been a sign of what was to come.

After the Friday evening show, I was talking to a woman who said she'd been to Craig's. She laughed, then said it was definitely an experience, but even so, she'd be glad to show us the way if we were going in a group. That news spread like wildfire through the Rex crew, and since the tent would be up for another few days, half the road rats were lined up and ready to go by the time I announced the excursion.

To my shock, Marge came over to the car as I was encouraging Marcel to get in. She wanted to go. The most doctrinaire of the Vegetarians, she declared that she wanted to see what the fuss was about. Fine by me, so I plopped her in the shotgun seat for the trip to Eads.

A caravan of cars left the circus grounds in the magnolia-scented night. Over the railroad tracks, past what appeared to be a tire factory, we traversed one industrial landscape after another, each looking successively poorer until our guide pulled into what appeared to be a half-vacant shopping center consisting of a series of mostly boarded-up storefronts. There was a hardware store on one end, a combo gun, ammo and vacuum shop in the middle next to an XXX video store, and on the other end was a rundown Winn-Dixie.

In the middle of the parking lot was Craig's BBQ. It had the architecture of a midwestern Dairy Queen with yellow bug lights and bulletproof glass. It did boast an extensive menu consisting of pork or beef ribs, rib tips, pulled pork sandwiches, burnt ends, beef brisket, chicken, hush puppies, corn fritters, red beans and rice, collard greens, peach cobbler and moon pies. While the choices were plenty, mine was simple. Pulled pork.

I ordered at the little window and placed my cash in the carousel thingy that took money in and sent product out. When it turned, a pulled pork sandwich wrapped in aluminum foil came out. This was a bad sign, one that suggested the risk of bar-b-que with a metallic taste. I unwrapped it and took a good long look. Foil, the standard white bread bun, something uniformly cubed and almost gray in color. On top of the suspect meat, coleslaw with slices of apple, a fact that I pointed out to Marge as a nod to her religion. Then hot sauce and the requisite white bread bun.

I took a bite. It was mostly okay. Nothing to write home about and certainly not a Payne's. But my displeasure was offset by my curiosity about what Marge would order and, more to the point, what she would consume. She ordered some burnt ends with a side of greens. We all congratulated her on the choice.

She began to eat, slowly at first and then with a quickening pace. Suddenly her head snapped back, her face flushed and her eyes rolled back in her head. I couldn't tell whether she had food poisoning or was having a religious experience. Given the look of Craig's, I was afraid of the former but totally prepared for the latter.

Marge leapt to her feet and bolted across the parking lot, running into the hardware store. To my amazement, she reemerged a minute later carrying a Husqvarna chainsaw followed by a clerk shouting for her to come back. She crossed the parking lot in record time and entered the Winn-Dixie. We pretty much abandoned our eats and rushed toward the store to see what would happen next. We didn't know what, but we knew it would be something to remember because that girl didn't lose her grip but once in a blue moon.

Entering the grocery store, we could hear the sound of the chainsaw ripping the shit out of something. Following that sound, I saw Marge standing in the dairy case cutting up something. Bits of packaging and what looked like cheese were flying into the aisle. There was a good-sized crowd gathered around her, some urging her to calm down, some with their mouths open.

Whomever I suspected was the store manager was saying, Madam, is there a paaaarticulaaaar reason that you've taken a chainsaw to my dairy case? I had to appreciate his tone of voice. You couldn't get much more politeness in that many syllables. I had to laugh.

Marge reached down and picked up a package of tofu, the bastard stepchild of an eraser and Elmer's glue. It may be nutritious, she said, but it sure ain't bar-b-que.

VX was repeating the line to Marcel in a stage whisper. Marcel was biting his hook to keep from laughing. Marge looked at them both, brandishing the chain saw: whirrr, whirrrr, whhiiirrrr.

When the police arrived to take her to jail, this moment would go down in the annals of circus history as the great Tennessee Tofu Massacre. That's the story I tell. Entertaining but not entirely true. First off, maybe there was no chainsaw, but if you didn't see the wink when I got to that part, my underlining won't help.

The Vegetarians had taken command of the communal cooking long before we left Alma and were loathe to give up any bit of culinary control, but the desire, or the necessity, of hiring a cook was always with us. The cost of paying for someone to cook for everyone just wasn't in the budget. We never had the facilities to do a rolling commissary, and even though we often used church basements and school cafeterias or gyms as staging grounds for the show, cooking was always a problem.

By time we got to Memphis, we were primed for a Payne's addiction. We were like junkies in need of a fix. Food and the procuring, making and eating of it had become a major focus of the company. There wasn't enough of this and way too much of that. Who cooked and when, where and with what was available in any given church basement was a conversation that never stopped. Factions appeared. Alliances were formed around pancakes and betrayed by bacon.

When we encamped in that fabled city, the logistics of hunger were fast becoming the death of us all. For reasons beyond me, as the Rex went into the heart of Dixie, the cost of food crept up while the cost of booze crept down. The fact we could get a case of beer in Arkansas for the price of two six packs in Illinois suggested that we should stock up. But the former, the fact that every bit of rice and beans, chicken or bread cost a few pennies more per piece or pound, was the Achilles heel of the Rex and indeed of any tour.

Do I repeat myself? It's worth the repetition. It's the difference between success and food poisoning. It's a truism that even for the Rex, or especially for the Rex, a lot of food needed to be procured, prepared, eaten and cleaned up after. We had no reliable mechanism to save or store anything that was not dry, so the operating principle was to get only as much as was needed for this meal or the next one. Eat it all at once. Reluctantly give away or throw away what is uneaten.

If we were someplace for a few days, you could think about putting up leftovers and rearranging yesterday's rice and beans as the base for tomorrow's soup. But when we were doing the old Option A, there was not enough portable refrigeration to hold enough for the thirty or forty or however many of us were there at the table from one meal to the next. Of necessity, what could go to the animals went, and what couldn't went to compost.

To his credit, Frank took my argument that hiring a cook could no longer be postponed to the Absent Owners and brought back what he thought was good news. They would bump for one at the same per diem as the rest of us were slaving for. It wasn't much, but it was something. All I needed to do now was find someone willing to do the work.

43—Archibald

That's when Archibald come to save us from ourselves.

I was at Payne's waiting on pulled pork and complaining to the ladies that I would miss their wares. I said to them, If I could, I'd take you sweet dears with us.

Miss Effie said, Lord bless us, travel with a circus? Miss our Wednesday prayer meeting? I think not.

Yes, Miss Effie, as much as I'd like to, it is probably not the life for someone as settled as yourself, with traveling being the heart of the matter. But I tell you by the prophet Elijah's flaming chariot, the circus is sore in need of a decent cook, and I can't think of two better cooks than your sister and yourself.

Miss Effie smiled and said, Now I know you're just sugarin' me. But if you want someone who is used to traveling and can cook almost as good as I do, you'd best be wanting my nephew, Archibald.

I would?

Come back this afternoon at five, and I'll introduce you. He's fresh out of the Navy and needs to stop hanging around my house. I love the boy, but really, he's got to do something with himself besides making biscuits in my kitchen.

I did come back at five. She did call him out from the tiny office in the back of the building. He came through the door—filled it up as he did so—and looked up at me from the angular lean of a big man trying to look small with the soft smile of a man who had a secret on the tip of his tongue.

I spoke first. Archibald, I presume? The name's Buzz, formally Doctor Buzz. I run that plugged nickel circus camped over on Mulberry.

I stuck out my hand, and he took it. When the handshake commenced, I noticed two things. First off, his touch was soft, but I could feel the muscle beneath the surface being held in check. If I was a praying man, I'd offer one prayer of thanksgiving and another for mercy because I could see that he was a lot bigger and maybe a lot meaner than he presented. I soon found out that I was right on the first but wrong on the second. He was indeed a looming presence trying to not attract attention, but over the remainder of the tour, I came to appreciate that Archibald didn't have a drop of mean in him.

It didn't take much to strike a deal. I had money and need. I didn't have a regular kitchen or utensils. He'd have to make do with whatever we found at every stop. It would be the same pay and the same per diem as the rest of the Rex team members got, though at the manifestation of this conversation, I still hadn't gotten what I considered to be the official okay by virtue of actual dollars. I'd have to give him what should have gone to Loren Red Beard or skim his share once a week from somewhere else. The point I was arguing with myself was that I couldn't afford to leave Memphis without a cook—in fact, without this particular cook, as he was present and accounted for.

He had time and skill. He had a big ass set of chef's knives and a few favored skillets and pots stuck in a cardboard box he was willing to carry along. He didn't have a car, but we had a bus. Most of all, he had the blessing of his aunts, and once on tour, he confessed to me that he was glad not to be making any more biscuits in Effie's kitchen.

When Archibald entered a kitchen, it was like Moses parting the waters. Everything moved aside. When he started to cook, whoever was there was enlisted for duty as he gave orders with the precision of a great general, plotted the campaign, marshaling these potatoes now, those carrots then, bringing the cheap chuck steak into action at just the right time to form a pincer movement under a barrage of spices. Even the hard-core vegetarians had to salute his skills. Besides that, he made rice and beans interesting again.

I'm going back to the story that started us off to remind the both of us that Marge did not take a chainsaw to the dairy case. I mean, how many hardware stores do you know that keep chainsaws gassed up and ready to use? If she had gone into the gun shop, she'd easily have been able to come out with a loaded 30-gauge shotgun or better. We were south of Mason Dixon, and I'd seen a full auto Mac 10 hanging on a pawnshop wall. Hell, that would have been easy. They do keep them loaded and ready in more than a few shops, but a chainsaw, not so much. I put it in there to just make the point that she had a life-changing experience there in Eads.

Now don't go complaining that I'm deviating from the facts. I told you from the get-go that I'd bend the facts to fit the story, and in this case, you have to admit it's a much better story with the chainsaw than without it.

But Archibald was another story altogether, one that would be told in every kitchen and with every meal the Rex sat down to for the next five weeks. I only wished I had known of him when we were in Alma. It would have made for a lot less bellyaching and a lot more confidence that we would get through this with our health in place, if not our happiness.

44—Rango

Somewhere during the Memphis sojourn, Marcel and Elijah met Rango. One strange dude, and here I'm not adding anything for the sake of the story. The facts were odd enough. He might have been a first cousin of Sun Ra, for all I know. He claimed he was not from this world and had come to Earth from some distant planet to run for mayor of Memphis. Had campaign signs that featured him looking very jaunty—shirtless and deeply tanned, wearing old-style aviator eye goggles. Could have been a trust fund baby gone off his meds for all I know, and that was certainly what I suspected when Marcel told me Rango wanted to buy the camel.

I said, He's joking, of course.

Why would he be joking, Doctore? He says that he knows their language, and our camel is asking for his freedom. Claims we keep him intoxicated and enslaved.

I grinned and said, The camel should be so lucky. I've not given him another beer since the incident in Peoria, so why would the camel say that? I looked at Marcel, who coughed, so I said, Tell me you haven't...

He's much more manageable with one or two while he eats. But Buzz, that's not the point. Rango wants to buy the camel. Real cash money. I've been thinking about it, and if he can have a good home, why not let the humped one rest from his dreary life of hauling pukes and rug rats?

176

I've been thinking about it myself, I replied. When we get to New Orleans, something would have to be done. Miss Red Boots takes the tigers with her, but the camel...

How much? I asked.

Didn't ask. After all, you're the money guy.

I'll have to contact the Absent Owners, but yes, I'm Johnny on the spot.

I made a call to explain the situation to Flat Frank, who in turn relayed it to the powers behind the curtain and then got back to me the next day, saying if I could get $7,200 for the camel, I could sell it.

In fact, I intended to ask for $7,500 for the camel and then another $1500 for the trailer. After all, what the hell did I need with a camel trailer once the camel was gone?

I was both surprised and pleased by how smoothly the agreement on price went once middleman Marcel introduced me to Rango. Tanned and wearing what looked like a blue silk bathrobe over florescent orange bike shorts and flip flops, he didn't look like he was from another planet but was decidedly out of place in the Peabody Hotel lobby. However, members of the staff greeted him by name, so I understood this was not his first time there.

Rango immediately said that he definitely liked the idea of buying a camel and was ready to give me cash or a cashier's check. That wasn't news, as cash or a cashier's check had been specified from the get-go. What was news was that there was no haggling. I said $9,000 is the price, and he replied, $10,000 sounds about right.

Okay by me, $10,000 it is.

I reminded him of the fact that once he took possession, I didn't want the camel back under any circumstances. We shook hands. He pointed at a briefcase sitting at his feet and shoved it toward me. All we had to do was deliver the camel to a farm that Rango owned. Directions to find it were in the briefcase. How hard could that be? I was ready to load the beast up and drop him off that afternoon.

Walking out of the hotel with a case full of bills arranged in neat rows of Grants and Franklins seemed a little strange, but a strange I could get used to. It felt like some kind of weird variation on a drug deal, and in a moment of paranoia, I expected the DEA to swoop in and arrest me for money laundering. That was not an unreasonable fear. That was also the moment when I wondered how Rango made his money.

The directions to the farm seemed easy enough. Hell, even getting the camel in the trailer wasn't bad. Three bottles of Rolling Rock coaxed him into place. Marcel climbed in the cab, and we headed toward the humped one's future retirement home.

Along the driveway, Spanish moss hung from a natural arch of old growth trees. The white columns of the two-story house gave it an old-school, landed gentry kind of aura. Off to one side was a series of barns in the Southern style—long and low sheds begging for tobacco advertisements painted on the side. There were attached corrals and a meadow rising up a gentle slope with some fine-looking horses strategically placed for maximum effect. Damn picturesque if you asked me, but Marcel wasn't asking. I had no need to comment.

We parked the truck and trailer next to the closest barn. Marcel climbed out and went around to open the door and ease the soon-to-be-gone camel out of the trailer. I stepped out of the cab looking for a welcoming party, or in lieu of that, anyone who would sign on the dotted line for delivery of the beast. I wished that it didn't matter whether anyone actually signed anything as we already had the money, but it never hurt to have paperwork that actually crosses the t's and dots the i's. There always was a chance that not getting it done right would come back to bite you in the ass later. I'd had enough of that from the camel to last a lifetime.

A three-hundred-pound African American guy with Rasta dreadlocks wearing bib overalls and a tie-dyed T-shirt emerged from the barn. He took a hit of a massive doobie and walked over to not exactly shake my hand. It was more a circular motion that ended in a half-wave of dismissal.

We're here with the camel.

What camel? He asked, looking at me with the puzzled visage that told me he knew nothing about this. Didn't ask for a camel, mon. I asked for a mule.

Not our department, I said. The mules come from somewhere else. Though I've got to tell you, if you're looking to plow a field, there are plenty of places in the Mideast where a camel in front of a plow is standard operating procedure. That said, I've got a camel that Mister Rango bought with the full faith and credit of US government currency, and in so doing, it has already been paid for. The trailer too. We're here to deliver said camel. You get it all—camel and trailer. Just sign here.

Rango, you say? He scratched his head as if trying to remember who Rango was before he brought the joint up to take another hit. No, mon, didn't say anything about this. He stared past me to look at the camel. Lord, that is too big.

Marcel had the camel half backed out of the trailer when it let out a fart. The smell of old camel pervaded the yard, overwhelming the smell of burning marijuana.

Marcel called out, Oh, baby cakes, that one was a stinker.

Mr. Take Another Toke agreed, then said, Say there, you fellows, just how big is that thang?

Marcel replied, Eight-foot something at the hump. Marcel now had the camel's lead in hand. Did the Doc tell you that in some countries, they use these babies instead of a mule? Do ten acres a day and fertilize it at the same time.

I already told him that, I said, giving Marcel a certified laser beam look of "please close your pie hole…"

Marcel spits out some chewing gum and said, Sorry, I seem to be a beat behind. Best let the Doctore do his thing, and I'll just hold this lead until you're ready to take it.

The camel blinked in the sunlight, then hissed at no one in particular. He let out a sound somewhere between a greeting and a belch. I couldn't wait to get the paper signed and head back to Memphis before he did something everyone would regret.

I said, Here, just sign this if you would, and my assistant will give you a quick run-down on the care and feeding of this magnificent creature. I pushed the delivery receipt toward the large man and pulled a pen out of my suit coat pocket.

Before he had finished his John Hancock, Marcel launched into a description of what to feed or not feed the camel if you want to avoid him getting the runs. Then Marcel said, He's happiest if he can have two beers a day. It doesn't matter when you give them. Time means nothing to a camel.

With that, I put the papers in my pocket, unhitched the trailer from the truck and said, Congratulations, the camel and this fine trailer are all yours. Marcel, get in the truck, we're late.

Marcel gave me the stink eye, suggesting that he was just warming up his camel instructions. Late for what? he asked.

I wanted to just get out of there, so while starting the engine, I said, For the afternoon's performance. Give the man his camel and get in.

This time Marcel understood. Sure thing, Doctore. He handed over the lead and, as he climbed into the cab, said, Be careful where you put your hand. He bites.

Fucking and fitting famous last words for the camel. As we pulled out of the drive, I felt a wave of relief wash over me. One burden lifted, and the Rex was now $10,000 to the good for the last two months of the tour. That would buy a few weeks of groceries to keep Archibald happy or to pay for the next unexpected breakdown.

For a moment, I thought that the wheel of fortune had turned once more. Happy days were here again.

45—Mississippi State Line

While Marcel and I were seeing to the camel's retirement, most of the Rex crew took the opportunity to do one of these three things in Memphis: Graceland, Beale Street or the Lorraine Motel.

I had no interest in Graceland. For my money, the King was best remembered in the catalog of music he recorded before he went to paranoid semi-seclusion amid the leopard print furniture or gold records on the wall. What was there to see in the end? It is a mausoleum of bad taste.

Billy Bones and Scott the Dog did go and reported that the best part was looking at the other people in line. Japanese tourists doing the Japanese tourist thing, older women who obviously were on pilgrimage and a bunch of black T-shirt hipster, graduate school historians doing some kind of field research. I must admit that seeing that crowd would have made it easier to take. The first time I ever went was the day they opened it to the curious. I could not believe that in the years since it had gotten any better.

I had gone to the Lorraine when it was boarded up. Spooky vibes rose like summer heat off asphalt. In those days, you could stand in what had been the parking lot and look at the balcony and then turn to see where James Earl Ray was when he pulled the trigger. It hadn't become a museum yet and was just a sad, sad reminder of what was lost. Even then, with the paint peeling and everyone arguing about what to do with the place, there were fresh bouquets left every day of the week. Looking at the scene of the crime falling slowly to pieces, I was reminded of what Big Daddy used to say, that there is always someone who takes their pain as your fault and thinks that hurting you will make it better.

Thinking about that sad, sad turn of time, I was reminded of a song.

> Come on down to the river. Lower yourself in.
> Don't care if you're Ophelia.
> Don't care if you're the creature from the Black Lagoon.
> The waters are dark, the current is uncertain.
> Let the healing water wash you in moonlight.
> Let the forgiving water carry you away.
> The big river will take your sorrow
> To the salty sea, to the great salty sea...

As I always say, if you believe, I cannot deceive. I wouldn't tell you wrong on this one. When I'm right, I'm right.

Beale Street was another matter. The original Memphis blues scene. It was once replete with gritty clubs and sporting houses, and the real "there" was Schwab's Hardware right in the middle of it all. Of course, they tore the whole thing down in the name of progress, built it up again in the name of tourism. Out with the old and in with the faux. Except for Schwab's. They didn't tear it down because it wouldn't be bought. Opened every day just like the sign said. It was a wonder to wander. Walking through the door felt right, smelled like an old boot, looked like a kind of mercantile of my forgotten youth, the kind of place that had a little of everything. If it went on the shelf, it stayed there until it got sold or crawled away on its own. If they didn't have it, you probably didn't need it.

I could give a flying fig about the modern clubs trying to give the feel of the long-ago real deal joints with pressed tin ceilings and sawdust floors where Frankie could meet Johnny. In the old days, you could drink something stronger than sweet iced tea, go upstairs for a bouncy bounce with a big-bottomed brown girl or even a skinny white girl down on her luck, then get shot coming down those stairs again. Maybe it was a boyfriend, maybe it was some tipsy river gambler who was looking to shoot someone else but plugged you instead. The new places all looked like they had crawled out of some "decorate your casino in plastic" catalog, hung with cute signs and fake antiques. I couldn't tell one from another by the decor or the menu. Schwab's was the only place with enough must and dust to make me happy.

The night before we left Memphis, which was the same day we sold the camel, there was a blowout party with the Rex crew and some local volunteers and folks who lived within spitting distance of the big top. Everyone was having a good time. The beer was flowing. Moonshine out the back door next to the line of Weber grills cooking locally made tube steak. Those were some better-than-average-tasting hot dogs and buns. Sliced tomatoes, fresh off the vine, not the hard, tasteless crap you so often find at the Winn-Dixie. Archibald had baked a couple of sweet potato pies that tasted of every good thing the South purports to be. There were eats enough for everyone to have their fill, and it was getting masticated with the joyful carelessness of fatty juices running down your chin.

Some kid, maybe nine or ten, was ripping the blues with the Rex band. I remember the kid because I got a picture of him with a red guitar half his size. I don't have a picture of the fistfight that sent Slim Jim to the hospital for stitches. I don't think I was even there when it happened, and I didn't find out about it until we were waiting for the tow truck in Mississippi. He had done what he did and avoided me until it was a day after, but by then, I had other fish to fry.

The hippy-dippy bus was ten miles over the Mississippi state line when it blew a rod. When I came down the road in the pride of Henry Ford, I could see the tie-dye was parked at an angle on the side of the highway, and a half dozen of the Rex crew were standing around smoking cigarettes or eating peaches they had bought at a farm stand. Billy Bones told me that the guy running the stand had let him use the house phone to call the sheriff's office, the sheriff had given him the number of a tow service, and now the tow service was on their way. Thank you, Billy, for initiative.

What hadn't happened was anything like getting the idle folks off the roadside and back on the road to the next stop. When VX drove up in Loren Red Beard's pickup, I flagged him down to load as many of the crew as possible into the cab and camper. He took four and their bags. We put another four in the Lincoln, and one of the Toms agreed that he'd drive it south and then come back to pick me up in Memphis at the Peabody Hotel that evening.

While we were standing beside a cotton field that was about ready for picking, the white blossoms like low clouds caught on the bare branches, VX told me about the fight. There was not much I could have done about it then, and there really wasn't much I wanted to do except to ask Slim Jim if he had insurance or used a fake name at the hospital or if I was going to see a bill somewhere down the line. Right about then, the tow truck arrived, and I had one of those more immediate things to attend to.

The tow truck hooked the bus up with a terrible groan as if the ghost of Wavy Gravy was lamenting his last ride, made a sweeping U-turn, dragging it over the closest row of cotton, and headed back to Memphis. Those plants would never be the same, and bits of cotton were stuck here and there all along the underside of the bus. The garage he was going to take us to was the only one he knew that worked on buses. Probably the only one his cousin owned. Same difference. It was where the bus would go. Once I sorted out the cost of the tow and the repair, I intended to retire to Peabody's lounge to wait for my ride back to the Rex, sipping a nice something and something. I hadn't had a mint julep since the turnips had come up, and that sounded about right.

Between the tow and the necessity of a rebuilt engine, the bounty of the camel's departure was already seriously eroded. Depleted, if I do say so, to the point where I could once again see the hole in the bottom of the moneybag. So was the schedule, at least as far as Billy Bones was concerned. He'd be tasked with waiting for the repairs to be done and then driving the bus down to Natchez or whatever was the next stop to rejoin the rest of us.

When we arrived at the garage, I gave Billy a hundred twenty bucks and told him to not drink it all at once because it had to last him until the repairs were done. Three days, I figured. I also gave him the name and number of Miss Connie, the local librarian who had been so helpful in smoothing over the bureaucratic bumps during our Memphis sojourn, with instructions to call her. He'd be able to crash on her couch if he promised to stay sober, but if he couldn't stay upright, she'd send him someplace else to hang his hat. If it was more than three days, he was to ask her to spot him twenty bucks a day with the promise that I would send her twenty-five for every Jackson she proffered him.

She knew I'd be good on my word. I had her address. We had gotten on pretty well for a man who was not interested in romance and a woman who knew the current mayor and chief of police.

Then I used the grease-slick relic of a phone in the office to call a cab. Yes, sir, Billy says, when life hands out lemons, you should make lemonade and add a little bourbon and ice. I didn't say it, and I didn't believe it. What I did believe was more along the lines of when push comes to shove, skip the lemonade and stick with the bourbon.

46–The Levee

There are levees pretty much the length of Ol' Man River from St. Louis to someplace south of New Orleans—high earthen walls rising thirty or forty feet from the water's edge. Usually, they're wide enough for a road of sorts on the top, officially to drive a car to inspect the works but practically to get to a favored fishing or drinking spot.

From the river, you see the rammed earth, rip rap or concrete, and whatever vegetation that has claimed space across the surface or between the cracks. Whatever is beyond—farm fields, houses, railroad tracks, woods—is assumed or imagined. The sole function of a levee is to keep the river on one side and ordinary life on the other. Mostly it works until the years or decades when there is too much of something, and the ever-changing, never-changing current finds a way to breach or spill over that singular function. Then lakes appear, seas even, mile after mile of river reaching as far as it is able, leaving buildings standing with water to the windows or worse.

And after, the cry to build a higher, stronger barrier.

As we went further into the heart of Dixie, the Rex moved from setting up in public parks and athletic fields to unclaimed spaces next to the levee. The river, the levee, the tent, the cars parked wherever, all became the scene. In some places, if you were on the river side, you could see the peak of the tent beyond the wall. If you were on top of the levee, you could look down on the backyard, as it was, and watch the performers making their entrances and exits and changing costumes behind the tent. If you were inside the tent, as I was, you could smell the river and hear the boats moving out of sight but not out of mind.

47–The Blues

In retrospect, trouble had come with every stop from the headwaters on down the line as we traversed the great ditch of time. This whole testimony is mostly the recollecting of the humorous, but what is comical now was often as not straight-up painful and grew fulsome the farther we got down the Old Muddy. The painful experiences began to manifest with the frequency of Walmart parking lots baking in the summer sun. There was the usual run of small inconveniences and accidents, some of which I have already recounted. I've skipped the sprained ankles when someone fell off stilts or the cuts and bruises that came with every putting up and taking down of the show.

Still, the bumps and bruises persisted whether I acknowledged them or not. The nicks and scrapes took their toll until every man Jack of us was hobbling like old men and pained from stem to stern, keester to noggin. It was like we had entered a different reality, one in which bad luck and trouble ruled, and you'd need to make a deal with the devil to get safely through to the other side. There were tales of many a man that met the devil at the crossroads and sold this or that for an end to their troubles. Most of those stories ended badly, but I was giving the prospect of making that kind of deal with each new hardship. If only I could know which crossing road would be the right one, I swear I'd have gone to take a look-see.

But the troubles I'm thinking about now were not the petty

inequities of the flesh. They were of a darker sort, an underbelly ache that I haven't dwelt upon previously or at least shoved into the corner of this narrative for a return visit. This is probably the latter.

The first of these was the fact that money was running out. It was not that the sponsors weren't paying, it was that they seemed to begrudge the amounts they had contracted for. In that regard, I was thinking it was time to go into the next vacuum and gun shop I saw and buy me a 9mm Glock to take with me when I went to collect the check. Instead, I started to have Scott the Dog or Archibald come with me when it was time to do the settling up. Not that they were going to do much, but they were big guys and could look like they'd just as soon break your arm as shake your hand. When they stood there, they didn't need to do much except say that they were glad to meet whomever we were meeting, then smile a big smile before looking the sponsor slowly and carefully up and down. After that, I'd remind the sponsor that the terms were as they had been—cash or a cashier's check Johnny on the spot.

Once in a while, a sponsor would try to postpone paying or haggle for better terms. The ones who held the cashier's checks leaned to the first, saying if I could just wait until Tuesday or next week to cash it, they'd be mighty appreciative. Scott would cough and look at me, then scowl.

I'd tell the sponsor, I understand your position. But you, Sir, must understand ours. Then I'd sweep my hand toward the tent before continuing with, There are mouths to feed, men, women, children, tigers, Sir—*don't forget the tigers*. On Tuesday, we will be in X or Y place, and of necessity, I will have to march this cashier's check into the first bank I come to Monday morning to keep the mighty Rex rolling down the river. While it may take the bank a day or so to process the paper, I will take this check in and take cash out. That is the necessity of it.

Those paying cash? Well, if there was any renegotiation to be had, it came in the counting out of the proceeds. It all depended on who collected the ticket money and if they were paying from onsite revenues. We'd sit together in the little cabin built on the back of

189

Loren Red Beard's pickup or one of the buses, put stacks of bills on a card table and total it up together as they went, 200, 400, and so on until they got to the number they wanted to end at. I would remind them that the objective was for both of us to make money, at which point I'd continue the count until we arrived at the number previously agreed upon. They'd usually sigh audibly, and we'd continue laying out currency until everything was right.

Either way, someone would often be unhappy, and I preferred it wasn't us. We were delivering the product, and the sponsors were supposed to deliver the fee. It should have been simple math for simple minds. But the fact was that even when we were getting paid what we were owed, too often, the expense dish ran way past the income spoon, and it was costing me more to replace the dishes than the Absent Owners, Flat Frank or myself had anticipated.

The second was that the seams were starting to show for everybody and everything. Folks were getting cranky. The Swede Girls had taken to talking to each other exclusively in Swedish. No one knew if that was because they missed the mother tongue or if they didn't want anyone else to hear what they were complaining about. Familiarity was breeding discontent as well as contempt.

Slim Jim had gotten into another fight with another one of the locals after a performance in some spit water town. Wasn't even in a bar, just some teetotaler sort of clapboard church space. Three more stitches worth of attitude adjustment should have taught him that fighting was a poor approach to disagreement, but it could have been worse. VX was Johnny on the spot breaking it up, but when I asked him what the hell that was about, he shrugged and said Jim didn't like the way the guy looked at Ruth. Give me a break! Every one of the locals was giving us the fisheye from the moment we arrived until the dust settled after we headed down the road. Those that lusted for Rex beauties were fewer than them that suspected we were the devil's disciples, even if the Kiwanis or Chamber of Commerce had booked the Rex.

We were not their kind. We were outsiders, strangers with exotic and probably corrupt, immoral, and certainly not visible Christian habits of prayer on Sunday and Wednesday nights. Not one of the performances started with a prayer, and most didn't even start with saluting the flag or playing the National Anthem. Local folk wanted to take a good long look at the differences we represented, but please, don't stay, and once you leave, half the town will pray for your redemption. Truth was, of course, the other half wished they had the gumption to go with us. For most of them, it would always be the wishing and not the going that mattered.

One in a hundred of the locals would actually ask about a job or at least a ride out of town. I had a soft spot for those boys in their ill-fitting selves wanting something other than the army as the exit card, or the girls who thought they were too pretty or not pretty enough for the locals and figured they could ride a sequined leotard as well as any of the Rex girls did. I knew the feeling. I knew what happened when you did what they so fondly wished to do.

More than once, I'd sit a kid down and say, this is not what you think it is. It is not a ticket to better. It's only a ticket to different. I'd look in their eyes and see if any of that easily dispensed advice registered and then hand them a Jefferson and say, if you want to go so badly, get on a bus as far as this will take you because the Rex is not your exit visa. Then depending on the circumstances, I'd start a positive review of their age, their sex, their sexual identity, a negative review of their lack of skills—anything I thought would give them hope that someday they could leave, but not now, not with us.

The crushing fact was that I didn't want the liability for taking a minor across state lines. Hell, I didn't want to take a minor to the next town. In more than one case, I was sure that their parents would have simply said goodbye, like mine, and been satisfied with their being gone. Still, the legal stuff, especially the entanglements that came with minors, required me to take a firm negative stand.

They were always young, mostly fifteen or sixteen, in high school, or sometimes tragically junior high and sick of being bullied. Those were the kids who could see their future in this slow decay of civilization and didn't like it. Kids like I had been back in the day. Kids hating their pa or ma, hating their schools and churches and

191

their bullying peers. More than one had suffered some kind of abuse and wouldn't believe for a minute that God or country would save them. They just didn't fit, couldn't pretend anymore, and couldn't wait another day to get the hell out. They desperately wanted us to be the ticket to anywhere better, and I couldn't do that, even though my heart went out to them. They were minors, and that was the sorrowful fact of it.

By the time they weren't minors, they had already left or had bit a bullet.

48–Bad Jazz

As we went further into the soft underbelly of the Bible Belt, the fetid heat clung more fiercely, and the kudzu grew thicker. The Rex became more exotic and more suspect as well. While the first half of the tour had been marked by sponsors eager to have us do parades and workshops—anything really, to keep us another day on the cheap to enliven the local scene—after Memphis, sponsors looked at the Rex and asked themselves what the hell they were paying for. None of them would cancel a contract because they had paid a deposit when they booked it and were not about to let that money go. Most were too polite to speak their anxiety, but I could see that some of them were reconsidering what they had decided that, yes, a circus is just what this town needs. Maybe it wasn't such a good idea after all.

Once we crossed into the nether regions of Fundamentalism, there also seemed to be an inverse ratio of audience to size of community or piety. The smaller the town, the more likely we were to get a full tent whether the local preacher used us as an example of the devil's handiwork or not. But in bigger places, getting butts in the seats was becoming harder to do. We were not big enough, exotic enough or reason enough to leave the ball game on TV.

It was Elijah who said, We should just play a little Bad Jazz on the street.

I like that, I'd said. You, me, and Marcel drumming up a little interest in the show.

193

And we did. Elijah on a snare drum with a high-hat cymbal, Marcel on a baritone horn or trumpet, and me standing in front and pitching the show, handing out "two for one" coupons to anyone who would take them.

The sound was mostly whatever tune Marcel could think to play, with Elijah providing a wide array of syncopated and propulsive beats. I'd hear the melody and launch in with rants and half-sung rhymes, mostly along the lines of:

Come on out, yes, come on out, we've got a show for you to shout about.
Big acts, little acts from far and near,
The strange and the wonderful Rex Terrestrial, Celestial & Nautical Circus,
At 7:00 PM tonight
Under a canvas sky, something to delight
Every eye at the old school grounds…

Yes, I looked like a man in a badly fitting suit with dark sunglasses shouting whatever rhyme schemes he could work into eight or sixteen bars with two skinny fellows in bow ties improvising or murdering a tune from some Broadway musical—all the while waving coupons.

We frequently set up on the busiest street corners we could find or somewhere on the near edge of the Walmart parking lot—not quite at the front door, but close enough so those pushing a cart to the far end of the row would have to pass us. We wore black suits, white shirts, the previously mentioned bow ties and hats. Hell, I wore some variation of that outfit most days, but for Elijah and Marcel, it was dress up. Elijah always had a straw hat, but Marcel and I were porkpie guys. We looked like a cross between old bluesmen, the ubiquitous Jehovah's Witnesses or Mormons, and some kind of demented store clerks.

Usually, we'd play in the simmering heat for a half hour or so, one tune after another, until dehydration set in and Marcel couldn't get enough spit to get a note. The handing out of flyers was hit or miss as more folks would not take them than would. Two-for-one meant nothing when lunatics are handing them out. There was a lot of head-turning to avoid eye contact and quickening of pace as they rolled their squeaky-wheeled shopping carts to cars baking in the sun.

Sometimes, someone from a store would come out and politely ask us to move along, or not-so-politely threaten to call the cops if we didn't leave post haste. More than once, the squad car would roll up and go past so slowly the engine would threaten to stall—the window would roll down and the officer behind his sunglasses would stare intently at the three of us cranking out decidedly off-tempo renditions of the Great American Songbook. They usually said nothing. When they did, it would be along the lines of, You boys are on private property and need to move NOW!

I'd say something like, Yes, officer, and by the way, can I offer you a ticket to the next performance of the Rex Terrestrial, Celestial & Nautical Circus? Now and then, I'd find an officer who was susceptible to gratuities.

There was no point in arguing with a cop, no matter how big or small the town. We'd finish off the phrase, a quick four beats to the bar or whatever, grab the drums and head on back to the Lincoln. Sometimes the cops would take the comp ticket offered but, even then, want us out of the sun and their sight. They'd shadow us across the parking lot and sit in their squads until we were packed and rolling toward the street. Then they'd follow us halfway to the Rex grounds just to make sure we weren't doubling back to start again.

49–Ghosts in Natchez

In Natchez, we camped on the grounds of an abandoned mansion—abandoned with good reason as the front yard and the street before it had departed the horizontal in favor of a long drop down to the Big Muddy. It was a nice house if you didn't walk two feet past the front porch. The place was uninsurable and in danger of dropping into the *ever-changing, never-changing* that was eating away Mississippi one flood at a time. Of course, the sponsor offered it as Rex Central because the likelihood of disaster on any given day was small.

At least, that's what the neighbor said. Her house was also uninsurable, but since she had lived in it the whole of her life, the white-haired Grande Dame was not about to let the ground disappearing beneath her feet force her to move one inch. She was a spry woman in her late seventies, a charm and a half in the Old Southern style, all sugar tongue and iron fist inside a velvet glove. She took a liking to the Swede Girls right away. They were cultured visitors from another country. But when she got a glimpse of Marcel, she made him her "special project" right then and there. I guess Marcel still had it when it came to women wanting to mother and smother him.

In the course of three days, Marcel had more over-sweetened iced tea, mint Juleps, sugar and molasses cookies, historical stories of the neighborhood's former glories and fortune-telling than he could stand. She came over twice a day to ask him to come to her house so she might have the honor of his company. He indulged her between shows because there wasn't much to do except sit on the porch and watch the towboats pushing barges or the sunset in Arkansas.

I was interested in the fortune telling. I wanted to know what the tea leaves portended for the Rex. To my disappointment, she said little or nothing about that and quite a bit about the kind of woman who would make Marcel's life complete. The first time she described his soulmate, while she looked into an actual crystal ball that she kept on the coffee table under a black silk wrap, it sounded like she was offering herself. But the next day, when she dragged her grown daughter over to the house to meet him, it was clear that it was the younger version of herself that she was promoting.

After the embarrassment of an awkward introduction, wherein the daughter grabbed Marcel's hook and began stroking it like she was polishing silver, they both blushed and tried in their own ways to steer Mom from her matchmaking. Miss Shelia hushed her mother every time the old woman praised her attributes. She was not a bad-looking woman, but to hear her mother tell it, she had been Miss Natchez two times running because no one had come close to her grace or talent.

For his part, Marcel suggested—without actually saying so—that he had a wife or girlfriend with him. Mom began fishing as to which of the ladies might be the one so she could size up the competition and, for all I knew, cast an evil eye on her. Everyone within earshot recognized that before Marcel could dig the hole deeper, a rescue was in order. I stepped between interrogator and unwitting subject to say that we needed to see a man about something right now. Marcel leaped at the opening. Attempting some graciousness, he went to kiss the Grande Dame's hand but gave it a glancing flyover as he backed away.

He spent the next day loafing at the performance site and then sneaking in the back door under the cover of darkness.

It was that same night that we heard the ghost or ghosts. And I don't mean that I heard or Marcel heard it, but rather that *everyone* in the house heard—music coming from the third-floor ballroom. Lush orchestral music in a twenties big band style that began just before midnight and continued through the striking of the chimes. It was still playing when Slim Jim and Ruth joined me in the hall, all of us looking toward the door at the top of the stairs. It was still playing when he went upstairs, opened the door to gaze into the long-abandoned ballroom. The music came to an abrupt halt when he crossed the threshold, which prompted a rapid-fire exchange.

How weird was that?

What did you see?

Nothing.

Marcel joined us and offered, It's the cotillion. She was right.

Ruth asked the obvious question. Who was right?

Marcel said, The Grande Dame told me the house was haunted. It's the daughter of the second family that ever lived here, or her unwelcome boyfriend, or maybe the both of them. Did you see them dancing?

Slim Jim said, Hell, no. I didn't see anything. I only heard what you heard, old-timey music.

Then Marcel told the story the way he had heard it from the Grande Dame, who had sworn it had happened when she was just a little girl. In those long-ago days, the house was occupied by a family named Watson, or maybe it was Edwards. Same difference. They had a daughter, Agatha, who they spoiled in every way. She was a beautiful but headstrong girl. Nothing was too good for her, and she expected to get what she wanted whenever she wanted it. The best dresses, hats, shoes, lessons of every kind. When she was about to turn sixteen, they were going to have a cotillion—a coming out party—and invite everyone, her friends, their friends, all the best Natchez society people for a night of dancing and fine food.

On the night of the party, everything was as beautiful as it should be. Everyone was having a swell time until he arrived. I'm not saying he was Black because no one knew that to be a fact. They knew he was some kind of mixed-race boy. Maybe Mexican or Italian with his dark skin and shiny straight black hair. Anyway, he walked right into the ballroom like he owned the place. Walked right up to Agatha, shoved the man in her arms away and began to dance with her. She should have slapped him for his rudeness, but she didn't. If fact, from the way they looked at each other while they danced, it was clear that she did not find him rude at all. It was also clear this was not the first time they had danced.

Before her father and brothers could grab that interloper, he took Agatha by the hand and ran out the second door, the servant's door. The two of them ran down the stairs, down the dark, wind-swept street into the night, laughing as they went. Her father and the other men raced after them. They searched all night but without any sign of them. Agatha was never seen again.

There were rumors that she and that boy had taken a steamboat to New Orleans, where a mixed-race couple might blend in. There were rumors that it was like Romeo and Juliet, that they had pledged their illicit love before leaping into the river. Or maybe that he had killed her, or that she had simply vanished. Was a real head-scratching mystery, it was. What was the end of the story was all a matter of who you heard tell it.

What everyone agreed on is that from time to time, about midnight, you could hear the band playing the song they danced to in that old ballroom. And if you don't break the spell, you can hear the two of them run down the stairs as the music stops.

Ruth said, Oh, Marcel, that's a good one. It explains everything and nothing at all.

Yup, Marcel said. Just like what we experienced. Hearing music in the middle of the night, and no one making it. Why shouldn't it be Agatha and her lover? It would be sweet if they were here with us. Let's get out the instruments and play them a tune.

Slim Jim said, You mean now?

Of course, now, Marcel said as he turned to find a trumpet.

It took a few minutes, but before the clock struck the quarter hour, a trio of trumpet, saxophone and Fiddling Mike on the violin struck up the sweetest of the circus tunes. The melody bounced somewhere between a waltz and a countrified two-step, swirled across the porch, through the house, up to the empty ballroom and out into the warm night.

I do not know that the ghosts heard it or if it reached the ears of the Grande Dame, who had told Marcel the story over iced tea and cookies. It made no difference. It was a sweet thought. If no one else heard it, we did, and it was a thing of beauty floating between the croaking frogs below and the silent stars above.

In, out, in, out, in time to the sound of the river, our little trio settled into a deep and satisfying melody. It seemed enough to lift the malaise. In the dark, our blues, like Agatha and her lover, found a way to disappear.

50–Marcel Gets Gas

Someone needed to drive the big cats from Natchez to Vicksburg. I don't recollect why it was not Billy Bones, but I do remember Marcel wanted to mount the wheel. I had a premonition that it was better to not have him drive alone, so I decided to go along. I gave the keys to my Lincoln to Miss Red Boots in case it was needed, instructing her to take care of my baby like it was her own. She replied that she, in turn, expected me to treat her babies, the tigers, like they were my own. Then, shoving aside old newspapers and beer bottles that littered the truck seat, I slid in beside Marcel.

Grinning, Marcel said, Danke, Doctore, we haven't ridden together since the camel's departure.

With that, he turned the key, and the engine groaned under the starter's pull, then coughed and ran rough. In the back of the truck, the cats called to us, to each other or someone else from their cages. I expected they'd settle in for another journey from one big dance in the center ring to another. It was part of the life they'd come to expect.

We hadn't gone but a few miles along a road flanked by Spanish Moss when Marcel said, Keep your eye out for cheap gas because this baby needs a fill.

I said, I'll pay and have a conversation later with somebody who should be doing a better job keeping the tank topped off.

Of course, you'll pay, Marcel agreed. I might be behind the wheel, but I don't have any money. In fact, I don't have a wallet.

About then, a gas station appeared, or rather the first of a series of signs alerting us in quick succession—gas, live bait, curios and a roadside zoo promising "fierce creatures direct from the jungle." Which jungle the sign did not say. What creatures that zoo held were also nothing more than garish red lettering, but once we saw the sign, Marcel and I both knew it had done its job. This was an establishment that we wanted to see in all its splendor, or more likely, given the general rundown look of the land, its squalor.

The gas station consisted of three buildings that I could see from the road. In front, a squat yellow building with a tin roof and two old-style gas pumps in front. There was no brand name, just the word GAS on the sign hanging beneath the roof. The same was true of pumps that had no indication of a brand or octane. Pump at our own peril, I thought.

Off to one side was a two-bay garage with partially disassembled cars parked in front of each opening. Behind was another structure with a curio sign pointed to an unseen door. The zoo was not visible.

Marcel eased the three-quarter-ton flatbed next to the pumps and turned the key. As if the silence was an alarm, a thin young man with a Mississippi mudflap of blond hair bounded out of the station, already talking.

Fill her up, mister? he asked, pushing up a pair of cheap aviator sunglasses to his forehead only to have them fall back to his nose to be pushed up again.

Marcel climbed out of the cab and walked towards the pump. I can do it, he said.

No, you can't, the kid said. It's the law. I have to do the pumping.

Marcel nodded and said, Well, in that case, where's this zoo? I want to take a look.

Out back. A real beauty spot. Soon as I pump this, I'll show you.

Marcel looked at me, then at the kid, saying, Why don't we look at it first, and then you can fill us up.

The three of us left the truck and walked toward a stand of trees thick with kudzu. We literally had to brush the abundant leaves back and step through the green curtain to see a collection of wire mesh cages of various sizes sitting on small legs about a foot off the ground. The first one we approached was empty, but the hand-lettered sign said GRAY WOLF.

Where's the wolf? I asked.

Died. Old age, I think. Or maybe Pa put her down.

The next cage had a pair of sleeping bobcats curled on top of some moldy cardboard and straw. There was a water dish and a bowl of what looked like dog food next to them. The third contained some monkeys sitting in the shade and picking lice off each other. The kid slammed the wire mesh of the cage to see if they would do something. They turned, one hissed and spit, then leaned back as the other resumed picking lice.

Marcel made a sound I had not heard before, a high-pitched stuttering. The monkeys immediately jumped up and began imitating him while pointing to each other and to the kid.

I had seen enough. I didn't want to know what was in the other cages because whatever it was would be miserable or sick or both. It was clear to me that this faux beach boy and his ilk didn't know shit about the care and feeding of animals. I turned and headed back toward the truck.

As I did, I heard Marcel say to the kid, Do you want to see some real wildlife?

What? Well, maybe, Blondie drawled.

Here's the deal, Marcel said. I've got something in the back of the truck that is worth more than this zoo and your entire curio shop, hell, more than this whole station put together. Something you just don't see in a month of Sundays. Something you'll remember until the day you die.

I was worried now. First off, Marcel was spreading it thicker than day-old oatmeal, and that meant he had something in mind. I could only guess as to what that was. And second, yes, we did have two large tigers in the back of the truck that—good God—the kid would never forget. Then came the catch...

Marcel said to the kid, Tell you what I'm going to do. I'm going to show you what I got in the truck for free. I'm going to do something that is so simple even you can do it, and if you can, I'll have the Doctore give you twenty bucks plus the cost of gas. But if you can't, I want you to fill our tank to the tippy top for free.

Blondie hesitated, then said, I don't know about that…

Marcel lifted the canvas flap to show him the tigers. The kid's mouth fell open, and he leaned in to get a better look.

Francis, the younger of the two tigers, turned to look at us, then got up, stretched, and approach the edge of the cage. The smell of big cat swept out, and let me tell you, it is the smell of your basic house cat times a hundred—a rich mix of fur, pheromones and kitty breath that comes from eating slabs of red meat instead of dog food. Francis stared at us with unblinking tiger eyes and made a guttural sound like a wah-wah pedal-powered purr.

As this happened, Marcel reached into his pocket and pulled out the padlock key. He opened the other cage door arousing Gertie, the older and decidedly more docile of the two. She rose, stretched and turned toward the open door as Marcel leaped up, jammed his hook on the steel crossbar and swung into the cage to lean against the bars separating Gertie from Francis. Gertie moved toward him a little faster than my comfort allowed and leapt up to throw her paws on his shoulders. He let out a whoooof as two hundred-plus pounds of not-a-housecat slammed him against the bars. But he took his free hand and rubbed the top of her head. She sounded louder than Francis, but it was still something between a purr and a growl. She slid down and turned to look at the open door.

The kid stood there, his mouth open, glasses hanging lopsidedly from his nose. I am conjecturing when to dive under the truck. If Gertie made a leap to freedom, there would be hell to pay, and not because she'd mauled some kid, but because I'm not sure we'd be able to get her back into the truck. If she got out, she would be free to stroll till she was ready to climb back in.

Marcel said, Heyyya hunga! You're my girl. Then, turning with one smooth motion, Marcel stepped past her, swung back down to the ground and closed the door. Gertie looked at us, then slowly turned and resumed her position near the cab.

Marcel turned the Blondie and said, okay, kid. Your turn.

Blondie said, To do what? To my eye, the kid was definitely a whiter shade of pale.

Marcel stepped over to Francis's door, inserted a key and said, I'll open the door, and you step in. Twenty bucks for you or a free tank of gas for us. He turned the key, and there was an audible click. Not seeing Miss Red Boots or any other impediment to fun, Francis leaned down toward the door, ready to leap if it swung open. In anticipation, he let out a surprisingly long and loud growl that made the hair on the back of my neck stand up.

I'm going to start pumping gas now, the kid said.

You sure? Marcel asked, rattling the lock against the hasp. Hell, you don't even have to get in there. I'll pay you to just to reach in and touch the kitty cat's paw.

You got your gas, Mister. Please, don't open that door.

Marcel slid the key out and pushed the bolt back into place. He reached through the bars with the hook and gave Francis a gentile scratch on the top of his head. Marcel stepped back from the cages and pulled the canvas flap back into place. There was a moment when the only sound was the gas pump filling the tank, then Marcel began to whistle a circus tune and climbed back into the cab.

I feel a little sorry for the kid, but only a little. Not sorry enough to pay for gas. Not near bad enough to forgive them for the deplorable condition in those zoo cages. For a moment, I'm tempted to buy the bobcats and monkeys, but what the hell would I do with them? I don't need either species in the Rex, and letting them loose was just another kind of death sentence. They should never have been there, to begin with. I swallowed hard, walked around the pumps to my side of the truck and looked at Marcel, who was wearing the goofiest grin I had ever seen.

The kid finished filling the tank and stood there staring at us with the hose in his hand.

Fuck him and his pa, too, Marcel said. He got better than he deserved.

I smiled and said, And why do you say that, my apprentice tiger tamer?

Marcel started the engine, then turned to me, saying, The monkeys said we didn't know the half of it.

I didn't remember the monkeys saying anything, just chattering excitedly, but it made no difference. This was the South, and I felt that way about everything that happened here. Always had, and every place the Rex stopped was like it was coming under a dark cloud. None of us knew the half of it. Whatever it was, we were no sharper than a cue ball on a crooked table. Whatever it was, by the time we found out, it would be too late.

51–Peking Opera

When we drove through Baton Rouge, the end of the tour was in sight. In anticipation of our last residency, we went straight to New Orleans. We settled into our allotted space and, between the first and second week of shows, went back up to Baton Rouge to do a single performance at the state capital. Easy-peasy. It would have been uneventful except for three conundrums that converged to make this performance a uniquely one-off affair.

The first conundrum was that for the first time in a long time, it was going to be an open-air show—no tent and no aerial rigging. All that stuff was back in the Big Easy. This was just the ring and a backdrop without bleachers. The audience would be sitting on the steps of some government building, and we would be performing on the lawn. Damn if I can remember what building it was. There was a wide stone staircase, marble columns at the top of the stairs and a substantial expanse of lawn at the bottom.

The second was that we were not the only attraction in Baton Rouge. I don't mean that we were competing with some country singer or them Cajun music performers playing in honkytonks every night. They didn't count. No, this was gigantic. It was the damn Peking Opera, and that was not something you saw every day. At least I didn't.

I wouldn't have even known they were in the big civic center theater if it hadn't been for the Chinese guys in dark suits and sunglasses standing on the steps as we were setting up the show. They watched us for a good fifteen minutes, conferred with each other before consulting with a large, square-shouldered white guy also in sunglasses. He was the one who inquired about who was in charge. VX pointed to me, and our course was set.

Are you the manager? the big white guy asked me

Who's asking?

Smith, FBI.

No shit. I looked at him with a new appreciation of his size and the government-issue opaque quality of his sunglasses. I asked, What does the FBI want with the Rex Terrestrial, Celestial & Nautical Circus?

I don't want anything, FBI guy said. But they do. He pointed at the three Hong Kong suits. FBI guy went on to explain: Those gentlemen are representatives of the Peking Opera on tour at the Civic Center, and they're interested in a cultural exchange with your company—performer to performer.

I waved at the suits, and they waved back. Really? I said. Where or when, and definitely, how might this cultural exchange take place?

FBI guy said, I believe they are inviting your company to come meet theirs, watch a rehearsal and share a meal. Then, depending on each company's appearance schedule, they would like to attend your company's next performance.

Four o'clock is our next show, I explained. Our *only* performance in Baton Rouge. At four sharp.

I'll inform them. He pulled out a little notebook, made a note on an empty page, then said, May I inform them that you will be attending their eleven o'clock rehearsal?

That's a half hour from now, I said. We won't be finished setting up by then. You're asking us to stop the set-up, go spend who knows how long on this exchange thing, then come back to finish in time for our previously scheduled performance.

FBI guy nodded, smiled, and said, Yes, exactly. Not asking, though. Suggesting—for the sake of international relations.

There was something about the way he said "suggesting" that made me think it wasn't a suggestion at all. Command was too strong a word, given his passive-aggressive smile, but I understood the intent.

A quick assessment of our progress combined with a fast calculation of how uncomfortable life might be if somebody was offended or embarrassed led me to this conclusion—we could afford a two-, maybe three-hour break for lunch, especially if the Chinese were buying. Besides, I could leave VX on-site to drive the road rats through the maze and just take the performing half of the crew.

Before I get to our lunching on Cajun blackened shrimp with the Chinese, I'll bring in the last and most unexpected conundrum.

You remember the little TV blond interviewer from St. Cloud? That was a long time ago and out of sight, out of mind, right? That's what I thought too, but damn if she didn't walk up mid-Fed confab with the same camera guy in tow. I recognized him right away. He still had the camera strapped over his shoulder and crossing his chest like it was a shotgun at the peak of duck season.

Doctor Buzz, she cooed like we were old friends, or worse, old lovers. I'm so glad to see you once again.

I feigned ignorance while I ran mental mug shots trying to connect face to name. And who are you again? The face is… err, lovely.

Betty Mercer. We did an interview in May when the circus was in St. Cloud. And thank you for that compliment.

Oh yes, at the campground.

I've convinced the station to do a follow-up, and, well, it took a little legwork to catch up with you, but here I am. She smiled as if it was obvious that this was a brilliant idea and waved her hand at the road rats hanging the backdrop. She continued: Rodney and I are going to shoot the circus in Louisiana.

I needed to fend her off or fold her in quickly because the FBI guy was starting to look nervous. I said, I'm not sure I'm ready for you or Rodney to shoot anything. Did you clear this with Lucy or Flat Frank?

She smiled benignly and answered, Your PR rep? Yes, I found her number on the old press release and spoke to her. She told me where she thought the circus would be about now. You're right on schedule.

I said, Of course we are. But I was thinking, Thanks a lot, Lucy, I'm not sure I needed this. I was feeling some unspoken but serious pressure from the FBI guy to get moving because the Chinese suits were now walking around the trucks, picking up props and laughing about the mosquito masks as they tried them on. I'd have to check Betty's answer out later to see what Lucy actually said.

I looked at Betty and said, Well, Miss Mercer, I don't really have time for this now. We're on our way to lunch with the Peking Opera and...

Oh, goody, she said. That will provide some great B-roll. She put her arm in mine and began to stroll toward the Chinese, who were now trying to walk on stilts. What the hell? That arm thing was one of my patented moves that she role-reversed on me. It looked like I'd been backed into a corner by a too-perky blond who was taking over my day faster than the largest of the Hong Kong suits falling off his stilts.

Let me tell you, though, the Peking Opera's rehearsal was pretty damn spectacular. Start with a troupe of twenty-four plus costumers, personal assistants, translators and what I would call handlers who seemed to have nothing to do except keep the rest of them from defecting. Superficially, the cast and essential tour support numbered about the same in company size as the Rex but were a lot more disciplined. I knew from rumor that these performers trained from childhood to do what they did better than anyone else. And I was about to have the blue tick truth of it proved.

That was clear when they began the warm-up. Where we would begin halfheartedly slouching into some semblance of order with mumbled conversations about who would do what, with a single whistle tweet they arranged themselves into two rows, facing each other with a small man—who I later learned was the movement director— between each line. He tapped his foot twice and raised his arms above his head, then loosely shook his hands five times. Then the arms went straight out from the shoulders for another five shakes, then each arm to the front, five, and finally down toward the ground for five. The entire company replicated each movement while enthusiastically counting off the fives. He then did four in each position, though not in the same order as the first time and at a faster speed. Three, throwing his arms into a new combo, and everyone moving faster, counting louder but still in unison, clearly following the changing arm positions. With the two count, it was like a series of lightning-speed kung fu blocks. But on the one count, everything slowed and was focused, very intentional, with everyone repeating the exact pattern of the original five count.

This was followed by a series of leg lifts and kicks, vocal exercises and facial contortions that went from trills to growls as they performed a series of tai-chi postures. Then they each reached across to the company member opposite them for paired stretches and bends, including backbends and lifts, rolls and flips. All of it was an unbroken progression from one set of gestures and exercises to another, picking up speed and physical complexity until I was on the verge of a sweat just watching it. The entire warm-up clocked in at twenty minutes and ended with a repetition of the arm flinging and handshaking that started it all. It seemed like a lot of work for a warm-up, but given their reputation, I suppose it was somewhere between scales on a piano and good habits.

The movement director bowed to the company. They bowed back. He disappeared and was replaced by a dour older man who barked out some instructions to the company, which broke ranks and began to get into costumes. The show, or at least the rehearsal for the show, was about to begin. Mr. Dour then turned to a Rex crew that had been standing in a loose circle around the edges of the stage. In heavily accented English, he invited us to take a seat in the first rows, explaining that they would present the classic story of the Monkey King, a tale that combined all their best features—melodic singing, graceful acrobatics, physical comedy and precise martial arts.

If anything, he was understating the mix of color, sound and action that followed.

About halfway through the performance, I glanced over to where Miss Mercer was sitting and saw that she had the camera in her lap pointed at the stage. The red light was on. The hair on the back of my neck stood up. No, tell me it wasn't what was. I heard a little voice in my head say, Trouble, oh we got trouble, right here in River City!

At the end of the performance, Mercer got up, and Rodney followed with camera in tow. They went down the hall, both of them slipping into the women's restroom. A few seconds later, Rodney and his camera went into the men's room, where I found him standing at a urinal.

I said, Say, what's up with shooting in the auditorium?

Without looking me in the eye, he replied, What are you talking about?

I saw Mercer with the camera on her lap, I told him. Pretty damn sure she was shooting, and if she was, we need to have a little chat. Right now. Because I'm also pretty sure that if the FBI knew she was shooting without having it signed off by the Chinese or the State Department, there will be angry alligators nipping at our asses.

He flushed, zipped and continued to avoid looking at me, but said, I don't know.

Give me the fuckin' tape that's in the camera. Now, Rodney, before I call those other guys in here.

Can't do that, he said, clutching the camera strap closer to his chest.

I'm telling you, Rodney—give it to me, and we'll forget anything happened, or you can give it to one of those sunglass-wearing morons who were so busy looking for something wrong they didn't see what was right in front of them.

I went over to the sink next to Rodney and started to wash my hands. Then I said, Of the two choices, I think I'm the better one.

I'll show you what's in the camera, he said, hitting the rewind button. There was a two-second whirr, and it stopped. Something that short did not bode well. He told me, Here, look through the eyepiece, and you'll see what's there.

I leaned in to look. He pushed the play button, and there was nothing but blank tape singing emptiness.

Maybe I made a mistake, I said. My apologies if I was in error, but you know, as my old man used to say, Life is simpler when you plow around the stump.

Outside the women's room, Betty was talking with Mia and Maya when it was my turn to put my arm in hers and steer her toward a corner of the lobby. She was looking at me with a smile that suggested either she had a secret or she really was my very best friend.

I trod the same conversational path with her as I did with Rodney. She feigned upset that I would even suggest such a thing. Yes, feigned is the right word, because as my ma used to say that just because a possum isn't moving doesn't mean it can't.

I'll collapse the back and forth and get right to the fact of it. She was lying, and she did roll tape. I saw it, but she intended to deny it from here to the editing room door. If it had just been her and me, she might have worn me out, but the fly in the ointment was that one of the guys on stage saw it too, told one of the Chinese handlers, who obviously told the translator who told Mr. Sunglasses. Before you could say, would you like to reconsider your story? the two of us were surrounded by a wall of dark suits. They didn't so much ask to see her bag as simply removed it from her arm. FBI guy slapped a pair of stainless-steel bracelets on her wrists while they were looking to see what was in the aforementioned bag.

First thing that came out was an industrial-strength commercial tape with the damn station logo on the label. No one said anything for a moment as it disappeared into an evidence bag FBI guy was holding. Then everyone talked at once without bothering to listen and kept talking until they decided they were talked out. That was when they unlocked the cuffs and walked away.

Now we're as fucked as stubble in the razor factory, I said, watching her massage her wrists. There's no way I can go back in there for lunch without having to ritually disembowel you or myself to make amends.

I'll make it up to you, she said.

I don't even want to know what you might have in mind. The way to make it up to me is to get out of my sight for a few hours, if not for always. You've been here for a little over two hours and have come this close to getting your pretty little ass slapped in a cell for provoking something that could easily be an international incident, or getting me tagged and towed for not doing something that would require a bail bond. So please, please, take your guy and get yourself out of here until four o'clock. I don't want to see you before show time. Hell, I don't want to see you at all, but if I've got to let you do a "feel good" piece, you can damn well train that camera on the Rex, and only on the Rex, when and where I say you should for as long as you're here.

Having said my piece and not choked her to twice past dead, I went back to eat the Cajun shrimp, rice, mushrooms and bright green peas. Betty went somewhere and did something, but God bless all of us, it was nothing I needed to do a thing about. We were all set for the Chinese to arrive for a happy gaggle of picture-taking after what was going to look like amateur hour if they compared ours with theirs.

For reasons that remained unexplained but gratefully acknowledged, they enjoyed the show and spent a good half-hour afterward walking around on stilts and trying on the buffalo costumes with much laughter and handshaking. In my estimation, we had skated on thin ice, and while it might have cracked, no one went in the icy water. Everyone came home safe and happy. Or as happy as could be expected in the situation.

52–The Prodigal Son

On the third day of performances in Audubon Park, with the New Orleans Zoo on one side and the river on the other, the dead rose again. Well, not the actual dead, but the dead to me. As I was looking at the list of available performers for the day's show, Loren Red Beard walked into the tent.

What do you need done? he asked like he just finished feeding the tigers or sewing up a rip in the canvas.

Where the hell have you been?

I needed a walk, Buzz, so I took one.

Trying my best not to utter a string of obscenities mixed with incoherent non sequiturs, I simply said, A walk? You are closing in on two months gone.

I had to admit that he didn't look much the worse for wear. Tan and rested, as they say. Maybe he had even put on a few pounds.

He replied, I'm much better now. He stroked his beard, shook his head like there was something buzzing around it—outside, or maybe inside. He said, Saw some interesting things, Buzz, but I missed the Rex something fierce.

Not enough to come back before…? I stopped and just shook my head. What did it matter what I was going to say next? It doesn't take a big person to carry a grudge, and it wasn't worth carrying this one another foot. The only question before the jury was whether I should take him back. I had never got around to replacing him in hopes that he would show up, and now he was back, so replacing him had become a moot question.

I looked at him and asked, Are you going to stay to the end or decide to take another walk?

Just then, VX walked by. Hey, Loren, he said matter-of-factly. Wanna help move the south prop box back into place?

I'm on it.

That was the end of the discussion. Loren Red Beard was back on the payroll doing whatever he did. It took about two minutes to get used to the idea, like he had never left, and the whole burning guitars in Missouri thing was just a bad dream or the kind of story you tell little kids to warn them about the dangers of standing in the rain.

I suppose you want to know where had he gone, what had he done. That was the question on every one of the Rex crew's minds except maybe for VX, who was more interested in when Loren would get around to asking when he'd get the keys to his truck back. After all, VX had gotten pretty fond of driving it, thinking he would be behind the wheel for the duration and maybe a ways beyond that.

In no particular order, it seemed that Loren had picked cotton the old-school way, dragging a sack down the rows, drank moonshine in juke joints; washed dishes at a Waffle House; stood at a crossroads waiting to see if anyone, devil or man, wanted to make a deal; ridden a freight to Mobile; gone fishing on the Gulf; tried to get a job playing piano in a Birmingham whorehouse; eaten Spanish Moss and roasted German cockroaches; danced the equinox with one or more Morris troupes; slept in the hayloft of a Renaissance faire blacksmith shoppe; and had his soul saved in at least two different revival tents. That was just what he admitted to.

Loren Red Beard walked in, whistling a tune, and picked up where he had left off. Need a rip in the tent sewn? He was on it. A buffalo missing a back end for the opening flurry of big ring action? I'd recognize those bowlegs anywhere. It was all the same to him, and from his perspective, the pleasure was in the tinkering, the puzzle of the jerry-rigged solution to the inevitable breakdown of the machine that had to last until you could replace the broken part. He had been stuck and now, apparently, was self-greased and good to go.

53–All About Betty

I should be so lucky. While Loren's return solved one problem, "The Betty" as I had come to think of her, had started off on the wrong foot and was now putting another one in front of the first. Miss Mercer seemed to have nothing better to do than interview the Rex crew at the most inappropriate times and shove Rodney and his camera into my sightline at every turn. She was as impervious to suggestion as a bucket of spit and deaf to my revolving array of pleading and threats.

I asked Archibald if he might slip something into the massive quantities of herbal tea she drank, something that would inconvenience her for a day or three while we were getting the show tight and right for the mayor's visit. He suggested that it was a low thing to do and unworthy on my part, but he understood the feeling. I wanted to take back what I'd said but could not regret saying it as a measure of how vexing I found Miss Mercer to be.

Marcel had a different, more favorable take on the pixie dust girl, which I considered using to whatever meager advantage I could muster before I lost control of the circus in the last week of the tour. He liked her, and from all appearances, the feeling was mutual—or maybe, I feared, a cynical ploy on her part to use Marcel to get me to back off. Something would have to be done. One of us was a shark, and the other was treading water. I didn't like the idea that after all these years, I was not the one with the fin slicing the waves.

I was coming out of the shower in the Rampart Street church basement that was serving as Rex Central when I saw Marcel on his way in. Spirit, I said, what's the prognosis for you and The Betty?

Nothing, Doctore, he said. We're just flirting a little, but it's not serious. You know, I'm not the marrying kind, and from what I can tell, she isn't either.

You two knocking boots yet?

That would be telling. As he said this, he flushed a delicate pink that ran from his ears all the way to the hollow of his thin chest.

I poured out my conclusion. So, you have. I laughed, gave him a pat on the back, and said, If you'll pardon the crudity, I hope she's more responsive to your attentions than she has been to my attempts to get her to stay out of the way.

Though Marcel visibly recoiled, I pressed on, saying, Can you talk to her, because to my view she's getting above her raising? Get her to not stand at the edge of the ring with camera boy for just this next show? After all, the mayor is coming.

He said, Might…

Might? No, not might—do it. Think of it as a favor to your long-suffering mentor. I held out my hand, and he shook it. I said, You're certainly entitled to your fun, and if she's fun, I say go for a second helping, but I've got to tell you, Marcel, letting the cat outta the bag is a whole lot easier than putting it back in, if you know what I mean. I know of what I speak, and you do too. Get her to be 20 percent more cooperative, and we'll both be happier men.

54—Jesus in New Orleans

Someone had suggested that the Rex might stay the winter in New Orleans. Why pack up and head north for another round of snow and ice? Stay a while. The audiences were still pretty good, and so the notion was put forth that if the Rex could find a suitable performance space, we could be in residence. We thought to pose the question on extending the run another two or three months to the whole of the Rex and the Absent Owners, but before we did, we needed to find a place.

Marcel and I had gone to look at a large warehouse that was available. While waiting for the realtor to arrive, Marcel noticed that one of the overhead garage doors was cracked open. He stooped down to peer through the obvious invitation to misadventure or possibly a charge of breaking and entering.

Suddenly, Marcel spoke up excitedly. Oh, Buzz, you need to take a look at this.

Marcel slid through the eighteen inches of open door. I bent down to glimpse a scene straight out of some massively Hieronymus Bosch triptych or maybe Dante's descent. One man's bad dream is another's evidence of a good time. Marcel, already inside, hit a switch. There was the sound of a motor laboring, and the door rose another foot before it jammed on something.

Fuck, Marcel said. Can you get through that? This son of a bitch ain't going up anymore.

Perhaps it was best that it did not. It was clear that the place had been rented for a massive Halloween party, and from the catalog of destruction, it appeared to be the kind of maximum fun event that we surely regretted missing. In the twilight of overhead windows, colored streamers and film that had never made it to the take-up reel were festooned over lights and hanging beneath the gridwork. The place smelled of booze, stale food, sweat and good marijuana. Marcel was already wading into the thick layers of trash, party favors, Mardi Gras beads, empty beer cans, balloons piled two feet deep from one end of the vast hall to another. Trays of broken bread and half-eaten fish lay on tables. There were squashed grapes and bits of cheese, grease-stained napkins and discarded plastic glasses underfoot. The smashed remains of large paper mâché and wood constructions were piled in heaps of layered color and glittering tinsel. Here and there, wet bars stood like lonely islands. Some still had liquor bottles at the ready. Marcel held up a full bottle of Johnny Walker Red.

Looks like there might still be some party favor here, he said. Then he picked up the garbage can that lay next to the bar, dumped the contents, and began loading unopened liquor.

I said, Perhaps you should limit yourself to the better name brands, Spirit. It looks like there's way too much to take everything.

Marcel stopped and said, Whoa, here's something. He reached down, and when his hand came up, there was a Nikon camera with a telephoto lens attached.

Does it work?

Don't know. Look's good.

The dutiful Spirit put it to his eye. He turned toward me and snapped a shot.

Sounds like the shutter works, he said.

He turned back, surveyed the debris through the camera, then focused on something, saying, Oh, Jesus, what's this?

What's what, Marcel?

More like who's that. There's a body over here.

I ran to Marcel's side, and he pointed to a mound of debris. Sure enough, there was a hairy leg with a bare foot sticking out. I leaned down to scatter some of the stained napkins and streamers to reveal first a hand, then a chest and finally a head. The face looked awfully familiar.

I said, Do you know who this is, Marcel?

Should I?

Doesn't he look like your basic Bible illustration of Jesus?

Well, the crown of thorns certainly helps.

I took a second look at the long dark hair matted around the too-familiar face from my childhood Sunday school. Indeed, this guy was wearing an ugly crown of thorns and dressed in a torn cotton robe covered with blood or wine stains. I glanced down at his hands. It looked like he had an open wound just about where the nail would go.

Marcel shouted, Whoa, Doctore, he opened his eyes.

Jesus stared at us, each eye focusing in different directions. Marcel and I helped him to his feet. That he could stand seemed a miracle, if not a full Lazarus.

Are you in pain? Marcel asked. Can you walk? Need a drink?

He pulled a bottle of orange juice from the garbage can. Jesus waved it away. Marcel put it back in the can and took out a bottle of scotch. Jesus waved that one away as well.

Shut your mouth. I'm telling you that this part is the whole truth—we were literally standing with Jesus, or a pretty good copy of Jesus, in the middle of some Big Easy version of hell's after-party, his eyes staring off toward some distant, better place. He attempted to speak, but no sound came out. He raised his hands as if to bless us but got lost mid-gesture and wound up staring at his still-bleeding hands. It was a little unnerving. Finally, he managed to get out a few words.

Oh, the price of our sin, he said.

Marcel countered with, Jesus, you can say that again. You don't look so good. Can you still do the miracle thing? Because you look like you need one.

Jesus turned to look at Marcel, smiled and said, No, it's not real pain. It will pass as all things must. This—he said, holding up his hand with what looked to be a serious hole in it—is an illustration of the internal state of our existence. It marks our separation from Love and Truth.

Marcel poked his finger at the hole in Jesus's hand and said, If you say so. This hole sure looks real.

Jesus winced and pulled away his hand, leaving Marcel with blood on the tip of his finger. Yep, looks real enough to convince me, Marcel explained.

As quick as the green ray at sunset, I totally saw the psychic history of this Dionysian geography and imagined the revels of the night before—the orgy of loosed passions before you die and the longing for a return to, as the church ladies say, blessed grace before you can be raised from the dead. I have always accepted the pleasures of the flesh leading to the morning after. You pays your money, you takes your chances. Here, in some Saturnalia of excess, it appeared that every inhibition had been abandoned and every thought of redemption postponed. My stomach clenched, and my muscles involuntarily ached.

I remembered all the times in my youth that I had stood like this Jesus in the light of the new day, eyes unfocused, brain searching for a language to describe the desolation within and the incomprehensible world before me. All those times I had sworn, never again. All the times I was feeling like half past Lazarus, three days in the tomb, and suddenly forced to re-enter life whether or not I wanted to.

Then Jesus turned his now smiling face to Marcel and said, Do you have the camera?

Marcel looked at me, silently asking, how did he know? I shrugged.

Marcel reached into the garbage can and pulled out the Nikon.

Bless you, Jesus said as he took the camera. May you be healed.

Marcel replied, The same to you.

Jesus turned his back on us and waded through the detritus into the shadows at the far end of the warehouse. We listened for the sound of a door opening or closing, but there was nothing. He simply disappeared into the darkness, leaving us with a garbage can full of booze.

I wasn't sure that either of us were the ones who needed to be healed. Marcel pointed at his hand and then ran his finger along his head where the crown of thorns would be. Man, oh man, Doctore, that must surely hurt.

55—Sin on Bourbon Street

From our vantage, there were strippers on one side of the street and bar-b-que joints on the other as Billy Bones, VX, Marcel, Archibald and I sat on a balcony above some bar on Bourbon Street. It was the night before Halloween. The city's excuse to party was already three days old. For some of the Rex crew, this New Orleans sojourn was fast becoming another night of too much fun before another painful next day. That "some of" looked to include me.

Halloween always was real New Orleans, men dressed as women, women dressed as animals and animals dressed as men. Our waitress was a case in point, dressed like a mutant crawfish. She looked like she had squeezed a size twelve body into a size nine red satin suit with little crawfish legs sticking out on the side, plenty of cleavage sticking out where the zipper gave way to superior force. Great, big, old crawfish antenna flopping like some loopy metronome keeping time on top of her head. Her hands were inside some big red claws, which looked great but made handling trays, beer glasses and money a chancy proposition.

Did we care? This is the Big Easy. Easy come, easy go. We had started on seventy-five cent martinis at one of the local watering holes on Rampart in the morning, and by the time we arrived at this location four or five stops later, the sheer volume of booze and the ingrained habit of drinking another one when the first was empty had taken on an indisputable logic of its own. We still had money. We could just keep on doing what we were doing. We'd drink, we'd pee, we'd pee, we'd drink. Every time the Crawfish Girl managed to maneuver through the mob of tourists to bring another round without showering one of us with beer, whoever was not in the men's room gave a little cheer and tossed another Washington on the pile of tips soaking up what didn't stay in the glass. She'd laugh, flirt and ask us to just whistle if there was anything else we wanted. We were too far out of cups to pucker and just waved her back to the table for another round every time she was near.

On Bourbon Street, they were cranking up the volume, pouring energy into the street until it hummed like some psychotronic magnet sucking every man, woman and child's secret admission of "what if" and "could be" into a vortex of the possible, right here, right now. October did nothing to stay the heat. The smell of booze, sex and latex shimmered in the air. The crowds surged like hurricane tide up and down the block, the lights blinking, the speakers pumping out the tinny jazz, the conventioneers looking this way and that trying to decide what to do next.

Down on the far end of the block, I saw an old couple coming down the street. They were older than the rest of the crowd by a good twenty or thirty years. All white hair and dressed very Midwest, reeking of Iowa or Illinois. He with a JC Penny's shirt and her with the nondescript print dress of a church-going woman and, I swear to God, a white sweater. She was clutching her white, plastic purse like it was her only lifeline to the known world. Probably here for a ministerial or teacher's convention and taking a break to get a glimpse of the Whore of Babylon in full stride before they go home to tell the neighbors just how shameful it all is.

Temptation and debauchery presented themselves at every door. Lust and depravity staggering down the street. Don't even ask about the alleys. Everything had a price. Everything was for sale. And crowded, whooweee! People of every class, every color, cheek to jowl, some in costume, some not, all of them having more than a good time with money flying out of their pockets like it would be worthless tomorrow.

There was a dwarf barker standing on a stool in front of one of the sex joints, his tiny fingers snapping a steady beat and his head on a swivel, like radar, seeking the next target for the bloodshot stare that dares any of them to say something.

Cooommmme on in! COOOOOOMMMMMON IINNNN!
Think you can tell, do you?
I don't think so. I won't tell if you won't.
Boys will be girls. Yes, Boooys will be girrrls!
They walk like an angel, they talk like the devil, but oh, they say the cutest things.
You, sir, you've never seen anything like this.
Real beauty. Real poise.
Not like Vegas, not in any city in America, not in the whole wide world.
This is the very best. No admission. No Cover. Commmmmon in!

The old couple stopped and looked at the little man, then at each other. They shrugged and, holding hands, went in. Fifteen, twenty minutes later, they came out again, the old man red-faced and shaking his head like he was waking up from a bad dream. The old woman stared straight ahead, but she had this weird smile on her face like she had taken a big spoonful of sugar that turned sour in her mouth, and she didn't know whether to swallow or spit it out.

Down a door or two, another barker was giving a pitch. This guy was dressed in a silver lame vest and a black bow tie. Might as well be blind, his wrap-around shades were so dark you couldn't tell if he even had eyes. His black hair was slicked back like a shiny vinyl skullcap, his mouth a blazing tunnel of gold teeth.

Hey, this is what you want, what you need. Girls, girls, girls.
Each one more beautiful than the next.
Got them creamy white, that's right.
Got them golden amber, for you gamblers.
Got them hot coffee beauties, real cuties.
Got them nut brown, make your head turn around.
Naked! Every one, just as God made them, naked!

All real, no plastic, no rubber, no scars. Naakked!!
No admission. No Cover, anytime. Naaakkkeedd!
No cover, anywhere. Naaaakkkkedddd!
We just want the pleasure of your company.
You can look at the rest, but these are the best.

The old couple stopped. They're hooked before he finished the pitch. They went in. Maybe they had a beer, maybe not, because fifteen quick minutes later, they were back on the street. The old lady still had that smile on her face, shaking her head. The old man was glassy-eyed like he'd just seen the impossible and then started laughing. She gave him a little nudge in the ribs, but he just kept laughing. She gave him a shot to the head with the flat of her hand. Not hard, just an open palm swat like she was going after a mosquito. He staggered back a half step, shook off the blow and looked at her. She laughed like a schoolgirl. He laughed too.

He took her hand. They must have been eighty if a day, but there was something so tentative, innocent and caring about how he took her hand that I put down my beer and leaned on the railing to do some serious watching. All the way down the street, they laughed at every temptation—the barkers, the sidewalk cons, the neon, the promises and the hype, like children hearing a familiar joke. It was carefree laughter fueled with white-haired understanding that what is important is untouched by the grime and stink that is all around them. It is as if they know they don't have much time left and have resolved to fear nothing. They are wide-eyed with giddy joy in a world that substitutes flash and folly for wisdom.

I imagined them at home, lying in bed with the moonlight seeping through the window. Their white hair is a tangled embrace, their soft fleshed hands touching each other's faces, counting the familiar lines, wanting to remember what it was like in case this is the last shutting of the eyes. They have been together for so long, they breathe in parallel, and just before going to sleep, one or the other says, It was fun.

What was fun?

New Orleans.

Yes, we saw it all.

I lean farther over the balcony to watch their progress through the crowded throng. They arrived at the next joint. They went in, stayed awhile, they came out, did the same at the next one, all the way down the street.

56–The Past Made Present

When I turned back to resume drinking, I saw her. Not the Crawfish waitress, but the other one who was working the balcony. I hadn't noticed her before, but when she came to the table, something clicked. Lord, have mercy—add something close to more years than I care to admit and change the location, but she looked like Bubbles. She looked like Bubbles would or should have looked after she gave up stripping. Maybe she still was peeling it off, because she still had her good looks and the sweet wiggle in the walk as she made her way through the room. The wiggle was all the more impressive because she was not a wide-hipped girl who naturally rose and fell in the rhythm of each step but more on the long-legged and lean, slightly boyish side of the beauty bar.

Her costume, such as it was, exuded some cross between a fortune-teller and tie-dyed gypsy. Three layers of lace and skirt that still managed to show leg halfway up the hip, a peasant blouse with enough buttons undone to offer a quick view down her blouse when she bent over to put down the drinks. It was very standard practice for better tipping.

The nametag on her blouse seemed fully out of place—LYNETTE. I mean, what fortune teller wears a nametag? Any clairvoyant worth a tinker's damn would know their own name and mine as well. Probably didn't use a stage name like Bubbles anymore. Maybe Lynette was her stage name—something generic to keep the frat boys and trade show conventioneers at bay.

Bubbles, is it you? I asked as she was leaning over the table taking our next round off the tray.

She looked like a deer in the headlights when she heard the name, then turned to stare hard, trying to place me. Clearly, the name was one she recognized but didn't hear often. Was I a local? Not likely. I must have been someone from her past, but she wasn't placing it.

Do I know you?

Used to, a long time ago. In Chicago, when you worked the Commodore.

I smiled at the thought that this was starting to feel like that Dylan song. What was it? *Tangled Up in Blue* came to mind. You know, that one where the guy fucks up and maybe gets redeemed in the end.

That was a long time ago. She straightened up and said, What did you say your name was?

I've had a few. These days its Dr. Buzz, but you used to call me Jelly Bean because you liked them, and I didn't. Still don't.

She left the table and went to the service counter for a whispering session with Crawfish Girl. They kept looking at us, their heads getting closer each time they glanced our way. By the time the next round came, she was fully there, and Crawfish Girl was not seen again.

With each trip to and from the table, we traded a little banter. Not about then. Then was an immense ocean best swum outside of public view. More about how Halloween in New Orleans compared with Mardi Gras and the Rex having our last three performances at the zoo. I invited her to come. She said she'd keep it in mind. Then, on the next trip, she asked me to write down the times and dates. Better than that, I pulled a flyer from my coat pocket and laid it on the tray with two complimentary tickets. After that, she asked if I had a phone number here in the Big Easy, but I didn't have my book and couldn't remember the name of the place we were using as a staging area. Hey, this was before every peanut in the world had cell phones, so don't worry yourself about it. Back in the day, getting a working telephone was a lot harder than getting a telephone number.

I told her it was a couple of blocks away, but it might be easier if I had her number.

She said, Will you call me if I give it to you?

There was something about the way she gave me the fisheye as she said it that made me think that, usually, the men who asked didn't call. Get drunk and lose it. Write it on something, and after it's awash in beer, not be able to read it again. Toss it away before the wife sees it. Who knows what their excuse might be. I wouldn't make that mistake. If she gave me her number, I would call her the very next day if I had to steal a phone to do it.

It would be my pleasure, I said, and meant it.

It had been more than a few years. There was a lot of catching up to do, and with the end of the tour in sight, I'd have some time to do it. Maybe a sojourn here in the Big Easy with Bubbles might be reason enough to stay a few days, or maybe a week or the winter. Or not.

Bubbles bent from the waist and, in doing so, gave me a glimpse of enough of her cleavage to make me remember what I had appreciated all those years ago. Not big tits. I've never really been a big-breast man. A champagne glass was the best, someone once told me. Whoever that was would then mix metaphors, talking about a half grapefruit being just about the right size and shape. Firm, but with enough jiggle to tell you them's natural, not a half-pound of sand packed in a baggie. Ironic, isn't it? I can remember the advice but not who said it. To their credit, it was a pretty fair description of my taste in mammary construction, and those grapefruits were pretty much what Bubbles offered, even after a few decades.

She handed me the number, and I was careful to fold it with the number on the inside and put it in my wallet next to the Ben Franklin that I carried to remind myself that I am not broke. At the moment, it was as valuable to me as old Ben. That was the moment when I knew that, though time was a thief, it just might be possible to steal back the dream of a happy ending. It was an irrational thought that surprised me, but once it was lodged in the frontal cortex, it seemed natural and obvious.

57—Circumstance

A roll of the dice will not abolish Chance.

It was Chance that put me there, and when the clicking dice flew out of the newly opened hand, it was sevens all the way to the table. I called Bubbles the next day, and to my joy, and maybe hers, she said that she'd like to see me again.

I had called, she had answered, I heard the sound of the rattling dice in my hand replaced by the joy of beating the odds.

58—Athena Redux

I was overflowing with desire to see Bubbles again. All the years of thinking about what might have been after she was gone were measured not by regret that I had missed my chance, but by the hope that gone wasn't really gone. Then here she was, back within sight, and I was determined to not screw it up this time.

My anticipation was fermenting one plan of action after another. I was no better than a leaky faucet because whatever was in my head—the day-to-day of getting what needed to be done when the end of the tour arrived—was constantly slipping away, and the only thing that stuck was the idea that I'd take her for the weekend to the Cornstalk Hotel just a couple of blocks from where she worked and get us the best room they had. Order up some champagne, maybe some oysters with a good horseradish, and we'd get properly reacquainted.

Mmmmm, yes—I was so confident that she felt like I did, so puppy dog anxious to bark up that tree, I was ready to reserve a room before I even asked her.

They say that the brain is a marvelous thing that works pretty well until you fall in love. Well, Marcel could tell that mine wasn't working as well as a guy trying to get an ornery mule to plow a straight furrow. It made no difference how I tried, that mule wasn't going to budge until it was ready, and then it was bound to go where it wanted.

What's up, Doctore? Marcel asked.

Got a thought about the future, Spirit, and that thought is shaking me to the very core of all that I hold to be my sure and true. A change is going to come.

Well, you might want to stop thinking about the future and take a look at the present, because you've got a visitor, and I don't think you expected to see her.

Sharon? I suggested.

Sharon who? A troubled shadow crossed Marcel's face like he was trying to match the name that slipped my tongue to a time or a face.

Never mind, I said. I don't know whence that came from or why it popped out. I was trying to change a subject that shouldn't have come up in the first instance. I followed up with, Where is this visitor for whom you're interrupting my contemplation of happiness?

Right here, said a voice that was still two parts Texas and one part whatever one of the Seven Sisters she had gone to. Smith? Wellesley?

The woman's voice added, And I would hope that the happiness you are contemplating is me.

Athena! I said it, and I meant it, I said. By all that is holy, what are you doing here?

Did you think I wouldn't want to see the end of the tour? Did you think we didn't have an unfinished conversation and I deserve an answer to my question?

I was happy to see her. I remembered everything that was right with her—her beauty, intelligence, wit, charm, the curve of her belly, the smell of her hair, and especially the taste of her mouth when it met mine. Especially that last time as she kissed me a kiss that brought me back to the second day of my too-short loft life in St. Louis. That delicious twenty-four hours when the Rex had gone ahead, and I had not begun to feel the separation. When my entire world was the woman named for a goddess.

It took about two seconds for me to realize that I was about to be caught in one of the two worst situations a man can be faced with—having to choose between two women. The dilemma glistened like the apple on the Tree of Knowledge before me. Oh, I can hear you asking yourself if having to choose between lovers is one of the two worst things a man can face, what is the second one? The other is having both women be in the same room at the same time. But mercifully, Fate had spared me that dilemma, at least for the moment.

Now is not the best time to have that conversation, I stammered. I suspected that she could tell that all was not right with my world, but she broke off the embrace.

She said, Later then. I'm staying at the Cornstalk Hotel. You should come by after this afternoon's matinee, and we'll have a tête-à-tête with some Kentucky gentleman—Jim Beam, Hiram Walker, one of those good old boys.

Well, that killed my thought of Bubbles ensconced at the Cornstalk, at least until I could get off this fence I seemed to suddenly be straddling.

As sure as the sun sets in the west, I walked her toward the edge of the park, which was dangerous in its own right, because in the space of three hundred feet, our gait synchronized, our arms found each other's waist, and being with this woman seemed like the most natural thing in the world. I'd need all my strength and perhaps a little cunning to not screw it up with both of them and wind up without the Texas redhead or the miracle of my lost dream's return.

When I got back to the big tent, Marcel was waiting and immediately said, This puts a wrinkle on the prune, Doctore. I mean, she came all the way down the river to collect the spoils. Wait, you're not spoiled yet—but you will be if she has her way.

Thanks for nothing, I said.

Sorry, Buzz. I've never seen you with one girlfriend, much less two. How did you manage that?

I don't believe I have accomplished that feat. I'm as dumb as a box of rocks when it comes to women.

I thought I had spent the better part of two years imagining I was courting Bubbles in Chicago and had nothing to show for it but a monumental bar tab and something like guilt that I'd rather not speak of. Now here she was. I felt as nervous as a blue tick hound at the start of a hunt just thinking about seeing Bubbles again. But then there was

Athena. She was the best thing about St. Louis, and I have to admit, I never expected to see her here. It said something about her. The girl knows what she wants, and I suppose that was me.

Marcel said, That Athena doesn't have the sense she was born with if she thinks you can be saved. How many times have you tried to settle down? Once? Twice? Okay, I know you married once you'll admit to, for what—four, maybe five years? Hey, wait a minute, wasn't your time in Chicago part of that sojourn? Bubbles wasn't your first wife, was she? Fess up, Buzz, was the two of you a priori?

Let it go, I said. That horse has been dead for a long time.

Speaking of horses, we both know, Doctore, that you're the kind of guy who's happy playing the ponies, drinking in dive bars and eating in greasy spoon diners. You might flirt with the waitress, might even do a little bouncy bouncy, but you can't really live with her. You're a sideshow barker, Buzz, a silver-tongued "come closer, have I got a deal for you" guy. Always was, always will be. It's your gift.

Dammit, Marcel, this is not the time to make sense.

Dammit, Buzz, you're right, this is not the time to make sense. That time came and went. As far as I can see, the guy who's driven this mess from Itasca to today needs to cure himself of one or both of these fever dreams and get on with the show. Get a grip. You and monogamy might wave at each other across the street, but you are not likely to end up on adjoining barstools or a double bed.

Spirit, I appreciate your advice, and I will give it careful consideration while I sit sipping my Scotch. I'm not saying you're being right or even horseshoe close makes this any easier. This whole world of wonders is three performances away from done. Then you and every other member of the Rex can say goodbye. You'll go to whatever next is, and so will I. Maybe back to St. Louis, maybe I'll winter over here, maybe I'll head on down to Sarasota and get me a job shilling for oddities at the circus museum. It's all grist for tomorrow's mill.

Both of us knew there was nothing more to be said, so we went to do whatever was in need of doing. I did appreciate Marcel's concern, and I would miss working with him after the Rex had run the last leg of the race. But the Damocles' sword of fact was that I would have to make a decision, and saying no to the both of these fine women made so little sense. I knew that I would have to choose one and disappoint the other.

59–When the Levee Breaks

After the show, I did go to the Cornstalk Hotel intent on having that unfinished conversation. As I've said before, when it is time to get on the bus, it is time to get on the bus, even if the bus looks to be headed someplace you may not want to go. There's as much chance it will turn around as it will end up in a ditch.

The clerk rang Athena's room, and it wasn't but a sneeze before she was in the lobby wearing something creamy and clingy, looking like Paris when it sizzles, a stop-you-in-your-tracks version of the goddess she was named for.

She narrowed her eyes and said, Good to see you, Buzz. Come up to the room, and we'll get comfortable.

It looks like you already are. Why not a drink in the bar?

They don't have one here, silly boy. Come up to the room. Mama knows what you need.

I'm sure she does, but I've never thought of you as Mama.

She laughed, took my hand and halfway up the stairs we were moving once again in sync. I considered it a bad sign, but trying to not walk in time to her gait would have been both awkward and unsuccessful. Once in the room, she was true to her word, though not quite in the way I expected. Oh, there was the getting comfortable with a drink to be had and an unfinished conversation as well, but neither of them was the first order of business.

Her first order of business was pushing me against the door to kiss me while she undid my belt and zipper. The pants retreated ungracefully to my ankles and the shirt followed. I stepped out of them rather than take a chance on falling flat on my face as Athena's right hand was working some familiar pathways down under. Her left hand was performing the disappearing act with the summer dress. As the kiss reached its zenith, we were both more than halfway to naked and the waiting bed. I could say that nature took its course, or that I was weak, and she was determined, but as they say, we found a way.

It was surprisingly good at the physical level, for if absence makes the heart grow fonder, between that last morning in rainy St. Louis and that October twilight room, my body missed her ministrations. Lips on lips hungry and attentive, hands touching, stroking, kneading, caressing, legs wrapped around legs or waists and heads resting against shoulders, we marched through the vocabulary of once-done-before positions testing the weight of her body on mine, mine on hers. Our breath growing shorter, until it was a kind of long shared moan, and thank all them saints with no names, there was no calling out of anyone's in the spent moment. That could have been awkward, and being limbs akimbo with her was awkward enough, or would be once we got to the untangling.

It was all as good as I remembered it. Better. Confusing in its familiarity. Time collapsed like it does when you have an accident, slowing down, thoughts still racing from detail to detail, to fix them for later. Whether we were in the Big Easy or some other place, I could not say. We were physically, if not emotionally, in sync.

I might as well have been a coyote opening a package from the Acme factory. She was the Athena I knew and yet not. I was, what? In my body, out of my mind, and emotionally conflicted. Light the fuse and climb aboard the rocket. Time means nothing to the dead and everything to the dying. In that hotel room on that afternoon, I was neither but might as well have been both.

That was the essential difference between Athena and Bubbles. Athena came into my life by way of the tour. It was the fact of the tour that brought me to St. Louis. It was the theft following the Arch show that created the space for us to dream about living in a new Garden of Eden. If I was Adam, she was Lilith, the first mate, the willful principle who proceeded the helpmate Eve, or maybe more likely, the forbidden fruit of the Tree of Knowledge.

Knowing what must be done, I decided I had best get on with it. I knew that when there was no more tour, there would be no reason for us. She was the "what if...?" that I had held out as a promise that made the last miles of the marathon bearable. Now, the question was how to say goodbye after my Johnny jump-up had said hello.

Bubbles was another thing entirely, and I was pretty sure that when I told her about Athena, and I would have to for my own peace of mind, she'd probably say, the past is past, and forgive me any transgressions before me, and she reunited. Or at least I wanted that thought to be true. Yes, I was already racing to a conclusion that had not arrived, but that wasn't any different than the way I thought of Bubbles and me from the git go.

She'd not be likely to forgive me any transgressions after we were reunited, but I had no intention of straying once Bubbles was back in my arms. Bubbles predated the circus. She was the fixed pole of the turning earth, the North Star lighting my dark nights. She was the siren song of my transitory life between Chicago and the Rex. If anything, she was the Holy Grail of happiness I had made for myself in the years of wearing out those old iron shoes.

If I spent two bits on the psychology of it, I could say most of those years itching to scratch a satisfaction with what was next was spent searching for her. Well, here in the Big Easy, them iron shoes were so thin I could read the newspaper through the soles. I was more than ready for the happily ever after.

When Athena had finally had enough, and I'd had more than enough, we lay naked and sweating in the bed. There was no speaking for a long time, just the heat of one body settled against the other, listening to our breath as soft as the wind moving the willow branches, and then she sat up and pulled a bottle of sparkling water from beside the bed.

We'll start with this. Then I'll ask you to open the champagne. As she handed me the bottle, she lightly stroked the line on my hips where the white meat met the tan. You've gotten thinner, and in spite of your dislike for Ol' Sol, it looks like you've managed to darken a shade or two.

Despite my fear, I plunged ahead. Athena, I said, I don't know where to start. I appreciate your coming all the way down here to see the end of the show. I took a sip and handed her the bottle before continuing. But I've got to tell you, this will be the last time, maybe the last time, I don't wanna...

She interrupted with, Are you doing lyrics? She turned to lean over me so close I could see the difference in color between her faded blue left and almost green right eye. What the fuck is that? You've never done that before. Spit it out...

We're done, I said. That's as plain as I can say it. I'm not sure we ever were more than your empathy and some fabulous sex. Really, I haven't had sex like that in... since I can't remember when. Maybe ever. I was headed for a brick wall at the end of a short alley and stopped short. I'm ready for some champagne now—to toast your beauty and to say goodbye.

Athena got out of bed and put on an iridescent blue silk robe which she didn't bother to close but let hang loose so that, with every step she took toward the bucket sitting on the desk, it fluttered like dragonfly wings.

Then she said, Do I have anything to say about this? She pulled the champagne bottle from the ice and said, Over, you say? What if I don't want it to be over? She didn't hand me the bottle to open but tore the foil and wire off with what looked to be more than a bit of anger.

She said, What kind of "how good to see you" is that?

The cork popped out.

Help me remember, my dear Buzz, what was my end of the conversation in St Louis? Was it go ahead, finish the tour? Did I say go, or did I say stay? Did I say that I should wait... for what? For a happy "us" after the circus when you would come back? No, that was your side of the conversation. You were the one asking to finish what you'd started. You were the one who made me the promise of later. Mine was, stay with me, and we'll find our way to make this work now. I was ready to jump, Buzz. Against all logic and everything my mother taught me, I was willing to buy the "here's the one man you've been waiting for" hook, line and sinker. The moment you closed the door, I thought about quitting my job then and there. I was an hour short of following you. I've never done that… I've never felt like I was living a damn romantic cliché before. But there I was. Much to my surprise, I cared. No, make that I do care. You callous asshole, I still care for you. More than I should. Obviously, more than you do.

Champagne spilled on the carpet and her feet. She looked at me.

You don't get to lick it, Buzz. Not after that statement.

I could offer an explanation…

I'm sure you could, but the question is why should I believe you? You're a silver-tongued devil.

She stopped waving the bottle and looked at me with an expression of a child on the verge of tears.

Oh, fuck that—you are who you are, and I'm… well, I'm who I am. Why kid myself? We'll have a glass and skip saying anything that we'll regret later.

She poured a glass and handed it to me. She poured another, then raised it to her lips, took a sip and said, If you're not going all in, if you can't see what a good thing you've got standing before you, I'd rather not have you diddle around the edge.

We raised our glasses but drank in silence. The irony was I did see what a good thing I had or could have had. How a week ago, I would have been all in and happy for it. But Fate or somebody's, maybe God's ironic sense of humor was such that different was now on the table. A Divine mystery, a damn miracle outside of whatever I could possibly imagine or expect had been made manifest.

The elemental Bubbles had appeared—a fucking parallel universe that was conjectured in dreams and, by all the logic of quantum mechanics, should not exist but did. It blotted out the world of Athena. Theoretical Bubbles was the black hole of desire dreamed on starry nights. Once conjectured and one proved possible, it pulled my heart into its gravitational field as surely and as swiftly as anything Einstein could chalk. Now, I was about to enter its true nadir, accelerating steadily in the force field of making dreams measurable. Once I passed through the gravitational shift that was Bubbles in my arms, it would open to who knows what, who knows where, but having waited half my life for this improbability to be manifested, I was more than ready.

Then, almost as an afterthought, I asked Athena if she was coming to tomorrow's performance. Athena put her hand on mine, leaned in to kiss me on the cheek and declined. It seemed she remembered an appointment she had in St. Louis tomorrow. She'd be leaving in the morning.

She said, Would you like to spend the night? One last dance?

No, best not to. As Big Daddy used to say, once decided, do not hesitate. Between the champagne and your perfume, the little man might want to play again, and then by the power vested in your radiance, the whole discussion, the whole decision would be back on the table.

You're giving me a lot of credit there.

I assure you, it is well-deserved credit.

As darkness fell, I stood up and looked out the window at the thickening crowd on Royal Street. If I stayed, I would surely falter. I dressed, and that was it.

Walking back to the Rex, I thought that this was an example of the lady and the tiger. The question is always, which door was the best one to open? Too late, I had already opened and closed one. The notion that I had made a mistake rose like the levee wall with the entire chemical soup of toxic waters behind it threatening to flood the newly cleared ground. I had said no to the woman I knew loved me enough to come looking. But what was behind the other door? I've said yes to a woman I haven't seen in so many years I've built an altar to her memory. Did that door lead anywhere?

Did I have any evidence that Bubbles felt anything for me? Besides giving me her phone number? I gave the question just enough time to imagine the levee's breach and then put on a mental lifejacket with Bubbles' name on it. It was the choice I'd made. I'd swim with or against the current as the waters rose. I'd find out soon enough whether I was a fool for love or just a fool.

60—Bubbles Redux

I called Bubbles, and she said I should come over to her place a few blocks up Dauphine. Now was fine.

I went over there, and the rest is nobody's business but my own.

Don't give me that look. You sat me down to tell you the story of the Rex, and I've been doing that all along. What's public is public, but even I, or especially I, have some things that are going to remain private. Oh, I'll nibble around the edges a little, but the real meat of how and what took me and Bubbles from the doorstep of her yellow house in the Big Easy to her in the other room cooking greens for supper is too precious for me to give you now or even after I get to know you ten years on. It is a story I've not told anyone who wouldn't take it to the grave upon the hearing.

Talking about Athena was easy because it really was, as I said, part and parcel of the Rex. I told you how she had come into the story and how she left. Rightly told, if I do say so myself. That served the larger story, and so I served up the whole embarrassment of it, at least as far as what I did and felt. But I think I've already said too much about Bubbles. She is the story that is written in the quickening pulse. She is too close to my heart to not say as little as possible lest it bleed out or be cheapened by repetition.

I said as much about our meeting on Bourbon Street as suited the telling, but this next piece is not so much a part of the Rex as it is the beginning of what came after.

I will say that our first hour together in the yellow house had as much silence as my last hour with Athena. We sat in hard-back chairs at a too-large farmhouse kitchen table. I suppose I could say the walls were periwinkle blue with a buttercream trim around the single window and doorframes, but the truth is, I saw the fact of those details later. That reunion night, the kitchen was dark except for flickering candles on shelves and countertops, so everything that was not in shadow was casting them.

We were sipping Jack Daniels from jelly jars. She'd ask about somebody who I didn't remember, and I'd mumble something to signal that I heard her. I'd take a sip and ask how she came to working at the bar. She'd answer with a few words as plain as a brown paper bag and take a sip. The more we drank, the less we said.

Then, when the jar was about half empty, I reached out and took her hand. It was small, warm, soft, reminding me of a thrush or house sparrow. I looked at her long, thin fingers like they were beautiful wings fluttering slightly and could feel the pulse of blood quickening beneath the translucent skin with its fine blond hairs and freckles.

She quietly said, You know, Jelly Bean, I thought of you after I left. Your kindness, how you did what you did without really knowing me. I realized there was so much more to it than you wanting to fuck me, and no man had ever done that before, been kind for my own sake. I thought about going back. I thought I should give you a chance. I didn't, and I'm truly sorry for that.

Then, to my surprise, and I guess hers, a big, fat drop of water fell on the table. I looked up to see if something was dripping from the ceiling and felt the next tear roll down my cheek. Surprised is too mild a word, but I didn't say a thing, just sat there holding her hand, crying. I hadn't done anything like that since my ma passed. Welled up and emptied out. Everything that had been held back, every sorrow, every remembering was in that leakage.

Maybe it was a maternal caring thing, not that I knew if Bubbles had ever been an actual delivered mother. She certainly didn't want to be a mother in the old days of our "not a courtship," but in the in-between, who knew? Made no difference, she did the right thing that night in that way that best comforts the afflicted. She let those tears roll for a good while, not moving or saying anything more to break the spell. She just sat looking at me, and it seemed she opened her heart to take in all my sorrow like she was filling a broken cup. Finally, I sniffed and let go of her hand to reach for a napkin to blow my nose. Loud. But since I had already sacrificed whatever dignity I had, I just honked and sniffed.

About then, she got up from the chair and came behind me to lean down, put her arms around me and nestle her chin on my shoulder. Squeezing me like she was giving me a Heimlich, she pulled me up out of the chair and turned me around to give me a full-on embrace. She didn't say anything, just held me close for a long time. Could have been minutes or hours, close enough to feel the give of her body through the cotton print dress. We held on till our breath was fully synchronized, and we were looking into each other's soul through the windows of our eyes. She was crying, too, in the way women do when they're feeling empathy instead of sorrow. There was such caring in that look I hardly knew what to do with it. I was on the verge of tears again when she stepped back.

That was the moment when I knew I had made the right choice.

I went to give her a kiss, but she turned her head, offering me her cheek.

Later, she said. That's for later.

I was afraid that I had made an error in wanting to kiss her and went to apologize, but she must have anticipated that as well because before I could get the words out, she put her finger on my lips and said, that's also for later.

I didn't kiss her that night and certainly didn't stay in her bed. That was all for later. We sat back down at the table and returned to me holding her hand, or maybe her holding mine, and drinking the rest of the Jack with long silences between what few things we did say. It wasn't much except for me to thank her for being there. I admitted that I did not know how to tell her how I loved her. Or why. But she said we could stand in the mystery of it. We sat as long as it took to do half a bottle—maybe an hour or two—then, as if by mutual mental telepathy, we left the kitchen and she walked me to the door.

When did you say the next show was? She asked.

Tomorrow. Then on Sunday, we bow out with all of us in our places with bright shiny faces. Tomorrow is at seven o'clock, the last one at three.

I'll come tomorrow, she said as she gave me a little nudge that sent me into the still, warm night.

That was our first night together, and that's all I'm going to say about my courtship of Bubbles. Well, maybe one more thing. Walking back to the Rex, I was drunk, but not on whiskey. There was plenty of that making the wobble in my walk, but this was something different. Something had lifted, and I felt that nothing, not Mercer and her camera, not the Absent Owners, not the damn river overtopping the levee, could put me off this feeling.

I deserved a cigar, and lucky for me, I had one in my pocket. When I lit it, the taste of Cuba was so sweet that I began to sing an old country song. "Stand by Your Man" or some shit like that. I'm a terrible singer, but I didn't care. I wanted to sing loud. So I did.

61–Witness

Bubbles came to the Saturday show just as she'd promised. Sat pretty in the third row, wearing a white cashmere sweater and form-fitting jeans that made her legs look even longer than they were. She oohed, ahhed, laughed and clapped when she should. Afterward, she came up to say that she thought I did a very good job. I was a natural, in her opinion, and much improved from the old days in Chicago.

If she had known that I was as nervous as a prom boy looking to pin the flower on the girl's bodice while her father looked on, she might have thought otherwise. Or maybe she did sense that and was giving me congratulations for having managed to get through the whole of the performance without breaking into a sweat or stuttering.

She leaned in and kissed me, one soft hummingbird touch, so light and quick it was gone before I knew it was on my lips. She took my hand in hers, turned it over to look at my palm. Your love line is here, she said. She traced it with her finger. She turned her palm up and, with the free hand, guided my finger over hers. Mine is here and welcomes our meeting.

She turned and left the tent. As much as I wanted her to stay for the sheer pleasure of knowing she was close, I was relieved that I could put my head down to turn my attention to the checklist for

Sunday, the last show, which was close enough to be imagined, though how we would feel when it was done could not.

When I looked up, it was Sunday, and the last show was in progress.

63–Goodbye Marcel

That last day, at one point, I looked out of the tent toward the levee. I could not see the slick brown waters of the industrial-strength river flowing to the Gulf, which was the inspiration for this one-ring wonder. In so many ways, it had been the source of every blessing and calamity that had followed us from Itasca to this conclusion. I knew it was there. I could see the top of a freighter making its way upstream to load or unload at some chemical plant or refinery. The boat moved through my visual field as silent as a fox closing in on a henhouse. Look directly at it, and it seemed not to move at all. Look away and back again, and you could measure progress by what portion of the background was now blocked out by sailors leaning on the rail pointing to the white circus tent on our side of a wall that was supposed to keep the wet wet and the dry dry.

If I wasn't in the middle of a show, I'd wave to them, certain that they would wave back.

Inside the tent, there was a palpable sadness thinly disguised as a loose-limbed, almost careless final performance of the Rex Terrestrial Celestial & Nautical Circus. In another fifteen minutes, we would be done in the Big Easy. Done with everything but the remembering of how bright and lively it was or was supposed to be.

The pretty picture I presented wearing my red drum major's coat with the white and gold trim did little to improve the scene. I certainly was not fooled. Every man/woman, man/man, woman/woman of them that was the Rex crew was working one act after another from muscle memory with a smile but with their heart not quite in it. Except maybe for Elijah. He always was in it 110 percent, even if he was in the middle of the swamp with an alligator chomping his ass. They all knew this was the last time they'd have to get it right. The fact that a good chunk of the audience was absent friends and family come to witness the last performance of their kith and kin only underlined the fact that this was the end of a particular time and peculiar experience. Unrepeatable and about to become legend.

Say what I will about the Rex, from start to finish, it had been a gut-scalding that left me more tender of heart than I'd care to admit. More physically drained as well. I started the tour at 195 pounds, and here I was, weighing in at 170 with none of my clothes fitting right. Hell, like the road rats, I was mostly drinking a six-pack a day just to keep a possum's shadow of weight on. I came to this state of necessity having vowed to Flat Frank and the Absent Owners that I would ride the raging bull of responsibility that was the Rex all the way to the bell with one hand waving and the other holding dear for tomorrow. That I had done. But the plain fact of it was between April and October, it had become more than the job Flat Frank had offered.

Call me Odysseus—the way home was beset with every kind of adventure that might test a man's endurance and wits. I was more than fond of the Rex crew and would miss seeing them in the day to day. Some I'd miss more than others, and none more than Marcel.

Even as one act was leaving and the next entering, I found myself remembering the conversation I had with Marcel two days earlier when I had come back from seeing Bubbles. It offered a classic example of why that boy was dear to me. He knew me as well as anyone.

Doctore, you look like the cat that ate the canary. Are you all right, or should I find a bottle of vinegar to put you back to yourself?

I am just fine, Marcel, bodacious even, as good as a man of my age and temperament deserves to be. I have made my decision.

He had then cocked his head, studying me to see if I was setting him up for a joke. Let me guess, he'd said. The red-plumed songbird has flown, and the snowy egret is nesting? You've declared your allegiance to long-suffering Eros even as you've turned your back on intemperate Bacchus? Am I warm, Buzz? I think I am.

So warm you'd burn your hand if you put it any closer to the truth.

It was then my turn to cock my head and study him. Nice choice of words, there, Spirit. Elegant even.

He laughed and said, I went to college. I can talk pretty or pretty well.

Spirit, what are you going to do next? This whole glorious mess that is the Rex is coming to an end. As sure as cash money, you must have a plan.

He scratched his head with his hook, looked around to see if anyone might overhear him, then said, I'm going to stay here with Elijah and his missus for a couple of weeks doing some street performances. You know, Buzz, a little bouncy bounce music, some tap dance, a little suitcase razzmatazz with the hat ready to catch the coins. The local boys seem to do pretty well, collecting nickels and dimes, and I can tap as well as any of them. We figured we'd try our hand at it.

Good luck with that one. As for myself, I'm going to park the Lincoln in front of a yellow house a few blocks past the Quarter and see if I can make what couldn't have been long ago happen now. I'm calling Flat Frank and telling him not to bother calling me back with anything that has me traveling farther than to there and back in a day. Then I'm mailing whatever paperwork is left over from the wreck of the Rex.

Wreck of the Rex! That's a good one, Doctore, sounds like a good B-movie title.

I'm mailing it all to Frank and that's that. After Sunday's performance, it will be goodbye, Marcel. I might see you around town, but no offense, I'm not going to be standing on the street corner with you and Elijah shilling for spare change.

We'll see how long that lasts, Buzz. I mean, I wish you all the happiness in the world with the skinny blond, but if I were a betting man, I'd offer up a Jackson that you'll be wanting to see an audience from the bright lights side of the stage before too long.

Marcel laughed. I'd say here's my number, he said. Call me when you can't stand domestic life anymore, but as we both know, I don't have a phone. All the same, we've parted ways before only to meet again, Doctore. I suspect that we've not seen the last of each other.

With that, Marcel stepped in to give me a hug and scratch the back of my head with the hook. Then he turned away and said in an offhanded manner, I got to see a man about a dog or a dog about a man.

63–Empty the Ring

As the Sunday afternoon show came to a close, the audience didn't so much applaud as drift out of the bleachers to join the final processional around the ring. It all began when one guy leaped into the line and snatched up a flower banner from Slim Jim to raise it high while humming along with the final tune. That he could do so was a testimony to either being a quick study of that jaunty little number or having seen the show before. I didn't recognize him as one of the volunteers who had helped along the way or one of the friends or hangers-on who had populated the farm in Alma. The guy did look a lot like Jim, so I guessed he might be a brother or cousin. Then a couple of thin women with long hair, pale legs peeking from beneath peasant skirts, grabbed the Swede Girls' hands to begin a dance along a serpentine path, collecting other performers and audience as they went. Soon, a turning line of long-haired, twirling-braids women were kicking heels up with every beat, hands waving to the sky or each other as they circumnavigated the ring.

The band came to the end of the march, hesitated and then started in again up-tempo. The bleachers continued to empty, some coming into the ring to join the mad throng and others just heading for the doors. They were the lucky ones because the rest were now subject to a whole mess of crying and hugging halfway between a come-to-Jesus revival and what I imagined a hippie love-in would be.

I went around and shook everyone's hand, thanked them for their work and reminded them that we still had to undo the bleachers and pack the tent in the morning. They could eat, drink and fornicate if they were so inclined tonight, but I would not be handing out cash until after the final teardown in the morning. They laughed and tried to pull me into the circling spiral. I stepped back quick as a hummingbird and headed for the door, giving Ben and the band the "cut it off" sign.

There was a beat, the blare of the horns, and the resounding crash of a cymbal. Then silence. The air so still that I could hear the river lapping the levee. And with that, the Rex crew took a collective breath, took off their costumes, and wearing the parade whites they had underneath, went off to eat, drink and do that other thing.

Miss Red Boots found me outside the tent and had the nerve to ask, Are you crying Buzz?

Me? I said. Not likely. Of course, I had my sunglasses off and was wiping my eyes on the sleeve of my jacket where the wet stain made me out to be a liar. Just a bit of dust...

To my surprise, she put her arms around me and pulled me into the most intimate hug I'd ever had from her. You know, Buzz, she said, we've had our moments. Good as well as bad.

I squirmed, but her grip could not be loosened without injuring someone.

And you know, I wish you well in whatever is next. You, the cats, VX, if you're headed in the same direction.

Yes, he's coming with me. It's the old family ethic. What's good for one is good for the other, she said, releasing her grip. For all that this tour has been, you've been a patient man. All in all, a fair man.

Don't say that. Or don't say that to anyone else. I have a reputation. God, if Flat Frank ever found out I was a fair man, he'd never offer me a gig again.

She laughed and said, As you wish, Doctor. It has been, quoting one of your favorite bands, "a long strange trip." With that, Miss Red Boots stepped back, shook my hand, and headed across the staging area toward the truck where her tigers waited.

255

I looked around to see if Bubbles was there. She had come to the next to last performance, so I did not expect her, but I was hoping she still might be present and accounted for. Of all the hugs that were being doled out, hers were the only arms I was wanting wrapped around my waist.

Later, I would swing by the bar to see if she was working the evening shift. When I saw her across the room, I realized that I was feeling uncharacteristically shy, so I turned around and went back down the stairs to the maddening crowd in search of cheap thrills on Bourbon Street.

In the between, I sat behind the wheel of the Lincoln and smoked a fat domestic cigar that one of the sponsors had given me along with the usual congratulations for a show well done. Not that I wouldn't have rather had a real solid five-dollar smoke, but beggars can't be choosers. No, that's not the right cliché. Every dog has his day? No, that's not right either. Don't look a gift horse in the mouth. There it is. This gift was in my mouth, and it smoked about as well as could be expected for two bucks, but what the hell, a smoke and a joke were what was called for, even if it wasn't a good cigar or a funny joke.

I didn't pay the "good show" talk much mind as I had heard one version of it or another all the way down the river. People said it even if they didn't mean it. You see a show once you make a decision as to whether you are pleased in the moment. If you like it, you say so. If you don't like it, common politeness, especially in the South, requires you to pretend you did. As long as I got cash or the check, I'd let you say what you will, then just smile back and say, yes sir, it's been a real pleasure doing business with you. We'd be happy to do it again next year.

Didn't mean a word of it. There would be no Rex next year. The fly in the ointment, as far as the Absent Owners were concerned, always came down to a simple proposition—did the show make money? And from the front seat of the pride of Henry Ford, the overwhelming answer to that was no.

Never once did I send money the other way. Every time we made a dime, it went back into getting us to the next check box on the schedule, the next town or the next accident. Even then, I had to call Flat Frank every five hundred miles and beg him to talk to the men or women behind the curtain to get another infusion of cash to keep the tigers fed and the road rats in beer. He'd hem and haw, but often enough, I got the telegraph that instructed me to head over to general delivery at the next post office, where they'd have a cashier's check in a plain brown envelope waiting.

I'll give the Absent Owners that—they were willing to cough up just enough cash regular as tick tock to keep us going.

If the circus was a tax write-off, it served its purpose. If it was art, you could argue that it was or it wasn't compared to whatever. It certainly was not Lincoln Center or even Ringling Brothers. Hell, I'm not sure Ringling Brothers was all that great anymore, what with the death of trains and the real canvas tent. But I swear, the very act of getting the Rex Terrestrial, Celestial & Nautical from there to here on a budget skinny as a zipper was more art than anything that happened in the ring. My art.

I don't count the bus or cars broken down with the regularity of Sunday services as negatives. They were expected additional costs, at least by me. And even then, we had managed to find enough of the almighty Yankee dollar to pay off the mechanics and put gas in the tank. I probably could count the Collapso, but I won't because, in the end, even that story ended better than we deserved.

On the plus side, I started with a camel and ended without one. Chalk that one up as some God's grace.

64—Lucy

Whatever it was, the tour was over. Flat Frank had sent Lucy to the last show. I was happy to see his number one assistant, the freckle-faced PR girl of the eternally cheery attitude, who had been my proxy with every bit of newspaper, radio or TV coverage along the route. I was glad she came, even if I wished that she had not put Betty Mercer and her faithful cameraman Rodney in proximity to the end of the tour. That was water under the bridge. At this point, there was no reason for me to complain to Lucy about them. She deserved as much as anyone to see that her labors were not in vain or unappreciated.

She was not there merely for the tearful goodbyes because the Absent Owners, in what appeared to be their custom or expectation, had prepared a disposition instruction package that Lucy handed me as I sat contemplating a second cigar, a decent hand-rolled Dominican.

The last will and testament, I said, turning the envelope over to unseal whatever instructions would be my last Rex responsibility.

Something like that, she said. I want to tell you that Frank is really happy with how this has turned out. He sends you his compliments and best wishes.

I laughed and said, Frank is always happy as long as he gets his 20 percent, which I must say is more than I've got to show for doing what he asked from the safety of his desk. Jesus Mary and sainted Joseph, Frank should try this sometime, and then he might appreciate me with a few Franklins bonus instead of best wishes. I can spend a bonus, but what the hell. You can tell Frank I appreciate what he did for the Rex, even if it was more than likely your intercession.

I opened the package and read the blueprint for dispersal. It pretty much came down to take it apart, pack it up and ship it to the four points of the compass. From the look of it, they had already begun the sell-the-Rex-off portion by portion before we had left Memphis, which pretty well explained why they were willing to let go of the camel.

You know, Lucy, I said, there are times when I think that you are the brains of that operation. Frank should be working for you instead of the other way around.

She blushed and leaned in to give me a peck on the cheek. After that, she turned to talk with the Swede Girls. To my surprise, she talked Swedish.

65–Pack and Go

Here is how the disposition went:

- Tent and supports, cables, stakes packed in the semi and driven to a warehouse in Dallas where it was to be unloaded by a local crew and the semi returned to Chicago from which it originated. Two road rats were required for the driving and paid for an extra four days travel upon delivery of the semi. Billy Bones and Finn got the nod.

- Bleachers were to be dismantled and left on site. One local crew would be coming to pick up three sections of bleachers at noon, and a second crew would pick up the remaining sections at one o'clock. To my surprise, both crews arrived on time, packed the bleachers into their respective trucks and departed without so such as a wham, bam, thank you ma'am… It gave me pause to wonder where the hell they had been the entire tour. Guys who come on time, do the job and leave without bitching or trying to renegotiate the deal. Would wonders never cease?

- Miss Red Boots and the tigers were to be paid their final fee, and she was free to take them where she pleased—to the next circus or no circus at all. When I asked her where that "where she pleased" might be, she shrugged and said that she was going to visit cousins in Florida. Good for her and good for VX, I thought.

I did not know which I would miss more, the skinny girl with the serious will or the skinny guy with the unserious wink of an eye for every occasion. I was pretty sure I would not miss the big cats, for while they were well-behaved, they were, in the end, tigers. I would not miss the necessity of feeding them meat that I would have dearly loved to give the crew or the smell of wet fur after a rainstorm. I would not miss hearing them vocalize that sound somewhere between a purr and a growl that made the hair on my neck stand up every time I heard it.

The rest of the to-do list was too banal for me to bore you with since a good portion of it involved paper. Useful as a bag of hair, it was a chore enough that it best be done then and not postponed for some later labor. Why even recollect it now? I'd take a day or two to push the paper, tally the accounts, sign off on the checklist, all the while wanting to say, Fuck you, Absent Owners, for not coming out from behind the curtain to introduce yourselves, shake my hand and thank me for getting the whole of it from there to the Big Easy.

But since we're taking an inventory of what was next and who was doing what, I'll fill in a few other blanks.

- The Swede Girls were heading west to Las Vegas or Los Angeles—it didn't make much difference to them. Someplace warm and dry. They said they had another three weeks on whatever visas they had before they would have to renew, leave or marry. Vegas seemed as good a place as any to find some work or a green card husband who could appreciate a big-boned girl that could bend that way.

- Scott the Dog was taking his wife and kids back to Minnesota. It was the same story for Fiddling Mike, Sissy and their two kiddos. They had all had enough and thought it was time to get the young ones back to school or grandma. When they heard the families were heading north, Marg, Rona and Big Bearded Jim looked to tag along. They were all planning on driving up together in their respective cars and bringing the tie-dyed school bus with them.

- Slim Jim and Ruth were fighting about whether to hitchhike back to Memphis and visit the folks they got close to or return to the cold-water farmstead in Michigan's Upper Peninsula that he had left when he married her. Given the match-up, I'd say that whatever she wanted was what he'd get. Their kids didn't much care about the future. They were crying about not being in the big ring chasing the stilt-walking mosquitoes with oversized fly swatters.

- Bandstand Ben was taking his electric guitar and the girl-friend he had picked up along the way for a stop in St. Louis to see her relatives. Maybe they'd announce their engagement or a wedding. When had that happened? Apparently, things had taken a turn from the serious to the more so about the time we were in Baton Rouge. It also seemed that I had not noticed that she had been the back end of a buffalo since be-fore Natchez. In my defense, all the back ends of the buffalos looked the same to me, two legs in black leggings stuck under burlap and a tail.

- Now that he was reunited with his cabin on wheels, Lo-ren Red Beard was going to head toward North Carolina to investigate some Bluegrass fiddle or clog dancing camps he had heard about on his walkaround. I wished him well and thought to myself that if I ever saw him again, it would be through the hand of Fate and the good luck of one or the mis-fortune of the other. The latter was his. I went to his funeral a few years ago, but that is another good bit of storytelling for another sometime.

- Claire with the twinkling blue eyes and long-nosed Tom were doing something. I'm not sure I knew or that they told me. They had said as little as possible about themselves the entire tour. Do the work and disappear into the camper or a museum or in Claire's case, any graveyard along the way to contemplate mortality or commune with the local ghosts.

- Captain Bobby had come down for the last gasp and was heading to someplace over Denmark way for a little of that slice and dice. When next we'd meet, he'd be she'd.

- Archibald was staying in the Big Easy to cook at some nuevo-Creole place around the corner from where Bubbles waited tables. She saw a lot more of him—shopping at the morning market or chatting up kids smoking cigarettes in the alley—than I did. She said every time she saw him, he was thinner and taller too. Before you knew it, I wouldn't recognize him, but I'd know his rice and beans anywhere. For a year or so, I'd go to that place just to order something I knew he would be likely to have cooked. I stopped going when I couldn't taste him anymore. I had Bubbles ask around if he was still there. He wasn't, but I was sure he was in some kitchen somewhere making food good again.

- You already know what Marcel, Elijah and Sonja had planned.

I did not want to work, at least not, soon. From my perspective, the next few months would be Bubble's alone. Us finding our way in this world. To her credit, and I suppose to mine too, we're still at it.

The plain fact of it was that everyone was ready to get gone.

That Monday morning was all about one last group effort to get this useful thing in that packing case in the back of the right truck or that bit of unneeded stuff to the trash pile that was steadily growing on the zoo side of the path. The blue flood fabric was going to a local church. The short stilts were going to local kids, the long ones strapped to the roof of a bus heading upriver. The buffalo were bundled and marked for delivery to some theater group that Rona had worked with before she took up the aerial arts. Piece by piece, everything that was the Rex had been accounted for, sorted, packed or discarded.

The clock ticked away until the only task left on the punch list was my handing out the last round of thin envelopes with ready money tucked in. It had gone quite well, though there was one little kink in the getting it finished when we discovered that the hippie bus had a dead battery, and we had to have a communal shove to get it started. That was more ironic and metaphoric than any of us might comment on, but someone took a picture of it. I got it here somewhere. In that half-focused picture, Claire is pushing Big Beard Jim's back while he, in turn, is pushing the bus. This was replicated by a good bit of the crew from one edge of the back bumper to the other, each trying to overcome the inertia of the bus. The collective will to work together succeeded one more time. The bus coughed and roared to life.

There was nothing left to do but for those who were traveling north to get on board and wave goodbye through the open windows.

66–Done Enough

A little after two in the afternoon, I was done, or done enough for me to fold the completed checklist and stuff it in the envelope that would go back to Flat Frank.

Bubbles had told me that she would be waiting for me to share some fresh crawfish and a cold Dixie. That was something to look forward to. Mmmm, I said. It would be past time for some of that old "bite the head, suck the tails" good eating.

I took the list of what had to be done I had carried next to old Ben in my wallet from Alma to the Big Easy, used it to light a Cuban. Then I got in the Lincoln and drove out of the park, saying to myself, that's goodbye to the Rex, and good luck for what comes next. And it was.

Epilogue—Where We End

What do you mean by what does it mean? Are you asking me for a moral to this story?

Did Jesus explain his parables or Vonnegut say what "Cat's Cradle" meant? Did Hemmingway say what the fish in the *Old Man and the Sea* stood for? It was a damn fish. Why not let the meaning be that a grumpy guy was in a boat trying to catch supper. Why do you need me to put some drugstore gloss on this thing?

Moral? Fill the crooked lines between the scattered dots and make your own briar bush to get tangled in, Brer Rabbit. Maybe there is no moral. Maybe it is as plain as the coffee grounds at the end of the day. Wet and used up. Maybe it just was what it was.

Or maybe the moral, if there is one, is the same as the Rex's invocation—Get better or die! That could be the goddamn moral of every story. We live, and then we die—so let us live as well as we can until there ain't no more.

Satisfied?

Now I'm going to tell you what I forgot to tell you before. It's not that important in the scheme of what happened, but it's important that I say it for me to know I told you everything that was worth saying. Think of it as a little leftover bit of sideshow ballyhoo. No sideshow slick would pitch this like I'm about to, but I'm going to let it roll just for the mouthfeel.

266

Maybe this is the moral—the why I did all this—so pay close attention to what comes next.

Step right up; don't be shy.
You don't want to miss it.
No, you don't want to say that
You did not partake of what I have here—
The rare, the beautiful, the precious grail that makes all new.
This is what you have longed for, have sought after,
What you have only dreamt of. What you did not believe was
possible,
The eighth wonder of the world, ancient or modern...

Yes, step right up,
Come closer and you'll see
I'm the kind of man who pays what is owed—
Cash on the barrelhead.
The kind of man who eats the crust of bread,
And gives thanks for the oven,
Savors the meat on the bone
And gives thanks for the fire,
Who takes a sip of something 'n' something
And gives thanks for the cup.
Two bits, four bits, six bits, a dollar
It's a small price for the knowing.

I'm the kind of man who believes that if time or money
Is all that stands between you and satisfied
There ain't a problem that can't be solved.

Step right up, come on in,
Don't be shy,
Even a blind man/woman can see
There is a welcome place for you.
This plain wood table is already set,
Sit down and partake of what love has offered,
Take your fill

Knowing presently,
Kindness shared with another can satisfy.

You there, what are you waiting for?
There is a chair empty for you…

Love is not a commodity, nor is trust,
Nor courage, nor mystery,
Nor grace, nor the prayers we pray
But something more
Rare and precious…

I'll say it again…
You get more than you deserve
At this groaning table
And you're welcome to it.
Give thanks for the blessing of abundance.
Say it true, now
That was some good eatin', some good sharing,
Well worth the wait.
Satisfying and satisfied at last.

Friends, there's comfort in the dark
When we turn out the lights.
With stars above
A pillar of fire in the wilderness,
A pillar of cloud beside the lane
To mark the way.
Follow on.

The circus tent is fled,
With it the story must come to its end,
The vacant lot returns tomorrow.

About the Author

Loren Niemi has spent forty-five years as a professional storyteller creating, collecting, performing, teaching and writing about what it means to be human. He has served as the Humanities Scholar in Residence for Northern Minnesota, been the ringmaster and tour manager of In the Heart of the Beast Puppet & Mask Theatre's Circle of Water Circus, and spent twenty-five years performing with Kevin Kling and Michael Sommers in the iconic performance art trio "Bad Jazz." In 2016, he received the National Storytelling Network's Lifetime Achievement Award. In 2020, he founded the American School of Storytelling, providing online classes in traditional, personal and applied storytelling narratives and in-person oral narrative workshops and performances.

He is the co-author, with Elizabeth Ellis, of the critically acclaimed *Inviting the Wolf In: Thinking About Difficult Stories* on the value and necessity of the stories that are hard to hear and harder to tell and the author of two award-winning books on crafting narrative: *The New Book of Plots* and *Point of View and the Emotional Arc of Stories* co-authored with Nancy Donoval. His collection of non-traditional "ghost" stories, *What Haunts Us*, won a 2020 Midwest Book Award for Sci-Fi/Horror/Fantasy/Paranormal fiction. His most recent book, *A Breviary for the Lost*, a poetic memoir of his seven years in a Catholic religious order, is available now.

Loren has a BA in Philosophy and Studio Arts from St. Mary's University, Winona, Minnesota, and a MA in Liberal Studies/American Culture from Hamline University, St. Paul, Minnesota. He taught storytelling for twenty-six years in the Communications and Theater Programs of Metropolitan State University, St. Paul, Minnesota, and at workshops across the country.

Made in the USA
Monee, IL
11 September 2023

42406402R00163